I0736357

Matilda

By

C.I. Garrett

JaCol Publishing Inc.

Copyright 2019 © by JaCol Publishing Inc.

Illustrations Copyright ©
2019 by JaCol Publishing
Inc.

FIRST PRINTING

October 2019
All rights reserved

JaCol Publishing Inc.
195 Murica Aisle
Irvine, CA 92614
818-510-2898
Editor-in-Chief: Randall
Andrews
www.jacolpublishing.com
ISBN: 978-1-946675-35-4

No part of this publication may be reproduced in whole or part, or stored in a retrieval system, or transmitted in any form, or by other means, electronic, mechanical, photocopying, recording, or otherwise without written permission of the publisher, except in the case of brief quotations embodied in critical articles and reviews. The classroom teacher may reproduce the materials in this book for use in a single classroom only.

Dedication

I want to thank God for my Father and Mother for always being there. I love you!
C. L. Garrett

Psalm 100:5—For the Lord is good; his mercy is everlasting; and his truth endureth to all generations.

Acknowledgement

I thank my Mother for sharing what she always wanted to know in the family. I had the research and was able to tell her what no one knew, I thank my sister for listening, and I thank my brother Todd for all the conversations we had concerning my writing.

I would also like to thank Aunt Alice for remembering all the information she was told by her Matilda, Uncle Joe, Mother Addie and her father William. Before she passed in 2017, I was able to read Matilda to her. Aunt Alice laughed and continued to laugh because it read like what she told me.

Thank you to my Uncle Curtis Ward. We call him Uncle Bubba. He did the research finding gravesites for me in Greenville, N.C. Uncle Bubba visited the Keeper of the Cemetery to get all the information I needed. Thank you, Uncle Bubba. Thank you, Aunt Jolinda, for trusting me with her family pictures. As I returned the pictures, surprisingly she sent me a new batch a pictures for me to copy. Thank you, Aunt Jolinda, Thank you, Aunt Debbra, for letting me know the family told you about the research I was doing. Once we finished talking, two months later, Aunt Debbra passed. Thank you, Aunt Annie Mae and Aunt Claretha, for the wonderful time we had at the family reunion in the summer of 1994. November 1994 Aunt Annie Mae passed and Aunt Claretha passed the summer of 2015. I want to thank my Uncle Gerald for telling me the information he knew about the family. Thank you Uncle Gerald.

Many thanks to Vernessia Proctor, Traci Simpson Robertson, Michael Bolton and Calvin Kidd for the gift of reading Matilda, you all were Awesome!

Special thanks to Carol Wright for taking my photo. God bless you, Carol!

I'd like to also thank my editor, even with all the back and forth, you never lost faith in this project.

Table of Contents

Chapter 1 1
Chapter 2 6
Chapter 3 10
Chapter 4 17
Chapter 5 22
Chapter 6 29
Chapter 7 38
Chapter 8 48
Chapter 9 54
Chapter 10 62
Chapter 11 71
Chapter 12 77
Chapter 13 88
Chapter 14 106
Chapter 15 113
Chapter 16 127
Chapter 17 131
Chapter 18 144
Chapter 19 151
Chapter 20 157
Chapter 21 168
Chapter 22 179
Chapter 23 187
Chapter 24 200
Chapter 25 219
Chapter 26 225
Chapter 27 230
Chapter 28 247
Chapter 29 254
Chapter 30 275
Chapter 31 281
Chapter 32 294
Chapter 33 299
Chapter 34 309
Chapter 35 335
Chapter 36 343
Chapter 37 349

Chapter 38..356
Chapter 39..363
Chapter 40..382
Chapter 41..402
Chapter 42..412
Chapter 43..420
Chapter 44..431
Chapter 45..439
Chapter 46..453
Chapter 47..466

Chapter 1

In my twenty-second year, I owed my great grandmother the courtesy of explaining how a newly graduated young woman could consent to marriage so soon before tackling the world.

Of course there are a few things you should know about my great grandmother, Matilda. Besides being the oldest living relative and matriarch of our family, she was a self made woman. At a hundred years of age, she still lived on the property bestowed her by the love of her life, the late Stanley Fleming, and I made the long drive down from the upper Atlantic to North Carolina to personally invite her to my wedding.

It was an early fall day in 1982. The greens were waning and a faint disposition of yellows filtered into the white oaks along the 13 to Greenville.

I had traveled from the sprawling highways of city to city to the pastoral highways of places the generations before me called home.

I pulled into a long rutted driveway of a home that remained fixed in a time I was unfamiliar with. A small well-kept home with acreage of a once sprawling farm invited me to take in the charm of southern hospitality.

A woman swept the porch, a slender middle aged white woman. I made sure I had the right address, but the woman waved me to come out of my car as I wondered if I had found my great grandmother's home.

"Excuse me?" I rolled my window down. "Is that Matilda Fleming's home?"

The woman smiled, "You must be her great granddaughter?"

I exhaled. My concern calmed and I stepped out with my hand thrust. "Cassandra. I'm at a disadvantage. I don't know your name?"

"I'm Nellie, Nellie Meyers, your great grandmother's caregiver."

"Oh no, is she in need of help?"

Nellie grinned. "Your great grandmother is one hundred years old, so one would think she needs help, but quite honestly, I'm more her company than her help." She leaned the broom against the porch post and waved me in.

"Matilda!" Nellie's shrilled in a song bird voice.

A soft voice echoed back. "In the kitchen."

My recollection of Matilda was scant. I'd never come to her home before, and our visits were all conducted at reunions at my Aunt Alice's. School and sports had taken me away from too many events and I worried Matilda wouldn't remember me.

I came around the corner and a feisty solid old woman, peered at me through thick framed glasses, eyes the size of fifty cent pieces. "I know you." She held a bony finger up. "You got eyes like your Daddy and thick hair like your Momma." She held her arms out. "Come give Tildy a hug."

I worried I'd hurt her, but as we embraced, for a hundred year old woman, she had the grip of a python. She squeezed me as though I'd come home, and I was hers. It felt warm, it felt comfortable, and it felt like love.

"What brings you all the way down here? Cassandra, right? I'm not dying am I?" She laughed.

"Yes, Cassandra and no I don't suspect you are dying. I wanted to personally invite you to an event I'm putting together."

"Not pregnant are ya?" She fixed her attention on me with a school teacher's scorn.

"No!" I was taken aback. "I'm inviting you to my wedding."

"You better be havin' it soon, you never know when I might go."

Nellie interrupted. "Matilda, you aren't going anywhere. You'll probably outlive me." She handed me a tea, and escorted Matilda and me to the front room.

She sat us, and in the chill of an autumn afternoon, I tried to scoot my chair closer to the fireplace.

"No further!" Matilda's mood hardened. "I'd prefer you not get too close to the fire."

I sighed. "Can I grab my coat?"

She motioned to Nellie, and Nellie pulled a colorful quilt off the couch.

When she handed it to me, Matilda added. "One of my quilts. It's yours now."

It was a beautiful patchwork, cream material with lavender and pink flowers. "It's beautiful."

She charmed me. "It pales compared to your beauty."

"Thank you."

I had come for more than an invitation, I'd come to gather history on my family. We'd spread out over the last few generations and I didn't know as many as I should. I honestly, didn't know much. "Matilda, would it be okay if I pick your brain about our family?"

"Oh Cassandra, I would expect nothing else. I hope you have a change of clothing. You're going to be here over the weekend."

I impishly grinned. I had brought my suitcase in hopes she would invite me to stay. "Yes, I do."

"Nellie, get dinner ready. Later, draw her a bath, and pull back the covers in one of the guest rooms." She inhaled and placed her hands on her lap. "Now, please begin with any questions you have."

I was about to discover that Matilda was an adult when she learned to read and write, and because of that, she'd committed her life to remembering things, and even more commitment to retelling them.

Chapter 2

"Has anyone ever told you anything about me?"

"A lot of things." Although in honesty, that wasn't true.

"Really?"

"Maybe not enough. Matilda, I've been away at college and--"

"A college girl are you?"

"Yes, ma'am."

"That's good. You are a good girl. Did you know you have two twin aunts who are educated? The first of our family to go to college."

Again, I was unaware. "Really?"

"You don't know your great aunts Araminta and Isabella?"

I shook my head in complete darkness.

She waved her hands. "Okay, it's lesson time. I see I have to go back to the beginning, child."

"Fair enough, I have all weekend, right?"

She winked, and set out to weave our family story:

Once upon a time, there lived an accomplished family. They lived in Greenville, Pitt County, North Carolina - in the country. The family consisted of a father, mother, and five children. The father's name was Stanley Fleming. Stanley was a farmer and a hobbyist cabin builder.

Stanley married his wife, Matilda. Matilda winked. *Stanley and Matilda had five children, four girls and a boy. The first born were twin girls born 1905. Their names were Isabella Maggie Annie Fleming and Araminta Jolinda Debbra Fleming. The twins, being the oldest, were considered the helpers of the family. Their names meant more to their mother Matilda, but she didn't know how she came up with them. The third child was a girl named Lillie Claretha Doris Fleming born 1908. The next child was Addie Maybelle Fleming born 1913. Addie was the only girl who had one middle name. Addie was different than the rest of her sisters-not better-but Addie was going to make a huge impact on the family, and she didn't need all those names weighing her down. Joseph Fleming came on the scene in 1917. Joseph didn't need all those middle names like Isabella, Araminta, or Lillie because he was the only boy.*

I gathered Matilda was more than a mother of five children. Matilda was a woman who, even though she couldn't read or write, was able to state Addie was going to make an impact on the family.

Matilda spoke of her family and herself in third person:

Where they lived was beautiful. The cabin was a first of its kind, mainly because of its big size, unique for that time in history. Stanley and Matilda bought the house from Mr. Aaron Simpson. Stanley's gift of cabin building allowed him and his cabin building buddies to take off the original siding and cut down trees on the property and construct a log cabin using chinky paste to allow the logs to bond permanently. The gift of this family was in the blood. It was passed down from generation to generation, and Matilda imagined it would continue to pass itself down through the generations to come.

Matilda's love of quilt making and sewing would be tested through her children and grandchildren. It was a Godsend to every generation who heard her story.

Everyone had some sort of gift to help the family pass on to the next generation, like Stanley's love of building things and passing them on to his children, grandchildren, and great grandchildren.

She studied me. "You know how to build, child?"

"I can hammer a nail."

She shushed me. "Please, your great grandpa would roll over in his grave if he heard that's all he passed on to you."

I urged her to continue.

"Let's see what Stanley could have passed on to his future blood relatives. Let's visit the cabin and watch him work."

Chapter 3

I wasn't sure what she meant. I wondered if she was going to get up and actually take me outside. I knew my great grandfather had been dead for quite some time and when she continued talking, I sighed relief.

The house was built from the wood in the wilderness of their property.

I interrupted. "You mean 'our' property right?"

She stared at me, and Nellie, who was passing through chuckled. "Your great grandmother likes to tell things in third person. You better get used to it."

Matilda dismissed the two of us and continued:

There was a creek about half a mile from the house. The bathroom was an outhouse in the backyard. Stanley wanted the house to have lots of rooms, and for being built in the early 1900s, it had plenty. It had a massive front porch with a swing hangin' from the porch roof and a dinner bell they barely used. When there was a bad storm or a blizzard, the dinner bell alerted everyone that something was a comin'. There were freshly cut tree stumps placed in different locations on the porch for extra seatin'. Matilda made fern green cushions to fit each tree stump. They looked like miniature trees on the porch.

Grandma started laughing as though her recollection of those seats were a source of conversation.

She had hangin' ferns and lots of plants going down each step. As you went through the front door to enter the house, you stepped up into a huge room, considered the parlor room. On the other side, a long narrow wooden dining table with two wooden benches, and two king-size chairs made up the dining room. The table could seat fourteen people. Matilda always had fresh wild flowers in a vase in the middle of the table next to a pitcher of water. The kitchen sat right off the dining room, tucked into a corner with a huge picture window that, in the morning hours, gave the room the sun's view. There were four doors off the family and dining room. Each door led to a bedroom.

My head swam as she gave this vivid image of a family that she spoke as though she was an observer and not a participant.

Her eyes would light up as she gave each detail, and the joy in her voice peaked as she dotted each person in her recounting:

The second bedroom belonged to the twins, Isabella and Araminta. The third bedroom belonged to Lillie and Addie. The fourth bedroom belonged to Joseph. The first belonged to Matilda and Stanley, it was considered the master room and had a fireplace and a door to the outside. Stanley built a little porch off the bedroom for Matilda to go out and drink her coffee in the morning, and sometimes she would comb the girls hair when the sunset over the horizon during the summer months. The porch was about ten by ten, with four chairs and an outside broom to sweep debris from the outdoors. In the summer, Matilda always kept flowers there. The porches, front and back, were gathering places and became social in the mornins' and evenins'. They had many talks out there while enjoying the scenery of the woods. It was breathtaking and beautiful, especially when the blizzards took over and covered everything with a downy white blanket.

It dawned on me. My great grandmother, whom everyone said had only learned to read and write in the last half of her life, had the poetry of a woman with many years of study. "Excuse me."

"Yes, child?"

"Where did you learn the word downy?"

She craned her neck and studied my face. "Do you think I'm dumb?"

"No, I didn't mean that at all, but from what I've always been told, and by your own admission, you learned to read and write late in life."

She reached across our seats and patted my hand. "One doesn't have to know how to read and write to know how to listen. My ears are quite good."

I'd been shamed, and I felt it. My utter lack of understanding could be chalked up to thinking school was the end all of wisdom. My great grandmother lectured me on wisdom.

"All questions will have answers in due time, child. May I continue?"

I nodded. "Absolutely."

The children's bedroom doors had to be left open in the winter so the heat of the fireplace could keep them warm. Sometimes Joseph would sneak in the living room and sleep on the bearskin rug and enjoy all that heat from the family room instead of sleepin' in his room. Matilda didn't mind. He was home and that was all that mattered.

Nellie called for a break. "Dinner, you two."

I washed up, and while I waited for Matilda to return, I canvassed the room. One wall had pictures from corner to corner. There was a picture of a woman who I discovered was Matilda's mother, Mrs. Lucy. She had long brunette hair and was pretty. The next picture, darkened, with cracks in the original photo, maybe a hundred years old, was Matilda's father. Beside that was Matilda and Stanley's wedding day. In faint handwriting, the words, 'January 18, 1905' were etched in the lower corner. Matilda wasn't smiling but it didn't shave any of her beauty away. Stanley smiled and looked into Matilda's eyes as he held her hand. Another set of parents turned out to be Stanley's mother and father. Stanley looked like both of them. Finally, a picture of the cabin as it was being built. As I viewed it, I realized it was the house we were in. New siding hid the logs and the interior had been paneled, and rooms had been rebuilt, but the shape was definitely this house. I was in a house that had stood for nearly 80 years and didn't seem to be any worse for wear.

Matilda came up from behind and startled me with, "That cabin was half way up when a traveling salesman came by taking pictures, hoping someone would buy one of his photos. That's one of his photos." She extended a wrinkled finger. "After all the helpers pulled their empty pockets inside out, the salesman gave Stanley a coupon for the picture and moved on. Stanley thanked the man, thinking he would never deliver the picture, but lo and behold, a few weeks passed and he came back with the photograph. Stanley gave me the picture to frame."

Matilda had left her third person behind, and for a moment I felt her expressing a side that wasn't storytelling. For a brief moment, she lived out a piece of time. Her eyes studied the picture, and she scanned to her late husband's photo, and sighed. "So many years ago." She reached out and we joined arms, she rested against me for support. "That picture hasn't moved in 77 years."

Nellie hollered, "This chicken and collard greens isn't getting any warmer."

Matilda's eyes widened. "Best not keep Nellie and her fine cookin' waiting." She turned me toward the kitchen and responded. "Hold your horses, we are a comin'."

Chapter 4

Matilda said grace, and I mean she said grace. She ran a little long, and when I peered from peeking lids, Nellie rolled her finger as though trying to speed up Matilda. When Matilda finished, Nellie let out an exuberant 'amen!' I snickered and Matilda gave Nellie the stink eye.

Matilda scooped into the greens and proclaimed. "I don't know what's worse, your happiness that my grace is over, or how you make collard greens. Hasn't anyone ever taught you how to make them?"

Nellie pitched her head forward and smiled. "Yes Tildy, you taught me, and if you didn't have to save the whole world in your sermon on the mount, the greens would still be hot."

I bit my lip as my eyes watered over. I wanted to smile but the chicken called. I pulled a fried breast to my plate and scooped out mashed potatoes and gravy. It was divine.

Matilda worked a drumstick. "You know, for a white girl, you sure know how to make chicken. Are you sure you aren't creole?" She grinned at Nellie.

"You think my auburn hair and blue eyes are very creole?" They continued their banter, forgetting I was there.

"How long have you two known each other?" I opened up the question for either of them."

Nellie replied. "All my life. I met your great grandmother when she was teaching my mother how to make quilts. People came from all over to see your great grandmother's quilts. I was this little girl she took in as her own, never paid much attention to the color of my eyes, just kept me in line. When my momma died she was the first one there to hold my hand, and to tell me that when people die, they don't leave, they just move on to another story. I guess Tildy and I are the next story."

"Do you have a family?"

"Husband passed away in the Korean War. One son, he's married and lives here in the area."

"A good boy too." Matilda spoke up. "You go to church with us on Sunday, and you will meet him."

"Meet him?"

"He's a preacher!" Matilda changed the subject. "You like greens?"

I shrugged. "There okay."

"Well, you won't like these." She winked at Nellie. "But I bet Nel's got a sweet potato pie around here you will."

"Thank you." Matilda kept sliding plates in front of me. "Grandma, if you keep feeding me, I won't fit in my wedding dress."

"Best to fill it out than to have it hang on you like a curtain."

I shifted in my seat. "I don't think that's going to be a problem."

Matilda pinched my tricep. "You are fine."

I quickly discovered Matilda set the pace for every conversation.

After dinner, I insisted Nellie let me help with the dishes, and Matilda stayed in the kitchen and drank hot cocoa and added bits and pieces of history about every dish and piece of silverware I touched. "Got that from the Goodfellows. They ran a pottery shop and made those dishes. Been with me for fifty years...Joseph found that butter knife fishing down at the river, back in 33. Pure silver...Got that glass at the county fair of 42, used to have a picture of the tin man on it from the Wizard of Oz, Stanley bounced a penny into it."

Nellie whispered. "She'll do this all night long. Still does it to me, and believe me, I've heard the same story over and over."

Matilda piped up. "I heard that."

Nellie continued whispering. "Oh, and her hearing is incredible."

Matilda didn't miss a beat. "Yes it is."

I turned my back to the sink and faced Matilda sitting at the table. "I'm so sorry I didn't get to know you better Grandma."

She smiled. "Well, think about it. You have two parents, four grandparents, and eight great grandparents. You can only know so many of them."

"True, but you are the only living great grandparent I have. In fact, you have out lived two of my grandparents. I should have come down here more."

"Nellie? Am I dyin'?"

Nellie didn't budge from her scrubbing, face down into her work. She muttered, "Don't think so."

"Then why is this child speakin' as though my foot is in the grave?"

Nellie continued, "Because you are a hundred years old, woman."

"Still here, aren't I?"

Nellie shook her head. "As I said before, you will outlive us all."

Matilda turned her attention to me. "Don't regret the past. We are here now. Live each second in the comfort that our time together is happening."

A hundred years had given her peace, it had given her wisdom, and I was a benefactor. "Yes, ma'am."

"Now hurry up so we can get back to discussing the past!"

Chapter 5

When we made it back to the front room, I noticed the room had cooled. Night had settled in and a nip in the air had brought a chill with it. Nellie stoked the fire and when I tried to work my chair closer, Matilda admonished me.

"I told you, don't scoot that chair any closer to the fire."

She motioned to the quilt, and I gathered blankets were preferred over the warmth of a fire. "Yes, sorry."

"Now, where was I?"

"You had talked about the picture of the cabin."

"Ah, yes." *The next morning when the sun rose, Matilda awakened. Her mood wasn't beautiful because an issue pressed on her mind. She was concerned over what took place on the route where they lived. A new law was in place for the county. All P.O. boxes had to have a name attached to it for better recognition and better service. Matilda couldn't understand what was wrong with her P.O. Box 516. They was goin' to add a new name plus the P.O.*

Box number to their address. They wanted--Stanley and Matilda Fleming, 516 William and Lizzie Rd., Pitt County, North Carolina.

Matilda said, "I can't understand who's gonna want to write that long name William and Lizzie Rd? It don't make no sense."

Stanley encouraged Matilda that it was the law, and they must abide by the law.

Matilda asked Stanley, "Who are William and Lizzie anyhow? It sounds like someone's parents. Who would name a country road William and Lizzie Rd?" As Matilda continued her fret about the name change, her neighbor a mile up and on another country road stopped by to discuss the same thing Matilda fretted about. Matilda's neighbor, Ms. Mildred Lee, had her route name changed the week before. Ms Mildred's country road was now called, 'Charles Shiver Rd.'

I shook my head. "Maybe I should get a pen and paper so I can record all this. I'm never going to remember any of it."

Matilda gathered me in. "Are ya' writin' a book about this?"

I laughed. "No, just think it would be good to remember."

She frowned. "Well, you should write a book. It's most interestin'."

I excused myself and found my briefcase in the car. I also brought in my suitcase, and Nellie was good enough to get me settled into my room. When I'd returned to the front room, Matilda patted my seat. "Hurry up and get in here, I don't wanna lose my train of thought."

I pulled my pad out and nodded. "Okay, ready."

Matilda eased back in.

Ms. Mildred kept askin', "Who is Charles Shiver?"

Matilda invited Ms. Mildred in for a cup of coffee. Stanley let the ladies go and fret. Stanley believed whoever William and Lizzie, and Charles Shiver were, they had to be special people to get country roads named after them. Stanley and Matilda's twins, Araminta and Isabella, heard their mother and Ms. Mildred fussin' about the street sign. The twins gathered in the bedroom with Lillie, Addie, and little Joseph. The twins started a talkin' about making the name make sense. They agreed they should go to school and find out who William and Lizzie, and Charles Shiver were.

As Sunday came to a close, and the sun rose on Monday morning, the children were anxious to get to school to do something for their mother. They thought it would make her happy if the people were 'good' people.

The children did their chores and Isabella pulled her little brother aside. "Keep quiet and don't yap to Momma that we are gonna bring Momma the history of those people. We want it to be a surprise."

Joseph nodded. He was more scared than anything. If he gave away the secret gift, his sisters would have no mercy on him.

Isabella and Araminta didn't know if they could find the answer, but they were willing to try. The girls walked to school, all smiles, so excited about their gift they could give to their mother. When the girls got to school they weren't concentratin' on learnin'. Addie's teacher, Mrs. Virgilena Henry, noticed Addie's impatience. Mrs. Henry was an excellent teacher, but if Mrs. Henry reported to Matilda and Stanley about Addie not concentratin',

Addie would be a sad little girl. She perked up when Mrs. Henry kept her eyes on her a little more than usual.

As school ended, the twins stayed after to talk to their teacher, Ms Eliza Nelson. She was a fair teacher who would stay after school to teach anyone having trouble in any subject. Mrs. Nelson loved the twins, partly because they were twins, and partly because they were so different. The twins explained to Ms Nelson about the new law, and Ms Nelson told the girls to sit tight and she'd do some snoopin'.

I stopped Matilda. "The twins? You mentioned them earlier. Whatever happened to them?"

"They're around, child."

"Where?"

She hesitated, put her finger to her lip and studied the ceiling. "One's in Paris and the other's in New York."

"Oh." I was surprised my Aunt Alice never brought up that I had a great Aunt in New York.

Anyway, while they waited the verdict, Isabella said, "I want to make sure Momma knows and understands why these people are getting this special attention. I want her to be proud of the road she lives on."

She was still smilin' when they heard a door creep open. It was Mrs. Nelson peekin' in with a glow on her face. She was always very pretty and smelled so nice. She told them being a teacher was the best job you could ever have because you build the world with what you do. The twins were inspired by Ms Nelson, and someday planned to build the world too.

Ms Nelson told them to take out their pencils and write what she said on a piece of paper. "First, William and Lizzie---"

Matilda lit up as Mrs. Nelson started the history of their road's new name.

"William and Lizzie were the parents of a son who had two sets of twins."

Matilda patted my knee as though that news was predestined. "Can you believe that?"

I shrugged.

"The teacher said, *"The Son's grandson had a set of triplets, and the son's wife's momma had a set of twins also. William and Lizzie had eight children but the multiplicity of his son's immediate family and the bloodlines that are still living today was a burst of excitement for the lines that* connect all these people together who still combine them to the original source who birthed the son, and who started it all in pairs and triplets."

Out of the mouth of this one hundred year old woman was a sentence I had to stop her on to gather what she meant.

Matilda and the twins thanked Mr. and Mrs. William and Lizzie Ward Sr. for their lives, for the parallel and good fortune having twins had blessed her family.

Chapter 6

"What about the other name?"

Matilda inhaled. "Patience, I'm getting there."

I hoped I got the Cliff Note version.

"Mrs. Nelson said, *"Charles Shiver was the oldest of his family. His Grandmother lived to see her nineties, and her mother lived to see her late eighties. What made Charles eligible for a road name was when his elementary classmate's granddaughter contacted Charles at the ripe young age of 92. Charles helped to tell the story about her grandmother and so many other names and stories that the next generation would never have known."*

I grinned. "Maybe a street should be named after you, Grandma. That sounds like you."

"Oh, bless you." She shook it off. *"The granddaughter of his classmate promised Charles she would finish a book for all to see. Charles would have to read the book in heaven, but before he left this world he knew what his classmate's granddaughter was puttin' together for the generations to come.*"

"What became of the book?"

Matilda turned toward the kitchen. "Nellie?"

Nellie hollered back. "Yes?"

"Where is the book that nice young lady wrote?"

"Don't know, Tildy." Her voice snaked back into the front room.

She turned to me. "I'll find it. You'll love it."

"Thank you." I snugged the quilt up to my neck. "So you make these?"

"Hundreds of them, child."

"They're nice." I traced the fabric, thick and smooth.

"Quilting was a passion, a desire that allowed me to create beautiful throws, blankets, and even curtains with useful or useless fabric for all to see."

"Well, you certainly perfected it."

I could see her drifting into another story. "Let me tell you about it." She closed her eyes and went somewhere in her past many years before. *The last Saturday in May was the annual church picnic. The quilters of the church discovered the theme for that year's entry. The quilters had to create a theme for one quilt and another quilt of their choice. Both quilts had to be at least eighty-five by eighty-five, and the theme quilt was 'The Color Purple.' The contestants could make any design of their choice as long as one of the quilts had the theme 'The Color Purple.' The contestants had 120 days to complete their quilts, and a chance to win a cash prize of ten dollars, a blue ribbon, and their name and picture in the newspaper the next day. The second prize was five dollars and a red ribbon, and third prize was one dollar and a white ribbon. Matilda loved making quilts. She made quilts year round and sold them to consignment shops for three-fifty a quilt. Matilda had also gotten requests to make pillow shams, and once, a pillow to complete a set. Matilda bought most of her fabrics at yard sales, fabric giveaways, and Estate sales. She had a generous supply of fabric, including the color purple for the quilt show that September.*

After the Picnic, Matilda started going through her fabric collection to start creating her masterpiece for the quilt showing of 1922. Stanley and the children started tillin' the garden for that summer's feast. Everyone helped, including all four of Stanley's daughters, and of course their son, Joseph. They worked in the garden until dark. The children had four more days of school before they were out for summer vacation. The twins wanted to help Matilda with her quiltin', but when you are two of four girls, with one brother who is the baby, your father needs you more than your mother, who was an excellent seamstress. Matilda prepared and finished her quilts every year by early July so she could help Stanley and the children with harvest time from mid-July and August. Matilda did a lot of her cannin' and sold them at local markets with Stanley and his vegetables.

On a June morning, Stanley got a visit from his brother Riley Fleming. Riley's farming business wasn't doing too well that year so he came to see if he could get some help from his older brother for a few days. Stanley didn't mind helping his brother, but who was going to till and plant Stanley's crops was the question. Stanley told Riley he had four daughters and a wife and only one son. Riley said he only needed him for two days, and he could come back.

Stanley talked it over with Matilda, and Matilda said okay, except Matilda knew those two days she would have to supervise, even work the land while the children helped. For Matilda to stay on schedule, she had to hurry to harvest the crops with Stanley and the children come late July and early August. Matilda knew the collards, turnips, and kale would be planted in early August for harvesting in early November. She was glad at the end of the two days so she could get back to her quilting. The next day, Stanley would be back, and her schedule would still be on time.

A week passed, and there was no sign of Stanley. Matilda didn't own a phone, and neither did any of her neighbors, but it didn't matter because Riley didn't have a phone. Matilda didn't know how she could get to Riley's home to find out if Stanley was all right because Stanley took the truck. Matilda tried not to worry. All the plans they made for the summer, Matilda refused to believe would be ruin because Stanley went to help his brother. 'Where is my husband?' Stanley's farming was his livelihood, and Matilda's quilting and canning was hers. Matilda had to figure out how to work the quilts for the quilt show and help the children with the garden. Matilda went into action since no one was sure when Stanley would return. The half of the garden that Stanley didn't till, Matilda would finish tillin' and have the children plant the seeds. While the children planted the seeds, Matilda could work on the quilts for the show.

Matilda had worked for two hours on her quilts when she decided to take the children some lemonade and cookies. She looked out the window and saw only four of her children. She couldn't see Isabella. Matilda rushed outside and noticed Araminta's trying to avoid looking at her. She knew her twin daughters. If one did something they should not do, the other knew about it. Matilda marched to Araminta, but before she could say anything, she noticed Joseph and Addie paying more attention to the barn than the plantin'. They too made haste and went back to diggin' holes and dropping seeds in when they were caught starin'.

Matilda turned Araminta. "Who's in the barn with your sister?"

Araminta knew a lie would make her life miserable. She also knew her momma never punished the truth.

I interrupted Matilda. "Are we still on the quilts?"

She hushed me. "I'm getting there, but with all stories, a few other stories are important, and right now, I need to get the twins out there, because my quilts played a big role in their private lives."

I braced myself for a late night. Nellie had entered, and I raised my hand. "Can I have a hot cocoa?"

She winked. "I thought you might need some." She had a cup in her hand. "This is yours."

I took the cup and sipped as Matilda continued.

Araminta said, "Momma, Isabella is in the barn with Jeff from school."

Matilda looked at Araminta and repeated the words slowly, "Isabella is in the barn with whom?"

Araminta bowed her head and her breathing shallowed.

Matilda reached out to Araminta's chin and lifted her face and they locked eyes. "How long has this been going on?"

Araminta said, "I believe awhile Momma'."

Matilda released Araminta's chin when Isabella headed her way alone.

Matilda walked toward Isabella. "Bring your Jeff to me."

Isabella's eyes widened as though she'd saw a ghost.

Matilda crossed her arms and tapped her foot. "Do as you're told, and I will be waiting for both of you."

Matilda turned to stunned faces of her other children. "Continue working." She told Lillie to go in the house and get the lemonade and cookies for everyone's break.

While Lillie followed Matilda in the house, Isabella ran up the hill after Jeff.

Araminta continued to work, but she knew she was in trouble with Isabella.

Addie watched Araminta.

Araminta turned to Addie, "Why did you and Joseph have to keep looking toward the barn? You know how Momma has an extra sense and picks up on everything."

Addie reminded her sister, "But you told Momma."

Araminta pointed at Addie. "Did you want me to live?"

Addie's eyes grew big as pool balls and she started digging. Lillie came back with lemonade and cookies. Araminta, Lillie, Addie, and Joseph sat under the tree and watched Isabella come over the hill with Jeff. They had a front row seat of the upcoming showdown - Isabella and Jeff...the beginning.

Chapter 7

For a hundred year old woman, she didn't seem to tire, and as much as I wanted to call it a night, she wasn't anywhere near finished.

"So, I'm gettin' to the quilts, but it really is the beginnin' of the twins becomin' young ladies during that time, so bear with me as I dance around the subjects." She winked. "I'm old and so I will plead a fading mind if you hold me to anything."

I grinned at my great grandmother. She might have been one hundred, but she was pretty cool. "That's okay."

"Good." She squinted. "Where was I?"

Before I could answer, she pushed on.

"Oh yes, the day we met Jeff."

"Isabella's sweetheart?"

She nodded:

Araminta tellin' on her twin brought out Isabella's ire against Araminta. Araminta dropped her head as Lillie told Isabella what happened.

Matilda came outside and Isabella and Jeff turned to face her wrath.

Araminta offered. "Momma has got to understand." Isabella knew Momma too, but the way Isabella looked at Araminta, she didnt think Isabella was too happy that Momma made her get Jeff.

Addie whispered to Araminta, "Who is Jeff, anyway?"

Araminta screwed her lips sideways. "He is Isabella's friend."

Addie turned and studied Isabella and Jeff. "Why would Isabella be mad with you about her friend?"

Araminta shook her head. "You're too young to understand, Addie. One day you're going to have a friend, and you're going to want to keep him all to yourself. Now stop asking questions, and let's all get back to work."

Araminta and Addie stood and headed back to the garden. Araminta took one last peep at Matilda, Isabella, and Jeff. As expected, Isabella still had her eye on her twin.

Matilda leaned into me and confided, "Araminta was born first, and Araminta had always been the responsible one."

"I see."

So, anyway, Isabella went after what she wanted and thought of the consequences later. Araminta knew once Momma found out about Jeff, he would be history.

Isabella introduced Jeff to Matilda as the three of them headed toward the house.

Matilda stopped. "Jeff that is my son, Joseph," she pointed to the only boy in the garden, "my daughter, Lillie, and my daughter, Addie, and of course you probably know Isabella's twin, Araminta."

Matilda speaking in third person made me forget she talked about herself. I wondered if that was how she spoke in all her conversations. "Matilda?"

"Yes?"

"You know you are talking about yourself when you say Matilda, right?"

"I know, child, I know."

She didn't seem to care that it came across as a story rather than history, so who was I to argue.

She didn't miss a beat after I'd interrupted:

Araminta couldn't believe what her mother said. "Family, Jeff is gonna finish plantin' the seeds in the garden and tend to them for the next few days. In the meantime,

Joseph, I want you to show Jeff the outhouse. Joseph, I also need you to get the six buckets and fill each one with water from the well for Jeff to water each seedlin'. Isabella and Araminta, I need you in the house, and Addie and Lillie, I need you on the porch to take some quiltin' pieces and lay the pattern on the porch."

Matilda turned to Jeff. "Welcome to our family, and if you need anything, just let me know."

Matilda walked in between Araminta and Isabella as the three headed to the house. Matilda knew what Isabella thought, and how angry she was at her sister, but Matilda also knew Araminta did what her mother asked of her. Matilda would try to sort it out between the two of them.

While everyone worked, a letter arrived. The letter was from Stanley's brother. Matilda gave the letter to Araminta to read, "since I couldn't read."

Matilda used "I" when she mentioned not being able to read. "Don't you mean Matilda?"

She frowned. "No, there are some things I have to admit up close. I didn't know how to read back then." She sighed. "Let me go on, and stop interrupting."

"Sorry, ma'am."

"Quite alright." She crossed her hands over her lap. "The letter read;

> "Matilda, Stanley had an accident and
> hurt his
> shoulder, he will be home in a few
> weeks once
> the swelling goes down and he is free
> from pain,
> I am sorry."
> Riley Fleming

Araminta said, "Momma, Uncle Riley stated Dad can't take that long ride home in his condition."

Matilda smiled. "Thank you, Araminta." She refused to react with her children in the room. "Since your father had an accident at Uncle Riley's farm and won't be home for a couple weeks, Jeff will continue to work the garden, and I will continue to make the quilts for the quilt show."

Jeff said, "Yes, ma'am, I would love to continue the garden, Mrs. Fleming."

Matilda didn't know Jeff and wasn't sure if Jeff was the right one for Isabella, but Matilda knew she wasn't going to separate them, not now. If Matilda separated Isabella from Jeff, Isabella would find a way to see him. Matilda believed in giving people a chance. She knew just because she gave Jeff a chance, it didn't mean that he had it easy. On the contrary, he had it harder than anyone because he wanted to be with her precious Isabella, and Matilda wasn't going to let anyone harm her. Matilda knew Jeff had a story to tell, and that night, at dinner, Matilda was going to have Jeff tell it. The only thing Matilda required of Jeff was to tell the truth from day one.

That night, after everything was out in the open, Matilda was able to tell what was going on between Isabella and Jeff. Was Jeff the ram in the bush?

Matilda asked, "Jeff would you like to say grace for us?"

Jeff spoke, "It would be my pleasure, Mrs. Fleming."

Matilda watched to see if he had a problem praying over the food. Jeff began a prayer that flowed as if he had been praying all his life. Jeff prayed as if he was forty years old. He impressed Matilda, and Matilda knew there was something special about this young man.

When dinner was just about over, Matilda, asked, "Jeff, since I knew nothing of you seeing my daughter, I would like you to be honest with me and the family about you and Isabella. I want to know how long have you been seeing Isabella, also I want to know all about you, and what are your intentions with my daughter? I will get dessert while you let that simmer."

While Matilda left the room for dessert, Isabella told Jeff, "I'm sorry about this,"

Jeff insisted, "Your mother is right, she should know all about me and you, and who I am. I agree with her, your mother sounds like a very smart woman."

My great grandmother puffed up like a peacock.

"He was a very wise young man, Grandma."

"Oh, there's more." She rolled on:

Isabella smiled at Jeff's admission. "Thank you."

As Matilda returned with dessert, Jeff stood, and his story flowed through his lips steady and swift, and tender at times. When it got rough, tears welled in Isabella's eyes, first a trickle, then a waterfall. Matilda's eyes formed glassy pools, and Araminta began to shiver with tears.

Jeff's story was emotional. He tried to answer every question for Matilda. "I met your daughter at school. I am a senior in Isabella and Araminta's class. I noticed your daughter at lunch one day, and I walked over to introduce myself. We have known each other for four months. Mrs. Fleming, I meant no disrespect to your family, we were only talking. I wanted Isabella to introduce me to you and her father two months ago, but she didn't think you would let her see me. I would like to court your daughter, Mrs. Fleming. I would like to ask her father, but I know he will not be back for a while, so I am asking you for permission. I work when I can, mostly at the general store up on Route 50, and I am the youngest of seven children from Virginia. I moved to Pitt County to live with my sister, Addrianna Myles, and her husband Keith, about a mile from here. My parents are deceased now, and I have been saving my money to purchase land in the area to build a house."

He turned the tables. "I do have a question for you Mrs. Fleming."

Matilda nodded.

"I would like to know if I could stay in your barn and work your land for you. The general store isn't many hours, so I can give you a full day's work to help pay for my room and board. I will let my sister know, and with your blessing, I can move in tomorrow. You don't have to worry about Isabella and me, as I haven't kissed your daughter and will not disrespect her in the least."

Matilda said, "Are you leaving something out of your story that you haven't told us?"

Isabella whispered, "I told you my mother can feel if you're leaving something out Jeff. You better tell her before she guesses it."

Matilda said it before Jeff could get it out. "Are you a future minister?"

Jeff smiled. "What gave me away?"

Matilda's eyes lit up. "Everything about you, the prayer, your work ethics, the way you look at my daughter, and the respect you have given me."

Jeff said, "Yes ma'am, I am."

I interrupted, to great grandma's consternation. "Are you psychic too?"

Nellie passed through. "She's got a knack about people. Never seen her miss a beat. So best you always be honest with her."

I bowed my head to Nellie. "Of course."

Matilda turned to me. "I knew that was a good boy." She went on:

Matilda stared at Jeff and told the children to start their chores. She told Jeff to follow her. Matilda walked out to the yard. "Jeff, yes you can stay in the barn. It is summer now, so you will not freeze from the winter and you can close the barn door for privacy. I see you are the ram in the bush. Dinner is at six every night. If you need anything, please feel free to let me know. Welcome to our home."

Chapter 8

"The quilts? What about the quilts?"

Matilda acquiesced. "Okay, on to the quilts." She shook off my persistence and continued:

Now that Matilda could concentrate on makin' her quilts, she was in such a good place. The girls didn't have to work the land anymore since Jeff lived in the barn, and they could take care of the house while Matilda got ready for the quilt showin'. Three weeks passed and Stanley was back home. Mr. Fleming was still sore and had to take it easy while he continued to heal. Jeff met Mr. Fleming, and Mr. Fleming thanked him for helpin' his family while he was away.

Stanley knew Jeff would be a big help even when he got back to work. Mr. Fleming was pleased. The field was nearly ready for harvestin', all the while Matilda finished her two quilts for the quilt show two days before harvest time.

Stanley took Jeff and Joseph to the market to sell the harvest that year. There was plenty left for winter, and the corn would be ready in two to three weeks, and the collards and turnip greens would wait until around Thanksgiving.

Jeff finished his chores early one day and asked Stanley and Matilda, "Would it be alright if I take Isabella to my sister's house for dinner?"

Matilda said, *"As long as you take Lillie with you."*

Jeff didn't mind at all, but Isabella wasn't happy about Lillie tagging along.

I questioned Matilda. "Why did you want Lillie to go?"

She looked at me like I was dim. "How old are you?"

"Twenty-two."

"And you have to ask why I wanted her little sister to tag along while they were away from the house?"

I smiled. "Point taken."

Weeks passed, and it was time to harvest the corn. Stanley took Jeff and Joseph to sell the corn and they picked more collards and turnips to sell as well.

The quiltin' contest was two weeks away, and Matilda had the girls look them over to see if they looked fine for the judges. Isabella and Araminta thought the quilts their momma made was perfect, considering the patterns she used was like her very own house - a log cabin.

Matilda and Stanley had so much on their plate that summer with Stanley gettin' hurt and unable to work the rest of the summer. Before Jeff came, the children were workin' the garden with Matilda. Then Jeff came to live with them, and Matilda had more time, like puttin' time into the twin's seventeenth birthday party.

The party was going to be special for Isabella because of Jeff. Matilda planned the twin's birthday party in the backyard. She would gather wild flowers as bouquets and use newspaper streamers hangin' from trees.

Matilda wanted the party to be a success. She had told the twins to invite their classmates to the party. Matilda had Jeff drive her to the paper factory to get two large pieces of cardboard and some paint so Lillie could paint 'Happy Birthday, Araminta,' and 'Happy Birthday, Isabella.' The supplies cost Matilda six cents, not leavin' her much money in her button jar. Matilda knew this would be the only seventeenth birthday party the twins would ever have and their last birthday party while livin' at home.

Matilda knew the twins would be in college or some trade school somewhere the next year.

The day of the party, Matilda had Joseph, Addie, and Lillie set up the decorations all over the yard. Lillie put out the cardboard posters and Jeff set up freshly cut tree stumps in a circular pattern so kids could dance inside a make shift dance floor.

Classmates arrived so Matilda told Lillie, Addie, and Joseph to have a seat out back because Araminta and Isabella were about to make their debut. The twins had on their prettiest homemade dresses. Matilda placed a flower in their hair and told them to make their seventeenth birthday the best birthday ever. In Matilda's excitement, she noticed Araminta seemed nervous. Araminta tried to play it off and smiled at her Momma. Isabella smiled from ear to ear and Matilda knew whatever Isabella had over Araminta's head was going to come out sooner or later. Matilda told the girls to go out back and entertain their guests while Matilda finished icin' the birthday cake and tossin' the salad. Araminta and Isabella greeted their guests, and Addie, Lillie, and Joseph were the perfect little helpers.

The party went well until Matilda caught a glimpse of a boy walkin' down the hill holdin' a bouquet of flowers. Could that be Isabella's plan? The young man only carried one set of flowers. When the young man reached the house, he didn't go to the backyard where the party took place. He walked up to the front porch and knocked. When Matilda answered, she was shocked to see the brightest grey eyes she had ever seen. She left his eyes and saw the biggest smile. "Can I help you?"

The young man said, "Good afternoon, Mrs. Fleming, my name is John Xavier Whitney. I come to bring Araminta a birthday gift."

I stopped Matilda. "Are we going down another rabbit hole?"

She smiled. "I have to get to this story before I can get to the quilts."

I resigned myself to the fact that my great grandmother would tell her story at her pace and her liking. "Is this man someone who plays a role in the twin's lives?"

"You are catching on."

Thankfully, she did have a method to her madness.

"So tell me more."

Chapter 9

Matilda wasted no time diving into Araminta's beau:

Matilda asks the young man, "Who are you?"

He said, "I am a classmate of Araminta and Isabella. Isabella invited me to their birthday party."

Matilda stood a little taller. "But it's Isabella and Araminta's birthday party, and you only mentioned Araminta's birthday gift."

John admitted, "Yes ma'am, Araminta doesn't know I was invited. Isabella knows I like Araminta."

Matilda said, "Did you tell Araminta that you liked her or was Isabella the only one privy to this information?"

John shifted his stance. "Mrs. Fleming, I have asked Araminta to allow me to visit her here, but she always says Isabella seein' Jeff was enough for you and Mr. Fleming to handle."

Matilda smiled. The boy was brave. She admired him for that. "John have a seat while I call Isabella in the house."

Matilda motioned Isabella as she walked in. John stood as she approached.

Matilda asked, "Isabella is this what you had over your sister's head?"

Isabella knew her momma wasn't happy. "Momma, John always liked Araminta, but Araminta wouldn't give John a chance because of me and Jeff. Araminta always said Jeff and I was enough for you and Daddy to handle, so I told John my momma said we can invite classmates, so I invited John."

Matilda was happy Isabella asked John. "You can go, honey."

Matilda went to the window and asked Araminta to come into the house. Araminta entered and her eyes widened when she saw John stand. Araminta's lowered her head and she held onto the chair for support. Araminta couldn't look at John or her momma. She didn't want this to happen.

Matilda on the other hand walked over to Araminta and hugged her. "Why are you looking away from Momma, do you recognize John?"

Araminta looked up. "Yes, Momma." Araminta's eyes went back to the floor.

Matilda raised Araminta's chin with a finger. "What's going on inside that heart of yours, tell Momma?"

Araminta was troubled and began to speak fast, trying to explain John to her momma. "Momma, I never wanted to hurt you and Daddy, I didn't invite John here. I talked to him in school, and I told him it wasn't good for us to get together. Honestly, Momma, I never told John to come, Momma I am sorry. John I do not know how you got here, but I am sorry you came all this way. I never meant to hurt you either." Araminta broke down in her mother's arms.

John approached Araminta, but Matilda stopped him and directed him to the sofa. She sat Araminta next to him. John watched helpless, wanting to comfort her. Matilda soothed Araminta's crying, patting her back.

Matilda eagle eyed me. "That boy took notice of my actions."

"And?"

"And it would play a role one day." She raised her hand and admitted, "That one could scheme." She shook her head and went on:

Araminta quieted and her eyes closed. Matilda knew she had to move Araminta before she fell asleep. Matilda reached up, moved her head and told Araminta to sit there next to John. Araminta's head popped up, and her eyes opened.

Matilda spoke softly, "Sit." Matilda gave her some tissue and smiled at the two of them.

Matilda assured Araminta, "I know you didn't invite John, baby. I told you and your sister to invite your classmates, and Isabella invited John."

Araminta whispered, "Oh."

Matilda continued, "Now, Araminta. Tell me about John."

Araminta glanced at John, and John reached out and placed Araminta's right hand in his.

Araminta looked at her hand in John's and sighed before turning back at her momma. "Momma, John wanted to come to meet you and Daddy a while ago, but because Isabella was seeing Jeff I---"

Matilda cut Araminta off. "Since you're having a hard time speaking from the heart, Araminta, and John appears to be the reason for it, let's ask John." Matilda turned to John, "John do you have a problem telling me why you came here today?"

John stood. "No, ma'am, I came here because I want to court your daughter, Mrs. Fleming. I told Araminta how I felt months ago, but she kept saying Isabella and Jeff was enough for her parents to handle and we didn't need to start something with one another until possibly much later. Mrs. Fleming, I know your husband is resting, and I wanted to ask both of you if it would be alright for me to come by to spend some time with Araminta." John spoke of his intentions for Araminta, while Araminta focused on the floor.

Matilda stared at her daughter. "John, ask your question again, but to Araminta."

This was a lot for me to take in. I felt like I was back in the stone ages. It was like they were arranging their relationships. I held my tongue as she poured out how she pushed her daughter into the arms of this young man.

Matilda said to Araminta, "Lift your head, Araminta, and listen to what John is asking you, and respond with what your heart is saying to you."

Araminta met John's gaze. "That day in school when I fell playing football, you were the first to run over and ask if I was alright. When I answered, Yes, I think I am fine, just a little sore, you took your hand and wiped the dirt off my forehead several times. I watched you, your eyes, how concerned you were for me. Then when the crowd started to gather, you grabbed your books and vanished. I tried to follow you with my eyes, but too many people blocked my view. Araminta, when I first saw you, I knew I wanted to get to know you; you have such a wonderful heart. The day the teacher asked you to stay after and clean the boards for her, I hid behind the school until the rest of the children left for the day, and when the teacher was in the next room with the principal, I came back to the class only to ask if you have seen my history book. When you responded you would help me look, I wanted to tell you then how I felt, but I didn't want you to think I was being fresh with just us in the class. I have seen you in class before, but that day when I looked into your beautiful brown eyes, I knew I wanted you. You did something to me. Do you remember when you were getting a flower on your desk every day for a week?"

Araminta's eyes flashed. She looked at John and whispered, "Yes...that was you?"

John nodded. "I wanted to make you smile, but every day I watched you hurry and take the flower off the desk before anyone else could see. I saw you stash the flower in your desk, and never take it out again. At the end of the week, I destroyed the first four flowers that were hidden in your desk because they had finally withered and died."

Araminta had wondered what happened to them.

John said, "That's when I knew how incredibly shy you were, and that made me want you even more." John noticed how Araminta's eyes never left his. Her breathing hardened and something had changed.

Araminta felt something for John and didn't hide it. Matilda noticed too, and she watched her daughter.

John told Araminta, "I decided to ask you to lunch with me four months ago to tell you how I felt. That's when you were telling me about Isabella and Jeff being enough for your parents." John knew he had to be patient with her because he felt Araminta was the woman for him, forever.

When Stanley woke up, Matilda would have a lot to tell him about these two wonderful men in their daughter's lives.

I kept telling myself, 'It was the times, it was the times.' I asked, "Did the relationships survive for very long?"

"You'll have to wait to find out. We still haven't gotten to the quilts!"

I raised a hand. "As much as I really want to get to the quilts, can we do that tomorrow? I'm so tired," more tired than I should have been. I had an uneasy feeling about my body, "and Nellie has been kind enough to turn back my bed."

"Yes, dear. Get some rest. We have sixty years to go."

Chapter 10

I woke to coffee and bacon floating in the air. I checked my watch and realized it was six thirty in the morning. Really? Someone was up cooking that early on a Saturday? As much as I wanted to rollover and dismiss the hour, the aroma of good breakfast won out. As I stepped out, my neck was stiff and my body felt unrested.

In the kitchen, Nellie had a three ring circus in full display. She had grits going, bacon on, eggs scrambled, and squeezed her own juice. "My goodness, is that all because I'm here?"

She smiled. "Only the amount. Tildy and I do this every Saturday."

"Why not sleep in?"

"Oh, Tildy is. She won't be up until seven thirty."

I shook my head. "That's not sleeping in."

She circled the table and set a glass of juice before me. "It is in Tildy's world."

I had to talk to her back and she left as quickly as she arrived, back at the stove dropping another two eggs onto a pan. "She's got a lot of energy for a hundred year old."

Nellie stirred gravy. "She lives for her stories, and having you here so she can tell them gives her spunk." She turned to me. "A lot more spunk than she's had in a long time. I think you are like medicine."

I sipped the sweetness of oranges. "I only came down to find out a little about our family. I didn't count on such a well rounded history."

"Well rounded?" She chuckled. "I guess you could call it that. Just keep in mind, Tildy sees things from a unique perspective."

"You mean the third person of herself?"

"She sees herself as a story, and she sees herself telling it."

Nellie didn't offer much else but a cryptic, "Know that she means well." She proposed, "Why don't you shower? The bathroom is free right now and if you wait, you might find Tildy likes to linger under the water, and you may discover all the hot water gone."

"Well, I guess I know where I get that from then."

I took a quick shower and met Matilda in the hallway.

"There still hot water?"

"Yes, ma'am." I had my towel wrapped around me.

She ran a finger along my arm. "Smooth skin. That's a quality the twins had." She continued on her way, slow but steady steps to the bathroom. She was aided by a cane.

"I don't recall you having a cane last night, grandma?"

She faced me as she turned to the bathroom. "I didn't. The mornings take a while for me to get these old bones circulated." She lifted the cane. "This is my morning booster." She winked and continued on.

After breakfast, Matilda insisted we start with the history lesson, even though I insisted that she should let me help Nellie.

"Nellie is fine. She does this every day, and I have yet to hear her complain."

Nellie shooed me away. "Just go, you remember what I said about medicine? Go be a dose."

Nellie must have been everywhere, because back in the front room, the fire burned, and I suspect one of

Nellie's duties was keeping it continuously going. Before I could sit, I got my warning about location.

"Not too close to the fire, please."

"I know." I found my quilt. It may have been September in the Carolinas, but at that time of the morning, a chill from the night before still lingered.

"Are you ready to pick up where we left off?"

We hadn't gotten very far in the story, and I suspected after this day was over, we still wouldn't be to the quilt story. "Yes, I'm ready."

She inhaled and exhaled, as though purging any forgotten thoughts. "John, the boy who came to the party, asserted himself that afternoon in this very front room. He said:

"Will you allow me to show you how very much I care about you?"

Araminta's tears seeped into her beautiful dress. She looked at John. "Yes, yes I will."

John looked at Matilda. 'Do you mind if I hug your daughter, Mrs. Fleming?"

Araminta turned to her Momma and realized Momma's dress was wet as well. John and Araminta walked over, hugged Matilda, embracing until Joseph came running through the back door, yelling, "Where's the birthday cake?"

When the party was over, Jeff and John sat on the front porch with Matilda, Stanley, Araminta, and Isabella drinking lemonade and talking about how their summer went, and how things have changed for all of them.

The next day was the day before the quiltin' contest and Matilda decided to make a chocolate cake to celebrate Matilda's win or loss at the next day's quilt showin'.

The festivities were a little different that year because they added a carnival along with the quilt show. Joseph and Addie were excited about the rides and getting some cotton candy.

Matilda broke her trance and interjected. "They called it 'Fairy Floss' back then." She slipped back in and continued:

Matilda entered her quilts, and she and Stanley walked around to see the other entries hanging up. Matilda gave Isabella, Jeff, and Araminta money to get on the rides at the carnival, and they kept Joseph, Addie, and Lillie close. When they entered one booth, they were surprised to see John. John was there with his father. The booth they were in was the 'Protect the Farmers of Pitt County Association booth.'

Matilda and Stanley hugged John, and John introduced his father to the Flemings.

Stanley said, "It's nice to meet you Mr. Whitney, you have a fine son."

After they met John's father, his father noticed Stanley's injuries and asked him if he was in a car accident? Stanley told him the whole ordeal and John's father stated to his son, "You never told me you knew someone who was hurt farming?"

Matilda said, "John didn't know my husband was hurt while farming, we just met John two days ago at my twin daughter's birthday party."

Mr. Whitney became excited, "This is Araminta's parents?"

John smiled. "Yes, Dad."

Mr. Whitney asked, "Is Araminta here too, I would love to meet my son's girlfriend?"

I stopped her. "Wait. Girlfriend? Didn't you stop them and correct them? I mean, they were just kids."

"I had a feeling about those two, so I had no problems with his presumptions."

I was dumbfounded. "I guess."

"It will all make sense. Let me continue."

The more she talked, the less sense it made. "Very well."

They all laughed and Stanley said, "She is with her siblings somewhere around the carnival."

Mr. Whitney asked Stanley, "Is it okay to turn your name into the committee to be placed on the list for enrollment?"

Stanley didn't understand. "Enrollment?"

Mr. Whitney continued, "Yes, any farmer over forty who gets hurt on their land while farming, no longer has to work his land. The county has a program to have helpers come and till your land and work it twice a week and harvest too."

Stanley and Matilda turned to one another. "I didn't get hurt farming my land; I got hurt helping my brother farm his land."

Mr. Whitney frowned. "I will be right back."

Matilda, Stanley, and John watched John's father walk to another booth. Matilda asked John, "Where is your father going?"

John squinted. "I think he's checking on laws."

Matilda was confused.

"My Dad knows you can't qualify for the program if you didn't get hurt on your land, but he knows I love your daughter, and he is going to the top man to make an exception."

I got this uneasy feeling my great grandparents had been leveraged with bartering for their daughter. "So did his father help you?"

"Hold on." She recalled:

While Matilda held onto Stanley, and Stanley tried to compose himself, Matilda said, "I guess you're that second ram in the bush that I didn't see coming."

Mr. Whitney came running with glean of joy. "I got the approval, you don't ever have to work your land again; it will be worked for you."

I tried to figure out how that could have been arranged so quickly, but I chalked it up to condensing the story, if that was possible with Matilda. "Boy, that was fast."

"Yes it was." She became more animated:

Matilda reached over and hugged Mr. Whitney with teary eyes, and Stanley shook his hand with a strong grip. At that moment, the announcer announced the quilt show was about to begin. Matilda and Stanley had to go.

Chapter 11

I found myself excited to find out about the quilts, and her foray into the twin's lives worked to keep the suspense. I urged her, "And?"

She cautioned me, "There's still some unfinished business. As I was saying," She smiled:

Matilda said, "Araminta will be at the quilt show if you would like to meet her."

Mr. Whitney stood a little taller. "We will be there, Mrs. Fleming."

Stanley and Matilda smiled and hurried to the show.

"Oh goodie. The quilts."

I think I annoyed her. I suspected the quilts, even as central to her life, weren't the most important telling of this part of her life.

She shook her head:

When Matilda and Stanley reached the quilt show, they still had fifteen minutes, so they waited with their children.

Mr. Whitney and John walked in lookin' for Araminta.

Matilda noticed. "Araminta there's John and his father, Mr. Whitney. Come on down so you can meet him."

Araminta was surprised to see John. "Meet him here at the quilt show, Momma?"

Matilda said, "Yes, baby, he's a very nice man, and he just did something wonderful for your daddy. Araminta, you have a wonderful young man in John."

Araminta said, "Alright, Momma."

When John and Mr. Whitney reached the Flemings, Stanley waved to his daughter. "Mr. Whitney, I would like to introduce Araminta Fleming."

John held Araminta's hand and smiled.

Mr. Whitney said, "John you were correct, she is beautiful."

Araminta was embarrassed, and her hand went to her mouth. "Hello, Mr. Whitney."

Mr. Whitney smiled. "Very nice to meet you, Araminta." He turned to his son. "John your momma will be upset that I met Araminta and she didn't; you will have to invite Araminta to dinner."

John bowed. "Araminta would you like to come to dinner with me at my house to meet my mom and brothers and sister?"

Araminta nodded. "Sure, that would be okay."

John turned to Stanley and Matilda. "Would that be alright for Araminta to come to my house for dinner?"

Matilda said, "That would be fine John as long as you allow Araminta's little sister Lillie to come with her."

I was wise to her methods this time and smiled.

Lillie's head snapped up, a frown on her face. "Again, Momma?"

John said, "Sure, Mrs. Fleming, we would love to have Araminta's sister for dinner as well. Thank you."

Matilda pulled Lillie close. "Your sisters should always be chaperoned when dating, Lillie; you will find out when it's your turn."

Lillie objected, "Momma, I don't like boys." Matilda smiled. "For now."

Somehow, I should have known that we wouldn't get to the quilt show too quickly and by my own curiosity, I had to wade into the oddity of such a perceived arrangement. "Grandma, don't you find that it was a bit forward of you to encourage the girls into those relationships?"

She shrugged. "But why? The girls were seventeen, and had not as yet had boyfriends. They were just a few years from marriage."

"You stated earlier that you wanted them to go to college?"

"And they did."

"So those relationships didn't continue?"

"I wouldn't have let them fail if I could help it. Of course they continued."

"You wouldn't let them fail? Isn't it their decision to let things fail or succeed?"

"That's the problem with the world today. We don't take an active role in our children's lives."

I wanted to object, but Nellie has bolted into the room. Her expression was one of uncharted territory, and she glanced with a wary look about fighting this fight. I took her cue and smiled. I bowed out of my objection. "Yes, you are correct. Many bad decisions have been made because children didn't listen to their parents. However, inside, I screamed.

Matilda went on as though my roadblock was nothing more than a speed bump:

The quilt contest was about to begin, and Araminta and John sat together with the Fleming family. Matilda's whole family touched their momma's arms and shoulders for support for all the hard work she did on her quilts. John and his father touched Matilda's shoulder as well.

The announcer said, 'Third place goes to Mrs. Cynthia Davison for her quilt the Purple Swan'. Matilda's shoulders tightened. She breathed in and out. The announcer continued, 'Second place goes to Mrs. Mildred Lee for her quilt the Plaid House.' Matilda breathed a little faster, and her eyes remained closed. The announcer proclaimed, 'First place goes to Mrs. Matilda Fleming for her quilt The Log Cabin.'

I found myself clapping. "Good for you, Grandma."

My great grandmother smiled as though the award was just handed out. Her pride overwhelmed her face, and she bowed her head to me. "Thank you."

"What happened next?"

Well, Matilda's knees wilted. She held on to Stanley, threatening to take him down too, so out of nowhere the two rams in her life carried her to the stand. Tears fell, and her eyes barely opened to see the blue ribbon and the envelope with the ten dollar prize. The newspaperman took a picture, and Matilda insisted everyone join her, including the two rams in the bush. That made the quiltin' show a true blessing and a success beyond measure.

Honestly, I could have done without all the ram in the bush talk, but I loved that she won. It made me appreciate her gift that much more, and I pulled it up around my shoulder and smelled the years of love woven into the fabric.

Chapter 12

"You mentioned the girls went off to college, so did they leave those boys back here in Greenville when they left?"

As though I'd opened a new can of worms, Matilda's eyes lit up. "I'm so glad you asked. I have that story to tell you next."

I looked at my watch. This might take us all the way to lunch. Oh, who was I kidding? This was going to go well into the break of day. "Okay."

She was ready and never broke stride:

Back home after things settled down, Stanley and Jeff surveyed the garden to see if they could harvest some greens for the markets. Matilda sent Joseph out to the garden, dragging Stanley's garden chair. Jeff and Joseph picked enough for the market and plenty for Matilda for Sunday's dinner. Meanwhile, Isabella, Araminta, Lillie, and Addie made plans for a birthday dinner for Jeff. Jeff's birthday was a month away, and Isabella had made plans for his sister to come.

Over that month, the two couples began to forge their relationships, as they spent most of their time together. One afternoon, as they gathered on the front porch, John pulled up and Araminta excused herself to take John to the backyard and let him know what great news she had. As they reach the backyard, they embraced with a kiss and Araminta's tittered with excitement.

John asked, "What's going on? You look so happy."

Araminta said, "I am happy, John, I have some wonderful news."

He rolled his hand. "Okay, give it to me."

She clenched her fist in victory. "The county representative came to the school today to discuss scholarships for our class. As long as the teacher recommends you, and your grades are up to par, we can get a two year scholarship to go to college. We can stay in the dormitory and have breakfast, lunch, and dinner in a real cafeteria, and come home on weekends and holidays. We can also---" Araminta paused at John's sad face. "John, what's wrong? There's nothing to worry about, I asked the teacher for an application for you too, and she has plenty."

John buried his face and turned away. Araminta reached for John's arm, but he pulled away.

She confronted him. "What's wrong, John?" Araminta put her arms around him. "John, please tell me what's wrong?"

John sighed and put his hands on her arms. "Araminta, I didn't know you wanted to go to college. I have been making plans for our future, and college wasn't in the plan. My father talked about college, but he knew the final decision was mine. All I want is to marry the love of my life, and that's you."

Araminta said, "But John, we've not known each other that long."

John shook his head. "A man knows when he has found his wife, and I have found mine."

Araminta tried to absorb his deep feelings. "Then all the more reason. College can help us with jobs and other things we may need for the future. It's for both of us."

John said, "I have to go, Araminta." He hurried to his truck and pulled out.

Araminta's mouth dropped. John drove off the property and disappeared. Araminta needed to consider the pressure. She turned and started her way up the hill to hide her worry. She rested next to a huge tree, drenching her dress with tears until her worry forced her asleep.

I couldn't help but cheer the notion that he had gotten upset, and assumed Matilda would stand by her daughter, and resent that he would try and pressure her to not go to school. "Good for her."

My grandmother did not have a 'good for her' expression and let me know it. "That boy was good stock. We weren't letting it go that easily?"

"We?"

"Stanley and me."

"Oh. Didn't Araminta have a say?"

"She was too young."

My blood pressure rose. "I see."

She continued:

Matilda excused herself and headed in the house looking for Araminta. Seeing John leave abruptly without a goodbye, Matilda knew something was wrong. Matilda couldn't find Araminta in the house, so she knew she had to be off somewhere aching. Matilda checked all the usual spots and she was nowhere to be found. Matilda walked to the woods yelling, "Araminta, Araminta. Where are you?"

The stillness terrified her. She knew John left unhappy and Araminta wasn't with him, so where was she? Matilda went back for help.

She gathered the kids and lanterns and headed back for the forested hilltop. They searched one side of the woods to no avail. They went to the other side, calling out, "Araminta, Araminta!" The night air changed as a cool air settled in.

Isabella noticed something shining off the moonlight. "Momma, look!" Up a slight hill, Araminta's white dress sparkled in the moonbeams.

She rested her head on her arms, sound asleep. "She had been crying and I was angry."

Matilda used the word 'I'. The closer Matilda got to her emotions, the more she slipped into herself. It was the second time she'd used first person to describe something close to her. I let it go.

Isabella and Joseph carried Araminta to the house and Matilda started hot water on the stove to make a bath. She nursed Araminta's hurt feelings with soothing warm water and tucked her into bed. Matilda rubbed her back with homemade cream, a menthol warmth. Matilda lay in

Araminta's bed until Araminta fell back to sleep. Matilda spoke with Stanley, and Stanley thought he should perhaps go talk to the boy.

Matilda stopped him. "John and Araminta will have to sort this out among themselves. Our primary responsibility is taking care of Araminta so she can be ready for school Monday morning."

I wanted to point out that her and Stanley had controlled everything up until then, why did she suddenly insist that kids should sort out a fight? Seems to me that a good parent should have cut bait and run. I gave a weak smile but I wasn't liking this John guy.

Matilda forged ahead:

Matilda awakened the next morning and noticed Araminta on the porch swing drinking a cup of tea. Matilda stepped onto the porch and noticed Araminta's hurting smile. Matilda kissed her daughter's forehead and sat beside her.

Araminta placed her tea on the table, laid her head in her momma's arms and once again started to cry.

"Matilda asked, "Did John hurt you, Araminta?"

Araminta answered, "No, Momma. I think I hurt him."

My jaw dropped. I guess women were conditioned back then. I didn't see how her decision to go to college should have hurt anyone. Had my fiancée told me I had to drop out to get married, he'd be dropped out, on the doorstep with his luggage in hand. I kept my mouth shut and went along. "And?"

My great grandmother pushed it along:

Matilda sat Araminta up in the swing. "What do you mean, you think you hurt him?"

Araminta said, "Momma, you know how excited I was about the scholarship." Matilda nodded and Araminta said, "Well, when I told John about it, he said he had no idea I wanted to go to college. As much as he watches me, and looks in my eyes, and tells me he loves me, how could he not see that? I know we haven't talked about it, and that's only because I had no idea I would get a scholarship to actually go. Momma, I would be happy if it was him who was going and he informed me."

"Matilda said, "I know you would, baby, but why was he so upset, did he have other plans?"

Araminta said, "Yes, Momma, he informed me, after such a short time of dating that he's preparing for our future. He doesn't want me to go to college. I told him college could prepare for our future too. I didn't know what else to say to him. He told me he had to go and left me in the backyard. I was so upset I took a hike into the woods. I'm sorry I worried you, it's just that John loves me, and I had no idea he would react that way."

Matilda said, "Araminta, you need to consider what he wants. He's the man in the relationship."

Araminta had enough. "Momma, I'm going to stop crying and go to school tomorrow, that's all I know for now."

The following Monday when class began, John walked through the door, and Araminta had no idea what to expect.

Isabella turned in her seat. "Whatever you do, do not let him know what your feelings are, ignore him. Do you hear me, Araminta?"

Araminta nodded. "Isabella, I don't think that's going to be a problem. I'm really confused."

Isabella said, "I'll help you?"

Araminta smiled. "Thanks, I need it now."

John sat in his seat behind Araminta. Isabella told Araminta to exchange seats with her. Isabella looked at John before she sat down, and John scowled at her move. When the bell rang for lunch, Isabella grabbed Araminta and rushed out the class and far away from the school. They sat in a small grassy area off a wooded area and spread a blanket and ate their sandwiches.

John knew how to sneak up on the girls. A few minutes later, John and Jeff were behind Isabella and Araminta. As soon as Isabella and Araminta stood, John had Araminta in his arms, and Isabella was frozen, taken by surprise. Jeff's presence took her attention away from John reaching Araminta.

When Isabella saw Jeff helping John, she couldn't believe it."

"Grandma. I need to take a break. I'm not relating to this at all. I'm sorry. Maybe a quick bite will help."

Matilda tilted her head. "What do you mean you aren't relating?"

"I just find this boy's behavior predacious. It's scaring me."

"Have I given that impression?"

Her words stunned me. She had to see that her daughter had no self determination. "You think Araminta made her own decisions?"

"Of course. We guided her, but ultimately she made up her own mind."

"Without the force of others?"

"We would never have allowed that."

"I still need a break. May we get some tea?"

"Feel free, child. Nellie will pour you some."

I felt this distant pain in my arm. Not bad, but aching, as though I'd been hit by something and it was just coming to realization. I stepped away from the room and entered the kitchen.

Nellie had a glass waiting. "Exhausting, isn't it?"

I leaned on the counter and whispered. "Is it just me, or does it seem like women had no say back then."

"Depends upon which women we are talking about. That woman out there in that chair had a whole lot of say."

"So I gather."

"Any more surprises I should expect?"

Nellie leaned in. "Oh, you don't know the extent of the surprises coming."

"Any you want to forewarn me about?"

"It is not for me to tell." She topped off my glass. "Besides, part of the fun is discovery, and I'm sure you will discover a lot in these conversations with Tildy."

Chapter 13

Before I could let Matilda continue with the explanation of how her daughters came to be with the men they were with, I had to decompress. As a black woman in the 70s, I'd fought hard for not only my color but for my gender, and gender defined my strength. I found it ironic that I viewed my great grandmother as having the fortitude of ten women, but that she found her behavior toward her daughter as acceptable. I had to reflect back to Dr. Ramsdell, a history professor my freshman year, who, upon pointing out that turn of the century culture made some pretty sexist laws, said that we have to consider the times, and what was considered acceptable behavior. I finished my tea, let Nellie top it off again, and made my way back to my seat.

"Are you okay, now?"

She didn't really want to know that answer. "Yes, thank you."

Before I could catch my breath, Matilda marched right back to that lunch in the clearing:

Isabella looked at Jeff. "I feel betrayed. Of all people, how can you go against me like this? Are you and John brothers now? You're supposed to be on my side."

Jeff said, "Isabella you never informed me of your plans to protect Araminta from John. I was sitting right next to you in class and you and Araminta talked amongst yourselves and exchanged seats. I knew nothing of your plans. So when John came to me to stop Araminta's protective sister---"

Isabella frowned at John's description of her.

"I was all for it because John came to me." Jeff grabbed Isabella's hand. "I need to talk to you."

Isabella still fumed. "I'm not leaving Araminta alone with John."

John had his arms around Araminta, rubbing her back in a circular motion.

I stopped Matilda. "Wait, isn't that the trick you used to cause Araminta to fall asleep?"

Matilda smiled. "I told you that boy was observant."

"That's grooming, you know that, right?"

"That's love, child."

I was infuriated. In the corner of my eye, I caught Nellie standing at the entrance of the kitchen. Her head swung left and right. She warned me to keep it in check. "Okay, it's love. Please, keep going."

Araminta told John, "You're going to put me to sleep if you keep rubbing my back that way."

Isabella said, "John will you let her loose so she can breathe?"

John disregarded Isabella and never left Araminta's eyes.

Isabella turned to Jeff. "Can you tell John to loosen his hold on Araminta so she can breathe?"

Jeff said, "I think John will make sure he doesn't hurt Araminta. He loves her." Jeff placed his arms around Isabella. "Can you please walk with me Isabella, I wouldn't leave your sister in John's hands if I thought he was going to harm her."

Isabella protested, "But he has harmed her, and I promised Araminta I wouldn't leave her."

Jeff understood a promise, so he asked Araminta if it would be okay if he and Isabella went twenty feet away.

Araminta nodded.

Isabella looked at Jeff and then to Araminta. She picked up her lunch and blanket and left with Jeff.

John held Araminta, cuffing her head with his hand close to his face.

Jeff said, "You have always been protective of Araminta, haven't you?" Isabella said, "I have to, I love her too much to let anyone harm her. Araminta will do anything for me, it's the least I can do. Protecting her is something she could always count on from me. Araminta is so fragile and that's why my mother still babies her when she's been harmed. Araminta and I are twins, but we are different in many ways. Araminta is more responsible, very easy to love, will do anything for anyone, smart, cries easy, and is very unsure she's ever needed."

Jeff said, "And you?"

Isabella laughed. "Well, I am not quite Araminta; you have to get to know me to love me. I will do for people, mostly if I know you, I'm very aware of my surrounding, I'm smart but I had to work at it, I don't cry, I am more sure of myself than Araminta, I'm outgoing, and I go after what I want."

Jeff stared at Isabella.

Isabella winked.

He grabbed Isabella's hand and stared passionately into her soul. "I know you think you and Araminta are different, but you and Araminta are more alike than you think. Doesn't your mother baby you when you've been harmed?"

Isabella said, "Of course not. I never show that side of me to my momma. I don't want her to worry, whereas Araminta tries not to show things to Momma, but my momma always catches it."

Jeff said, "Well what are you going to do when Araminta gets married and moves away? Will you let her husband take care of her?' Jeff thought Isabella had that extra sense like her momma.

Isabella said, "Jeff you know something about Araminta and John that you're not sharing with me?"

Jeff said, "John is telling Araminta about his feelings for her."

Araminta meanwhile was trying to remove John's hands, but John said, "I'm not moving from you." John had a serious command to his voice.

Araminta pleaded, "John, I want to go back to class."

John reached down to Araminta's chin and lifted her head. "Do you think I would have made all these plans if I was to lose you to an accident? I know I hurt you, but if you let me explain, give me a chance to prove how very much a part of my life you are." He whispered, "You'll see that I am worth it."

Araminta worked to get loose. "Well, okay, but lunch is over, and the bell will ring in a few minutes, and--_"

"Can I walk with you to class?" John kept hold of her hand.

Araminta gave in. "Yes."

John released her. They walked and John started to tell a story. "Araminta, when I left you last week, my head was everywhere. First, I want to apologize. Please tell me you forgive me, I will make it up to you."

"I forgive you, John." Araminta said what she knew he'd approve of.

John said, "Thank you. I will apologize to your entire family for upsetting them and having them search the woods for you. I would do nothing in this world to hurt you, and I am glad your sister is very protective of you. I can't be mad at her for that." John kissed Araminta on the cheek. He realized why he fell in love with her – it was her forgiving heart. "Jeff came to my house and told me your family had to search for you and found you asleep. I know I'm going to have to make this up to your mother and father."

Araminta said, "And Isabella too, she was the one who spotted me in the woods."

John said, "I will, I can't have your family hating me. I love them all."

Araminta said, "My family is fine, John. They love you."

All the preparation's John and Jeff made for Araminta and Isabella were for the girls' benefit, their future. How could anyone stay mad with John? John worked on Saturday and sometimes after school with his dad. Since the first time John met Araminta, he had started preparing for a future with her, and he didn't know her, other than when she asked him if he was alright after a football accident. John always thought anyone that sweet had to be his. He had saved so much money for a house and land for them. John told Araminta all this after he heard Araminta's story about going to college. Later, John told Araminta how he and Jeff talked about his plan and how they secretly searched for a house and land together for the twins.

Isabella had no idea what the two of them were up to the past few weeks. Only John's parents knew, and he wanted to keep it a secret until Christmas. John knew Araminta's favorite holiday was Christmas, and he wanted to propose to her on her favorite holiday in front of the entire family. When Araminta mentioned the college representative that day, John and Jeff knew the money they saved was being placed on land that Jeff, John, and John's parents were signing that afternoon. He didn't know what to tell Araminta. He had to try and stop her plans.

John asked Araminta to ask her momma and daddy if John and his parents, along with Jeff, could meet her family that night to discuss the future, and what happened.

Araminta relented, "Okay, I'm sure they will want to have your parents over for dinner."

John said, "Are you sure that will be okay with your momma?"

Araminta said, "I'm sure, it's fine, dinner is at six, but of course you know that. I will let my momma know about the meeting as well. Can you come fifteen minutes before six to try and calm my daddy down about the woods? If we can't calm Daddy down, then there will be no need for a meeting."

John said, "I will be there early." John kissed Araminta goodbye as Araminta broke away and hurried back to class.

When class ended, John insisted the twins ride with him and Jeff. When they made it to the house, Araminta jumped out and ran inside.

Jeff told Isabella not to tell Matilda, as Araminta had to focus on how to pull that one off. The truth was, Araminta did tell Matilda, and Matilda was very happy the two had patched things up, but Araminta didn't want her relationship with John to stop her from college.

I shouted, "Good for her!"

Grandma shook her head at me:

Araminta decided that if everyone wanted her with John, she'd have to figure out how he could go to college too. How could he when he had to work to pay off the land?

John was ahead of her though. He knew he had Matilda wrapped about his finger, and he was sure buying a house and land would make her daddy fall in line as well. That land and house was worth more than a girl going to college.

I shook my head. "So you wanted them to get married and settle down on land rather than go to college?"

"Hush now, child. You don't know that. I had no intentions of those girls not goin' to college. I just needed to figure out how to get those boys in college too. They were plannin' for a future, and how they would care for them."

There was nothing I could say. She clearly didn't see the harm of her actions, and she definitely didn't see John as a predator. Somehow I saw this story having a miserable ending, but as I had quickly discovered, I wasn't going to find that out anytime soon. "So what happened next?"

Matilda smiled:

It was about five p.m., and the Whitney's would arrive before six. Isabella was in the barn with Jeff and Lillie discussing what was going to happen that night. Matilda didn't know what the meeting was about, but she wanted to talk to John and Araminta for a few minutes before dinner. At five-forty, John showed up. Matilda had just finished the food and extinguished the fire in the stove's belly. She placed the food on the table. Matilda told the kids to wash up for dinner. She put her apron over a chair and told Araminta to come with her to the front porch.

"Good Evening, Mrs. Fleming," John hugged Matilda and Araminta.

Matilda looked at John, knew that there would be hell to pay with Stanley about Araminta being left in the woods alone. Matilda had already forgiven John, but she needed to make sure John never hurt Araminta like that again, so she could go to bat for him with her husband.

John asked, "Araminta can you sit down." He moved with Matilda to the swing. Araminta had to let this play out.

She knew that the more John talked the more he was going to win over her parents. Maybe if he could, maybe he was the right man for her. He cared about her; he never let her out of his sight when they were together.

John and Matilda laughed a few times. John had assured her that he was going to take care of not only the family he created with Araminta, but also for her parents.

"John gave a deep apology. "Mrs. Fleming, I am so sorry about what happened to Araminta. I love her with all my heart, and I would never have left if I had known she would be that upset. I have been making plans for my future with your daughter since the day I fell playing football. Did she tell you about that?"

Matilda smiled and nodded.

John said, "Anyone that sweet to talk to a dirty football player was someone I had to pursue. I know Araminta is sensitive, and very fragile, and there's no way I could ever take advantage of that. I told my father about Araminta after the football game, and he said he would support me in anything I needed for Araminta."

He stood and walked over to Araminta on the steps. "Can you walk down the dirt road and wait for my parents?"

"Yes, John."

Matilda looked at Araminta. "When you get them, please have everyone seated and say grace and make sure the food is ready on the table."

Araminta said, "Yes, Momma."

"Araminta ran down and waited. When John's parents arrived, she led them back up to the house and past Matilda and John.

John admitted, "I sent Araminta to walk my parents up because I didn't want her to hear what I was about to tell you, Mrs. Fleming. I told my Dad I wanted to marry Araminta someday, and I needed help trying to purchase land to build a house for us. Mrs. Fleming, my Dad worked for the county for so many years. He knows a lot about doing things that are free for county residents, and I knew he could let me know how I could pull this off. Mrs. Fleming sometimes men have a one track mind, and I thought I knew your daughter. That day when she told me about college, I didn't know what to say. It threw me, and I didn't see that one coming. However, I spoke to my daddy, and we will help you and Stanley out if you can see to it that Araminta gives up this nonsense about college. I can make her life ten times what college can." He stood, "I have plans. I'm going to own hundreds of acres before long. Daddy and me have a plan."

I interrupted Grandma. "I am perplexed. I know you told me that they went to college, but the road you are leading me down, isn't sounding like it."

Matilda smiled. "This is what I told that boy."

John, I wholeheartedly support you marryin' my daughter, but you want a smart woman, and college woman is a smart woman. Don't stop those dreams."

John shook his head. "Now you pert near know she can't go to no college if we get married. I can't have my wife away from the farm."

Matilda said, "Then go with her."

John stared. "Go with her?"

Matilda nodded. "Yes. Get some farmin' classes or those fancy animal classes where you fix them."

John hesitated, "You know that might be doable." He stopped Matilda. "I need to ask my father something. Let me get back to you."

John went in and he had a private meeting with his father, came back out all smiles. "I can't tell you now, before we have the meeting, my dad will explain in detail about it. There is a way for Jeff and me to go to college with Araminta and Isabella. Mrs. Fleming, I don't want to have this meeting if you feel I'm not the right man for Araminta. I hope you can continue to grow and love me as your daughter's husband someday."

John formed tears. He stopped and took Matilda's hand, studying the wedding ring on her finger. "Where did you get Araminta's wedding ring, Mrs. Fleming?" She pulled her hand away and held it up between them. 'This? This is mine. Stanley bought this for me eighteen years ago when he ask me to marry him."

John shook his head, puzzled, and pulled a box out of his pocket. He gave it to Matilda.

Matilda looked at John. "What is this?"

John said, "It's for Araminta."

Matilda opened the box and Araminta's ring fell onto her lap. John and Matilda smiled as she picked up the precious jewel and laughed at the moment. Matilda said, "Now how could I not let my daughter marry a man with good taste. You picked the same ring for Araminta that my husband picked for me."

"You got played, Grandma."

"Excuse me?"

"He saw your ring and duplicated it. This kid manipulated all of you."

"You take that back." She scolded me. "He did no such thing. Now I might be kinder to him than you think I should be, but that boy put his heart and soul into Araminta."

I was wrong to say what I said, and I knew it, but my instinct bled of creepiness about this kid, who would now be close to sixty years older than me. "Forget I said that. I was just caught up in the moment."

"You have nothing to be forgiven for. When you hear the whole story, you will understand."

I wasn't sure about that. So far, my great grandmother had not said anything about John that I liked. However, I had to take her at her word. "Fine."

"Now, where was I?"

Did she really want me to say where?

"The ring, yes." She held up her finger and showed the pattern in question.

John said, "That was a surprise to me too, but I don't plan on asking Araminta to marry me until Christmas."

Matilda asked, "Then why do you carry the ring around with you?"

John said, "Knowing it will be with my future wife someday, I carry it to remind me every morning when I wake, and every night when I sleep, now and then this ring will be there."

Nellie defused the moment. "Hey, why don't you two break for lunch?"

I turned to Matilda and noticed how alive she'd become. Nelly was right, recalling these events did give her a boost. "Is that good with you, Grandma?"

"Oh yes, let's eat first.

It would be good to slip away from the past and talk
a little here and now for a bit.

Chapter 14

Nellie dished up breaded pork cutlets with redeye gravy and spooned out some collard soup. There's nothing lady like to sipping collard soup, and even though I did my best, my two hostesses didn't seem to care. Nellie could cook, and I was happy she was there for Matilda. "This is really good, Nellie."

She slid some cornbread toward me. "Thank you." I avoided sparking up any conversation about the history of the Flemings, opting to wait and let Matilda spill it out in her own unique way. I kept circling back to her insistence that John was a good man. I supposed, if Araminta married John, she had a lifetime of getting to know him, and perhaps time changed the perspective on him. I was astounded by her recollection, down to some minute details, of events that happened sixty years before.

I think Matilda rehearsed for our next session because she was overly reserved at lunch, and Nellie didn't bother her train of thought. For me, I followed suit.

"Don't run off you two, I have pecan pie too."

I teased her. "What do you do in here all day, cook?"

"Matilda enjoys good food, so I guess the answer is yes. I probably do more cooking than cleaning."

Matilda chimed in with a friendly dig. "She's better at cooking than cleaning anyway."

I scanned a spotless home. "She must be an incredible cook than."

Nellie grinned. "Thank you."

Matilda lifted off her soup. Thick glasses gave her eyes an owl like quality. She faced Nellie. "Yes, yes she is. She is a gem, and gems are hard to find."

Nellie waved her off. "It's the company I keep that makes me who I am."

I interrupted their good will toward each other. "I want to get back to the story, but would it be possible for me to take a walk first?"

Matilda piped up. "Absolutely, but I can't go with you. I'd only slow you down." She cackled at her joke.

"If you want some company, I am due for a walk myself." Nellie offered.

"That would be wonderful."

We walked out back of the property, and up into the woods. The afternoon sun had warmed the day and Nellie gathered I hadn't come prepared for the south. "You're a little overdressed for our temperature changes."

I had on a thick wool sweater. "It shows, huh?"

She smiled. "I hope you have a shirt under it, or this walk will be short."

I did, and I removed my sweater and tied it around my waist. We turned and took in the valley.

"You know, Tildy talks fondly about this area. In her stories, you will hear about the farming, the hills, the old barn that used to sit right there." She pointed to the clearing between the house and where we stood.

Seeing the house from the backside triggered something. "I had the weirdest dream last night."

"About?"

"Well, I saw my grandmother Addie in that house as a young adult. She was surrounded by children. Matilda didn't recognize them, but they appeared to know Addie. Matilda seemed horrified. The children did adult things. I kept wondering if these were the siblings of Addie, the ones I've never met."

Nellie turned and studied my face. "Did Tildy talk about all her kids?"

"Not yet, just the twins."

"The twins?"

"Yes, Isabella and Araminta."

She inhaled the fresh clean air of a Carolina fall day. "I see." She smiled. "Maybe those are the children you are seeing."

"She discussed them as adults."

Nellie's head tilted, as though curious. "She did?"

"Yes. Is there something wrong with that?"

She wanted to say something. I could feel it, but she rubbed my shoulder and pointed up the trail for us to continue. "So tell me more about the dream."

"A child stood on a chair cooking dinner."

"That would have been Lillie."

"A little boy sat at a chair and pretended to be a newscaster, reporting an upcoming storm."

Nellie walked alongside me. "Not sure who that was, unless it was Joseph, but there wasn't television back when Joseph was that age."

"I didn't gather that it was back then. It felt current."

"Have you discussed this with Tildy?"

"No, should I?"

"If you do, you know you will be in for about five hours of explaining what it means? She will tell you why her kids have come visiting your dreams." She grinned and urged me to keep up with her. "Keep going."

"They were young but had the vocabulary of professors."

"I'm sure you are blending your college life with the stories Tildy has been weaving for you."

"Probably."

"Was there more?"

"A little boy played a trumpet, and a little girl twirled a baton. The little girl had a majorette uniform on and marched to the sound of the trumpet."

"You have as active an imagination as Tildy."

"Maybe not. I think the trumpet player was my dad. He plays the trumpet, and my Aunt was the little girl."

"You don't have a fever do you?"

I sighed. "I actually feel sore, but I'm fine. Just all the intake of information is flooding me with childhood memories."

Nellie gave a cryptic response. "Yeah, but whose childhood?"

"There's more."

"Okay."

"There was a man against the wall in an Army uniform holding a boy's bike and a girl's bike."

"Hmm."

"What?"

"That sounds like Joseph. He was in the army."

"Nellie, what does it all mean?"

She laughed. "Maybe my cooking didn't agree with you."

"Well, if I really want to know more, I suppose we both know who will have some suggestions."

She chided me. "Careful what you ask for. You might be down here a month with us if you do."

"That might not be too bad. I certainly have enjoyed Matilda's recalling of her past."

Again Nellie hesitated. "Yes, well, make sure you keep things in perspective. She is a hundred and sometimes she isn't completely straight on the facts."

"I'll keep that in mind. Thanks."

We completed our loop and found ourselves heading back down the hill to the house.

Chapter 15

When we made it back to the house, Matilda had moved my chair farther from the fireplace.

She offered, "I assumed you worked up a lather so the fire might be a little too warm."

She was right, but I suspected that wasn't her motive. "Thank you." I excused myself to take a shower first, and when I returned she had the anticipation of a schoolgirl, sitting with a wide smile and ready to return to her recollections.

"Okay, Grandma, let's go." I settled in, clicked my pen, and opened my tablet.

"So, we were discussing the night John and his family came to the Fleming house for dinner."

John and Matilda knew they missed dinner. It was seven o'clock, and the meeting was about to start. John hugged his future momma-in-law and kissed her on the cheek.

John said, "I will take good care of Araminta."

Matilda kissed John on the cheek as well. "I know you will."

John thought his future momma-in-law would never be a momma-in-law to him, but a just momma.

The meeting started after Matilda hugged the Whitneys. Araminta got John a plate of food, and Isabella got Matilda the same. John and Jeff stood and asked Stanley and Matilda, and John's parents, "Would it be okay if Araminta and Isabella, and the kids not sit through this meeting? Mr. and Mrs. Fleming can they go to the barn."

Matilda understood why, but Araminta and Isabella thought it was unfair. Araminta felt as though her feelings wouldn't be addressed.

Isabella said, "I waited all day for this."

Araminta added, "John please, I waited for this meeting as well."

Araminta stiffened as John kissed her on the cheek. "I will come out to the barn and get you as soon as it's over."

Isabella agreed but Araminta refused. "This is about me; we are part of this family too."

John grabbed Araminta's hand. "For me?"

Araminta turned to her momma who gave her a nodding wave to leave. Isabella sighed, "Let's just go, sis."

Jeff kissed Isabella's forehead, and she pulled Araminta along with the rest of her siblings.

John promised, "We will make this as quick as we can."

Matilda said, "Take a quilt, and when you come in bring some firewood to the porch for the fireplace and stove."

Jeff interrupted, 'We will do that after the meeting, Mrs. Fleming."

I interrupted. "You let that boy dictate the meeting? Didn't you find that a bit insolent?"

"Child, he was one of the rams in the bush."

If I had to hear that term one more time, I was going to scream. "I see."

She moved along:

After the kids left, Mr. Whitney stood up and gave the details of the meeting. He said, "John, Jeff, myself and Mrs. Whitney purchased twenty-five acres. The land has five houses and a foundation built for a church for Jeff."

Stanley and Matilda were shocked at the amount of land bought. Jeff and John never told Matilda or the twins of their lofty goals.

Jeff stood. "Mr. and Mrs. Fleming, I love your daughter Isabella, and I want to marry her someday. I want to make one of the houses hers and share the land with John and Araminta. There are five houses there, and we will offer the houses to each of your daughters and son. We will farm the land, and one day take care of your grandchildren. We can build a house in case you want to live there too. We ask nothing of you Mr. and Mrs. Fleming."

I begged to differ. "Excuse me, Grandma, they were asking that you hand over their daughters without their permission."

"Child, in that day and age, to have such a prize of a man come into your life was a blessing."

"For who? You?"

Matilda froze. Her thoughts adrift. She turned to me. "For everyone."

I wanted to cry for a woman I had never met, but who seemed so vulnerable in a world dominated by men, and without her mother as her armor against it all. "I have a hard time with that."

"Let me continue." She exhaled:

John stood. "This is our gift to show you how much we love your daughters. Mr. Fleming we wanted to know if we could employ your log cabin acquaintances to help us add on and build up the houses. We will help of course."

Mr. Fleming said, "Sure, boys, whatever you need, it's yours."

Jeff said, "Mr. and Mrs. Fleming, do you object to me marrying Isabella?"

Stanley and Matilda shared a moment and turned back to Jeff. "No Jeff, we think you would make a wonderful husband for Isabella." Matilda continued, "We love you Jeff as our son already."

Jeff eased a joyful smile. "I wanted to propose to Isabella on Christmas along with John if that would be okay with you?"

My contemporary woman roared, "Shouldn't that have been Isabella's decision and not you and Stanley's?"

Matilda just stared at me and didn't miss a beat:

Matilda began to cry. "Anything you want, Jeff."

Stanley said, "It would be fine with us Jeff."

When John stood to join Jeff in the request, Stanley had a few words for him. "I do hope that if you are planning to make the same proposal that I won't see a repeat performance of the other night, young man?"

John nodded. "I've told Mrs. Fleming how sorry I am for what happened with Araminta. Had I known she would do something so foolish, I wouldn't have driven off. She certainly needs a responsible man who can guide her behavior."

My head jerked and tilted, but Matilda didn't notice my irritation by his complete lack of respect for Ariminta.

Stanley said, "Matilda told me about you, John, and if I have your assurance, I accept too."

John smiled. "You do, and thank you, sir, I am honored. I love Araminta very much."

Stanley smiled, pleased that his daughter had met this young man with so much promise.

John said, "That's basically it, if anything comes up we will let you know. Jeff and I would, well, we want to keep the engagement a secret from Araminta and Isabella, can we agree to do that?"

I waved to Matilda to get her attention. "If the girls don't know then how is that an engagement?"

"They made the plans with us."

I held my tongue.

Matilda had no intention of letting me derail the story:

All the parents agreed.

John said, "We wanted to start new jobs with the Wilson Firm next July, but that was before Araminta told us about the college scholarship. My dad has informed me of something that may make everyone happy."

Mr. Whitney stood. "Mr. and Mrs. Fleming, I know the firm that John and Jeff will be working for, and they said they have opportunities for people to go to school with scholarships. I've done a few favors for them as well, and I am certain that they will cover scholarships for the boys. They will make it a company improvement scholarship, and they will pay for school starting next August. They will also pay them as if they were physically on the job at the Wilson Firm. They welcome college bound students who are willing to study agricultural science and help build the corporation for years to come."

Jeff looked at John. The news caught him off guard. "That's great news, John."

John whispered, "But my father tells me that we will have to wait for four years before getting married."

Mr. Whitney nodded. "Yes, the scholarships require that the recipients be non married."

Matilda wondered how that would affect the plans to build on the farmland.

Jeff wasn't happy about waiting to marry his love. John too had concerns, but knew the alternative was worse. "Jeff, Mr. and Mrs. Fleming want their daughters to go to school." He pulled Jeff aside. "But if they should find school doesn't agree with them," he winked, "then we could always get married sooner."

I uttered, "So did they sabotage their college careers?"

"Hang in there, child." Grandma smiled:

John started to think about what Araminta told him about the college program, and how he responded. He knew to keep his mouth shut and let Araminta and Isabella's parents make the call. He and Jeff were just holding on waiting for their answers. They knew their majors would be agricultural science for John and seminary for Jeff.

I had to offer, "The girls are going to be going off to college not even aware that they are being married off."

Clearly, great grandma and I were not seeing eye-to-eye on the rights of women. She put her hand out to settle me down and continued:

Stanley and Matilda spoke among themselves, while everyone waited. John and Jeff waited, worried what might be the outcome.

Mr. Whitney broke the silence. "Mr. and Mrs. Fleming, we know this is a surprise to you as well as it is to John and Jeff. We know the outcome is on you because John and Jeff will have to attend for four years regardless." John's dad looked at John and Jeff. "They don't have a choice in the matter. I also know how you feel about college for your daughters. No one here can decide what's good for your girls, I feel like they are my girls too, but you have to decide. If you want to wait another day or days, we can set this up for another day."

John looked at his dad in disbelief. He didn't want to wait that long.

Stanley stood for the first time. "We didn't know we could send our children to college at all, because of the cost.

When Araminta came home to say they could go to college for free, well we were very excited. My wife and I cannot read or write, but we are so excited that our children can. I know our decision will affect the children's future with each other. Mr. Whitney I love your son and I have told Jeff that about him on numerous occasions, I love you as my own son. What my wife and I decided will be one we hope John and Jeff can help us with."

John and Jeff remained hopeful.

Stanley said, "First, John and Jeff, what I'm about to say is something I hope you can keep to yourselves and not tell Araminta or Isabella. I need your answer before I can go on."

John looked at Stanley. "Uh, yes, Mr. Fleming, we promise not to say anything."

Stanley proceeded. 'Well, we don't want to make any of you unhappy, but one thing we do know is that if Araminta and Isabella can receive a college education for free we prefer them to go for four years."

Mr. Whitney agreed.

Stanley said, "My suggestion, and the help from you that I need is for you and Jeff to come up with a plan that will make me and my wife know that if we agree to a summer wedding in 1929 when the four-year college is over, you two will promise, not only me and my wife, but your mother and father that the girls will graduate on time. I mean the graduation of 1927, and I expect to be seated in the audience seeing my two girls walking across the stage receiving their degrees." Stanley choked up.

Matilda took over. "I know if one of my daughters gets with child, it may be difficult for them to finish, but my husband and I can't control that. We are just asking for your help. We want you to help us continue to make you happy because you are our sons too." Matilda looked at Mr. and Mrs. Whitney. "Does that sound fair to you?"

John interrupted, "What if they decide they don't want to continue?"

Matilda shrugged. "I hadn't thought of that, but if it happens, then it happens."

Mr. Whitney looked at John's mother and nodded. "Yes, that sounds very fair." He turned to his son, "Mr. and Mrs. Fleming have been very fair to you. If you didn't know they loved you before, you should know it now. I know you and Jeff will make the right decision for

Araminta and Isabella during those four years. Okay, it's up to you. Today is Monday."

Mr. Whitney looked at Stanley. "Can we meet back here Friday at seven to see what the boys have come up with?"

Stanley nodded. Matilda said, "That sounds fair, I will take care of the children in the barn again."

John and Jeff stood, realizing how heavy a weight this was on them. John said, "We will start planning today."

Stanley said, "Remember you are not to discuss this with Araminta or Isabella. We agree?"

John and Jeff agreed.

Mr. Whitney said to his son, "If you feel this is too much for you, we can always plan a wedding for summer 1929."

John said "Okay, Dad. I want to get Araminta, Isabella, and the kids back in the house before it gets too chilly for them."

"Mr. and Mrs. Whitney hugged the Matilda and Stanley and left for home.

Stanley asked Jeff, "How is the kerosene furnace working out in the barn, is it keeping the place warm?"

Jeff said, 'It's better with the furnace, I enjoy it, it's so warm now, thanks.'

Matilda said, "If it gets too cold you make sure you come in the house and sleep in Joseph's room."

Jeff said, "I will, thanks."

Matilda added, "Take some extra quilts before you turn in."

Jeff said, "Yes Ma'am."

John went with Jeff to the barn and told Araminta to wait for him in the house while he and Jeff brought wood up.

Araminta obeyed. "Okay."

The young men brought plenty of wood to the porch. They ran back to the house to see Araminta and Isabella.

"Time out" I had to take a break. Matilda liked to cover the minutiae of her stories, and I needed to digest the overall gist of what had just taken place. "So these two young women are unknowingly getting married to their boyfriends, is that right?"

"With the loves of their lives."

"You mean the loves of you and Stanley's lives?"

"That too."

It just wasn't making Matilda sound progressive. My tone must have alerted Nellie because she dropped in with some Chamomile tea. "You look like you could use something relaxing."

"You mean I sound like I could use something relaxing." We exchanged winks.

I had to take everything in. I jotted down notes for the future, names, places, questions. If I thought the quilt story took awhile, I knew we were in for a long story on this engagement and college one.

Chapter 16

I tried to work a lonely kink out of my neck. It had stiffened something awful. "So did the girls get to college?" I tried to move the story along.

Matilda reminded me. "Oh, so much more has to happen first. Just wait. We are getting there."

Patience would be a virtue.

She ripped right into where she left off:

John told Matilda that he and Jeff would chop wood that weekend. He said, "You can never have enough wood. I will be on the porch with Araminta."

Matilda said, "Okay John, but only for fifteen minutes, it's still a school night."

John said, "Yes Ma'am."

Jeff kissed Isabella on the lips and told her he would see her in the morning. Jeff ran to the barn.

John grabbed Araminta and kissed her as well.

Araminta couldn't feel the cold air against John's stature.

He had ten inches on her, and bent as he ran his lips across hers. She was warm, and so was he. They sat on the swing for a few minutes, and he told her the meeting went well. "Araminta what if I told you I was going to college with you for those four years? Would that put you at ease about our relationship?"

Araminta's head lightened. He was going to go with her? "I guess."

He had a puzzled look. "You guess? You mean of course it will. We'll be together."

She smiled. "Yes, yes of course."

John's eyebrows raised. "I will be in the men's dormitory, across the way from your dormitory, but I'm sure there will be times I can sneak over."

Araminta nodded, "And I suppose we can eat breakfast and lunch and dinner together, and study in the library too."

John was elated. "I will drive you home every weekend, and bring you back on Sunday night." He hugged her. "I want you to go in the house and stay warm. I will see you in class tomorrow."

Araminta hugged John, and he planted a kiss on her before he left. She waved. "Goodnight, John."

John said, "Goodnight, my future."

Araminta exhaled and turned to leave. John moved around her and opened the door for her and shut it behind her. Araminta watched him through the window as he drove off.

As much as I had wanted to object, I found this odd union developing. I couldn't say it wasn't Stockholm Syndrome, but if Matilda was telling the story as it actually happened, then it appeared Araminta was giving in to John.

On Friday night, the kids were herded in the barn, and John and Jeff stood in front of the parents with their answer. John spoke first, "Mom and Dad, Jeff and I thought this through all week, and we feel we can get married in 1927 and go to college and have everyone graduate in 1927. It's a challenge we are willing to take. Mr. Fleming you will be at that graduation in 1927 to see all four of us marching across that stage. I speak for Jeff when I say we will not let you down. We are so glad we have a wonderful support system."

"Grandma, did you really think that being engaged in college was a good thing?"

"In the twenties, if a woman went to college, they might very well have been married."

I thanked my lucky stars I wasn't from the twenties.

Jeff stepped forward. "To have my future wife's parents watch her walk across that stage is a dream of mine I wish my own parents could have seen. I promise it will happen for Isabella. Thank you for trusting me, I won't let you down."

The parents all hugged Jeff and John, and John and Jeff promised to never discuss with the girls until after graduation. The wedding would be the summer of 1927.

I put my pen down and took a long steady drink of chamomile. I needed it.

Chapter 17

"Matilda, I'm not sure what you like about that John boy, but I'm going to assume he grew on you, because everything you've mentioned so far makes him seem kind of domineering."

Matilda reminded me. "Men were domineering, good God fearing men back then, but there are reasons I speak highly of John. I know the rest of the story." She leaned in, "Did you know he saved Araminta from a kidnapping?"

My curiosity piqued. "What?"

"Uh huh."

"Carry on then, I want to hear this."

Matilda smiled:

Jeff's surprise birthday party was a complete success. Jeff's oldest brother, Clifton, was there, and his sister Katie, too. Addrianna was there with her family. Everyone ate so much food they were all taking turns using the outhouse. It was John's turn and Araminta was next. Araminta headed out there when John came back into the house. They kissed and she continued on.

When Araminta came out of the outhouse, someone put a bag over her head and muffled her attempts to scream. Someone said, "Put a note on the door." They dragged her away, and threw her into a truck. Two men drove off with her.

John thought Araminta had fallen in the outhouse and came out to look for her when he found the note. His heart raced as he read it.

You stole our jobs. We would have
had those jobs if you and your buddy
hadn't come along with your daddy
and he knows the boss. I know they
would have given us the jobs if you
didn't come in the office that day.
Well we have your girlfriend, so
either quit your job or pay a ransom,
you have two days to decide. If you
choose the ransom, you will deliver
it alone at the window factory, on
Sunday, $200.00, leave it in an
envelope under the third gate

marked 'south.' Remember no

police.

Fear shot across John's chest. How could he tell Araminta's mother her baby had been kidnapped? John was angry his baby was in the hands of mad men, angry at the world because they couldn't get a job. If they hurt her he would get his revenge. John stopped his thinking. He knew Araminta wouldn't want him to get upset; he could hear her talking to him. How could he be without his life for two days? They wanted him to hand over two hundred dollars and they would return her. How was he going to come up with that kind of money and not let anyone know she was gone? John didn't know what to do. He didn't want to take the chance of Araminta being hurt. He heard Jeff go into the barn, and ran after him. John told Jeff to read the note.

Jeff looked up at John. "I remember those two guys."

John said, "I do too, but I have no idea where they live or who they are."

Jeff said, "We could go to the Wilson firm tomorrow and inquire around."

John said, "Jeff, I have Araminta's daddy I have to deal with tonight. The last thing I told him when he forgave me for leaving his daughter in the woods was, 'I will take care of her.' What can I tell him now?"

Jeff said, "I'd worry more about her momma. She'll likely skin your hide."

John shook his head. "Let's go see my dad."

He turned and said, "You tell Isabella that Araminta is with us and that we will be back. I know Mrs. Fleming is going to fuss about the school night, but I can deal with that much." While John and Jeff drove to John's parents, John began to realize that he couldn't hide the fact that she was missing, not even for two days. Matilda and Stanley's daughters had never been out of their sight for a day, let alone two days. She needed to be back with her family. He needed her.

John and Jeff reached the house. John's dad was about to retire for the evening when John burst in and said he needed to talk to him. After showing his father the note, John's father got dressed and said they would have to tell the Flemings the truth.

"What were you thinking son? You can't keep that from her parents."

John raised his voice, "But I feel responsible."

His father raised his voice louder, "Doesn't matter, think! Use your head." Mr. Whitney gathered his wife and the four of them headed back to the Fleming household.

After telling Stanley what happened, and showing the note, Stanley said, "We have no choice, we have to go to the police."

John protested. "This is my future wife, and we will do what the note says. I'm in control here, this was meant for me."

Stanley stepped close enough for John to feel the heat coming from Stanley's anger. "You will do as I say. Are we clear on that?"

John wasn't bending. "Who is the note to?"

John stepped closer. "I don't care. Who is her father?"

Mr. Whitney stepped between the two. "Mr. Fleming is correct, son. This is his call."

John began to cry. He needed to be the one to save her; he was her knight in shining armor.

Stanley took the note, turned to his wife and said, "Stay here in case she should make it back."

Mr. Whitney went with Stanley, and his wife stayed to comfort Matilda.

John, however, had other plans. He grabbed Jeff. "Come on, we are going to drive around and see if we can find something suspicious."

John headed out route 50, not sure where to go, but checking every car they passed or came up on. Anything that looked out of the ordinary, he was going to check.

Jeff offered, "You know, if they headed out this way, they might need to get gas. There's not much else after the Perry gas station. Maybe they saw something?"

John turned. "That's a good idea." They drove the half hour to Perry's and pulled in, a lonely pole light gave an ominous glow to an otherwise dark night. John got out of his truck and went to the gas attendant. "You pump gas for two black fellas like us?"

A wiry old man with weathered skin and salty hair nodded, "Sure did." He eyed John. "Why you ask?"

John said, "They took something that belongs to me."

The old man smiled. "You mean a young lady?"

Jeff's head snapped around and John closed in.
"Yeah, you saw her?"

He smiled. "Saw her? While they used the restroom,
I helped her out of their truck and stuck her in the shop.
They came out mad as hornets, and looked and looked for
her, but I hid her pretty good."

John asked, "Is she still here?" The old man
motioned for the boys to follow him. "A lady came by, and
I asked her to go get the police. They should be here any
time. Your girl friend is still here."

When Araminta saw John, she breathed relief. "A
face I know. I'm so glad to see you."

The words felt good. John felt the hero. "You're
okay now, I'm here, baby."

Jeff kept an eye out for either the police or their
two unwanted guest.

When the police showed up with the woman who
went and got them, everyone met in the gas station to find
out what happened.

Araminta said, "I shook off the blanket and the gas
station man saw me. He looked down and whispered, 'You

need help?' I nodded and he helped me up. He rushed me into the back of the shop and hid me in a closet."

The officer asked, "Did they hurt you?"

Araminta shook her head, "No sir."

He turned to the woman, "And you happened to come along afterwards?" A nice white woman with three kids bowed. "Yes, and Mr. Perry asked if I could go get the police."

The officer asked Mr. Perry if he could describe the men, and John interrupted. "If he can't we can. We know who they are?"

He turned to the boys, "Who are they?"

Jeff said, "We don't know their names, but they lost out on the two jobs we got over at our work."

The officer took all the information the boys could give them and then said to Araminta, "I'll need to take you to see the chief, and so that we can get a hold of your parents.'

John insisted. "We will drive her, officer."

The officer shook his head. "No you won't. She will ride with me, you can follow."

John tried a smoother approach. "It just seems she would be more comfortable being with her boyfriend.

The officer escorted Araminta by the arm. "Too bad."

John fumed.

Araminta was grateful to everyone who came to her rescue. Before she got in the car, she asked the woman and her kids who they were. "Excuse me, ma'am, but I didn't catch your name, and my parents will want to thank all those who helped."

The lady smiled. "No thanks needed."

Araminta said, "You don't understand, they will want to thank you properly, especially my momma. Can you please tell me?"

The lady said, "My name is Jackie, and these are my three children Claude, Carmen, and Risé. We were on our way home when we stopped in for gas. I will leave my information with Mr. Perry. I'm just glad you are okay, young lady." She hugged Araminta, and waved as Araminta sat in the car with the officer.

They arrived at the police station to report the kidnapping. Araminta told the police everything she knew, *and then Jeff and John filled in the rest. As they gave the account of the note, Stanley and Mr. Whitney arrived, surprised and elated to see Araminta and the boys together.*

Araminta told the investigator, "My father is here, and he says he has the note."

The Captain came in the room with the note and gave the investigator the paper. "I think we can wrap this up pretty easy, Don."

The investigator nodded. They motioned that the boys could go with the adults back home. "We'll be in touch. We will let you know how the investigation goes. In the mean time, please be careful."

Araminta thanked God for Mr. Perry and all the others who helped. Ms. Jackie, the investigator, and the captain were so nice. Momma always told her to pray, even when she didn't need God.

John put his arm around Araminta. "You are safe now, I'm here. No one is going to hurt you." Araminta had seen her life flash before her eyes. Hearing John assure her everything would be okay, sounded so reassuring. She patted his hand. "Thank you."

Jackie, the woman who had gone for the police, waited at the station to say her goodbyes and well wishes.

Araminta hugged her one more time. "Please don't be a stranger, I truly believe people are where they are for a reason."

Jackie said, "I wanted to remind you that Mr. Perry, who has owned that station since they started putting gas in cars, is a very nice man, and I hope you thank him the same way you thanked me. He's a very special old man."

Araminta smiled. "I will make sure he knows how grateful I am."

John tried to cut in with, "Well, we were right behind those men, so they weren't getting far."

Jackie gave a weakened smile. "Yes, I'm sure you boys were, still, he really risked his life."

Araminta nodded, "Yes, John. He was special."

I asked Matilda, "I thought you said John saved her? It sounds like Mr. Perry did."

"But it was John's rapid concern that put everything into motion. He was truly concerned about his Araminta."

There was no logic to that, but this was all going according to Matilda, so I just sat back and let her continue.

Matilda made Araminta go with her to the doctor the next day to make sure the guys didn't hurt her. Araminta told Matilda and John she was fine, but Matilda and John wanted to be sure. None of the kids went to school the next day. Araminta felt like she was under constant surveillance, especially when she went to the outhouse. She knew she could probably never go there again without someone waiting outside the door. They caught the two guys who kidnapped Araminta with John and Jeff's help of their description.

Matilda turned to me, "That's where John proved himself, he caught the guys from his keen observation."

I let her have that one.

Araminta had to go to court and testify against the two men, and they were convicted of kidnapping. Araminta was a local hero in the paper, along with Mr. Perry, and the authorities said everyone involved were brave to do what they did. Araminta didn't think so. To her, Mr. Perry was the hero and was glad she had a friend for life. Araminta was happy to be alive.

"That's a really fortunate thing. Did you remain friends with Mr. Perry and Jackie?"

"Of course, Jackie's kids became friends of the family as well."

"Are they still around?"

"The kids are, but no, Mr. Perry and Jackie is no longer with us. Not too many people my age are still around, child, and Mr. Perry was pretty old when we met him."

"No, I suppose they aren't." I smiled. "But at least you are." I offered, "And because of you, everyone is living on through your history."

I only hoped the next story would make me like John a little more.

Chapter 18

The engagement still intrigued me, and I had to ask, "Matilda, you mentioned that the twins would be asked by the boys if they would marry them that upcoming Christmas. Did that go off as planned?" I kind of knew the answer but by asking at least I could direct some of the story to the points of interest.

Matilda's eyes lit up when I asked. "I'm so glad you are following me."

"Well, I'm really interested in my great aunts. I know so very little about them."

It was Christmas and Araminta saw John acting strange. It was their first Christmas together, and John and Jeff's family were all comin' over for the biggest Christmas dinner ever. Matilda told Araminta that it was for such a wonderful year; in the boyfriends they had, in the college offers they had, and in the ordeal of the kidnapping. However, Araminta suspected something else was up. Isabella thought so too, but they didn't question it. Araminta and Isabella met more of Jeff's siblings. There was Jeff's sister Shelby, Vaughn his brother, and Fred his other brother, they were so nice. Araminta and Isabella enjoyed the hugs from new family. Araminta had warmed to John, they still weren't the item Jeff and Isabella were, but she tried. She suggested to John that they make each other gifts that year, even though John would walk away when she would bring it up. Araminta had hoped John heard her because she made him a knitted scarf. Araminta did it late at night because John was always around. When Araminta helped Matilda cook, John would be there. When she studied, John would be there, when she walked to school, John would be there.

Matilda didn't mind John's constant appearance. Matilda said, "Let that man do what he got to do." He'd become such a fixture that nothing surprised Matilda anymore. He made himself at home in their home.

That Christmas would be very nice, John and Jeff cut down four Christmas trees. One for Matilda and Stanley, and one for John's parents; one for the Mr. Perry's gas station, and one for Jackie, who'd become an occasional visitor to their home.

John and Jeff also hunted turkeys, giving them out to all the family members who wanted one. Matilda suspected they hunted a dozen that year.

Matilda had twenty five quilts in the house. She would make quilts as gifts, but because of everything happening with the end of the twin's senior year, she didn't have time. Matilda took ten she'd made a year before, washed them up, mended any loose threads and gave them as gifts. Jackie got one, Mr. Perry got one, all four of Jeff's siblings, John's mom got two, and she wrapped two of them up and gave them to the local shelter. Matilda always thought about other people.

John and Jeff stood in front of the fireplace and told everyone to gather. There were so many people in the house; what a beautiful site. John called Araminta to come forward. Jeff called Isabella to do the same.

John looked at Jeff and said "It's your show."

Jeff smiled and turned toward Isabella. He knelt in front of her and poured out a story to Isabella that everyone wondered if it was true.

I couldn't help but wonder if he took after Matilda. I grinned with impishness, and I thought she caught me because her head swiveled.

Jeff said, "Isabella, this ring is the very ring my father Clifford Jordan Sr. placed on my mother's hands on October thirtieth, 1884. My brother, Clifford Jordan Jr, inherited this ring from my mother, giving it to me since he hasn't married and I am the first male in the family to marry."

My ears perked up. "Wait, I thought they were just getting engaged. Are they getting married at that moment?"

Matilda laughed. "Sorry, he said, engaged. I was thinking ahead."

"Well, she let the cat out of the bag about what would eventually happen. Too bad, I was so hoping the girls would say no."

"It is also a gift of forgiveness for our family struggles. My siblings and I welcome you to the family, and I want to tell you of the conversation I had with God concerning you. It was an awesome surprise to me as it will be to you as well. God told me to let you know you are an

essential part of my family, as not only a help, but a huge part of what's to come during the devastation."

Matilda Gasped.

Jeff continued, "You will be the first to know once God informs me of the appropriate time, but for now there's this question that has been on my heart."

Isabella smiled.

Jeff said, "Isabella Maggie Annie Fleming, you have crossed my path for a reason, and I am curious to see where God takes us. God brought us together and on that note I would like to ask you a very important question. Isabella will you take this engagement ring to marry me one day?"

Jeff declared his love for Isabella, and Isabella who wasn't the emotional one, broke down and shook when Jeff placed the ring on her finger.

Isabella said, "Yes." As Jeff placed the ring on Isabella's finger, everyone clapped and hugged Jeff and Isabella.

For as happy as Matilda was telling the story, I wasn't too happy about all the indoctrination. It just felt like my female antecedents didn't stand a chance to make their own decisions. I got that Matilda said they were happy, but it seemed like they were coerced, and didn't know any better. I was staring at not one generation gap but three. This all took place sixty years earlier, and it felt like hundreds of years earlier.

Matilda could see something on my face because she stopped. She reached across and took my hand. "Don't be disappointed in how your twin aunts were married. They really did love their men."

"Grandma, you of all people, being a God fearing woman, should understand free will."

"What wasn't free about their relationships?"

"You and great grandfather Stanley pushing them into relationships they may not have actually wanted."

She challenged me, "The man you are engaged to, do your parents approve?"

"Yes, but they never encouraged me to marry him. They let it be my decision."

"Life was a little different on farms, child. Family was a family affair, and family didn't move far away. They stayed and worked the land."

"So?"

"So, relationships had to work for everyone."

She made a valid point, and my only response was, "Well, I guess I'm glad I wasn't born back then."

She wasn't offended by my rebuke. "And you shouldn't have been. Your destiny is for this time and place. If you happened to slip back to that time, I'd shoo you away and tell you to come back to your own reality."

I sat back. There was so much more for her to tell me.

Chapter 19

I clicked my pen and wrote Araminta's name. "I'm guessing we now have John's proposal?"

Matilda nodded:

Araminta walked over to hug Isabella too, but John pulled her back. He asked, "Do you mind hugging your sister later?"

Araminta had a pit in the bottom of her stomach. She was pleased for her sister, but hoped this wasn't a dual event. "Oh, okay."

John knelt down. Araminta's eyes grew big. She thought this was all about Isabella, and having John kneel before her was alarming.

I interjected. "I bet. I'd be shocked."

Everyone turned to John kneeling down as John spoke from his heart. He said, "I have never thought I could meet one of God's most precious creatures to ever walk this earth, until I met you."

Stanley grabbed Matilda as the entire party could hear Matilda catch her cry with her tissue.

John said, "Araminta you have showed me what a wife looks like by walking in a room. I loved you from the moment I met you on that football field many moons ago. I love you, and I hope you know I will do my best to take care of you for the rest of your life. Araminta Jolinda Debbra Fleming, will you do me the honor and make me the happiest man on earth, will you accept my engagement to marry me?"

Araminta scanned the room, her mother was so happy, everyone wanted this to happen. She couldn't believe John felt so certain about the two of them. Araminta remained stone faced. Her words fell from her mouth with a slow realization that anything else would be frowned upon. "Yes."

John hugged Araminta and wouldn't let go. "I am so grateful to have you in my life." John started to bawl and Jeff had to pull him off Araminta as the tears progressed into a mountain of sobs.

"That's not normal, Grandma. That's what guys do to guilt you into loving them."

She just waved me off:

Isabella and Araminta hugged each other. The twins looked at Matilda, who cried almost as much as John.

Stanley looked like he didn't know how to talk. He was so choked up and blamed his injuries that past summer for why he had to go lie down, but they knew better.

Isabella and Araminta sandwiched Matilda on the couch and rested their heads on her shoulder.

Maddison bought Marilyn over to sit next by Matilda. Jeff and John knelt down in front of both mothers and said that was the best Christmas of their entire lives. Jeff's brother worked at a photography shop. His gift to Isabella and Araminta were pictures of the engagement party. They stood in front of the fireplace, some seated some standing but all smiles thinking about the Christmas that almost wasn't.

"Don't you have those pictures? It dawned on me, I didn't see any pictures of the kids, anywhere."

Matilda shook her head. "No, unfortunately, the fire took all the picture I had but the ones you see."

"The fire?"

"We had a fire years ago that burned up a lot of our precious memories. Thankfully, I still have them locked away right here." She tapped her forehead.

What a tragedy. I did an inventory of all the pictures I had, and if they were safe in case of an emergency. I had to make sure I had duplicates made, just in case.

Matilda went on, "The engagement turned into a blessed event."

"They were still in high school, weren't they?"

"Yes."

"And you didn't worry about other things happening?"

Matilda shrugged. "Other things?"

"You know, like, you know." I pointed to my stomach.

"You mean pregnancy?"

"Yes."

The laughter from her lips brought Nellie running into the room. "What's happening?"

Matilda put her hand to her lips. "My lovely great grandchild was worried about the chastity of my children."

Nellie didn't find it as funny as Matilda and returned to whatever she did in that kitchen.

Matilda turned to me. "You have brought us to a big issue with the twins and their men. I suspect we will be here a long time as we unravel the mystery of our girls and their understanding of where babies came from."

"Are you telling me you were marrying off your daughters and they had no sex education?"

"Child, what era do you think this was?" Kids weren't as promiscuous as they are today."

Somehow I felt like that was directed at me, but since I was aware of sex at a bit younger age than that, it was hard to disagree. "Yes, well. It still seems a bit premature to offer up the hand of your daughters before they were even graduated from high school."

"This was black America in the 1920s, child. The norm was to get married young and not make it through school. Not a lot of kids finished high school, and black kids had an even lower rate. Our girls were making it through school, and you might not like our methods, but by being right there in all the decisions and helping iron out the wrinkles, our kids did graduate. So regardless of what you think, we succeeded."

Her observation was spot on, and I found myself forgetting she hadn't learned to read and write until later in her life, because she had an articulation that went beyond someone who wasn't that learned. I backtracked. "You know Grandma, you are correct. I might disapprove of how involved you were, but I can neither speak for the times, nor for my aunts." I winked. "But I'm going to ask them when I meet them."

She smiled. "I would expect nothing less."

Chapter 20

We took a break for dinner and I tried to make a call to home, but I got a disconnected tone. I tried again and got the same response. So I called my fiancée and got the same thing. "How strange."

Nellie responded. "What's that?"

"Neither my parent's home nor my fiancée's home is working."

"What do you mean?"

"I mean I keep getting a disconnection response. Like the number isn't any good."

She waved her hand. "That happens down here occasionally. That's not on them, it's on us."

"Well, I really need to speak to my mother. I promised her I'd give her a call while I was down here."

"You might have to go into town and use a payphone."

"Maybe after dinner?"

Nellie motioned to Matilda. "I think Tildy is gearing up for another session. Are you sure you don't want to go tomorrow before church?"

I doubted one more day would hurt. "I suppose."

Matilda ate with expediency, and I could see she really wanted to continue my lesson in my family's history. There was no avoiding it, and besides, for all the frustration I found in their attitudes, I was drawing a clearer picture of who they were.

We reconvened in the family room, and I noticed my chair still on the far side, away from the fireplace, even though the temperature had dipped. I wasn't going to get that heat from the fire, so I provided myself with the quilt. It's warmth a constant reminder of a time gone by.

"Are you okay, child?"

I refocused. "Yeah, I'm fine. Just my mind is wandering to home."

"I heard you can't reach anyone. Well, you have us, and until you can get a hold of someone, let that comfort you."

"Thanks, grandma."

"Now, back to that fateful year of the twins and their beaus."

"Yes, let's get back to it."

I cheered up. "Okay!"

As a new year was upon them, the old year was quickly departing. New Year's Eve was found to be a comfortable place to be at home. Matilda was in the kitchen fixing a turkey. John's mother Marilyn invited the Fleming family to a New Year's Eve dinner, and John would be coming back with Araminta to the house to make sure he had a chance to kiss her as 1923 entered the world. Mrs. Whitney told Matilda not to bring anything, but that was like telling Joseph apple pie wasn't good for you, he would eat it anyway. Matilda told Marilyn she was bringing four sweet potato pies, and an applesauce cake. John and his three brothers were in the backyard chopping wood as the Fleming family pulled up.

Joseph jumped out and ran to meet John and his brothers. Lillie was crazy about Julian, but Julian had a girlfriend and wasn't interested in Lillie. His girlfriend was supposed to be coming to dinner as well. John's brother, Jamison, was a hunter and inventor. John said Jamison had all six of the girls in his class chasing him. Araminta saw Jamison at school and admitted there was a girl with him most of the time, but Jamison wasn't really into girls like Julian. Jamison liked taking radios apart and putting them back together. He loved watching his dad work on his truck. He wanted to be an automobile mechanic when he graduated. Mr. Whitney told him that was an honorable profession, but as long as the county sent students to college he could be anything he wanted to be. Jordan was into building things. He loved working in the yard with his dad.

Last but not least, John had a sister, and her named didn't begin with a J. Ella Julia Whitney was named after Mrs. Whitney's mother. Her middle name was a tribute to

Mr. Whitney's dad. Mr. Whitney's dad was named John Xavier Whitney also. Mr. Whitney's older brother was John Xavier Whitney Jr. John's father wanted to name all his sons with the letter J, and he gave them all Xavier as middle names.

Ella and Addie were the same age and hung out in her room playing with dolls. Addie said Ella was her forth sister. As the family reflected on the past year, 1922 ended with the family stuffing themselves with ham, meatballs, turkey, stuffing, salad, and sweet potato pies.

"So, did anything eventful happen that New Year's Eve, Grandma?"

"Well, we got to know the Whitney's better, and that would bode well for the future."

"And the twins?"

"They got ready for spring finals, and they had to go to the orientation at the college they would attend."

"How did that go?"

It was a few weeks before Isabella and Araminta would head to the college for orientation to meet with their counselor to register for the fall session. Isabella and Araminta had never been away from home for a week.

Araminta said, "I guess this will prepare us for when we are really in college this fall."

Stanley and Matilda were going to take them to the school on a Monday and pick them up on a Friday. Araminta was glad Isabella was going with her. She didn't think she could go to school alone without Isabella. When Isabella and Araminta talked to Matilda those few weeks before the girls left for school, Matilda seemed worried. It was probably Matilda missing the girls before they had left.

John wished he could register all over again, but John and Jeff had already registered with the Wilson firm, so only Isabella and Araminta could attend that orientation week. John said that was the only part of the entire college experience he didn't like, and that was a week without Araminta.

Araminta knew John was having anxiety over the separation, she however, felt an odd sense of relief. When John came over for dinner the week before they left, he wanted a heart to heart with Araminta. John wanted some kind of reassurance that everything would be alright with Isabella and Araminta being forty-five minutes away. Araminta told John she would have her protective sister Isabella with her; what could go wrong? John wanted to go with Matilda and Stanley when they took Isabella and Araminta to school, but Matilda wanted Isabella and Araminta to have a break from all of the family, and do what they came there to do so they could get back home. John didn't agree with Matilda, but she said if John wanted, he could call Araminta at the dormitory. Matilda knew that would be a different adventure for John and Araminta. John accepted that.

"See, I knew that guy would be the jealous type. You described him as one, and you still are." I scolded Matilda.

"We all have our weaknesses, and he certainly had his, but his heart was in the right spot."

She frustrated me to no end, justifying his behavior.

After Stanley and Matilda dropped Araminta and Isabella off at school, Matilda only cried a little.

Matilda winked at me.

Stanley had to watch and listen to his wife cry the entire forty-five minute drive home. Stanley tried to reassure her that the girls would be fine.

I wanted to know. "How did the orientation go?"

When the resident assistant knocked on Araminta and Isabella's door at seven thirty Monday night and said Araminta has a phone call, Araminta felt so important. This was the first time Araminta ever received a phone call in her life. Araminta ran to the phone, Isabella racing behind her, both smiling as Araminta said, "Hello."

John said "Baby."

Araminta asked, "John? What are you doing calling?"

John said, "I am going out of my mind missing you."

Araminta relayed, "I just had dinner with you last night, and you kissed me so many times, wasn't that enough?"

John said, "It's never enough with you. So tell me what have you and Isabella been doing all day?"

Araminta said, "Well, when Momma and Daddy left to head back home, we sat through an orientation about school policies and rules. I have never seen so many people our age in one place. We don't have this many people in our school. They seem friendly enough."

John's voice rang out over the phone, "What about the boys, are they friendly, too?"

Araminta worried this might have been why he was calling. "No more than anyone else."

He pried, "So how many have you spoken to?"

Araminta played innocent. "Girls or boys?"

He answered with a curtness, "I think you know what I mean."

Araminta sighed and thought why not. "The boys are the friendliest. They stared at Isabella and me, wanting us to go to eat with them and walk to the library. One nice young man even wanted us to go with him to show us where we can buy things we may need off campus. He was really kind to us, and told us we can go off campus, but the school will try to keep the freshman under their thumb.

Isabella and I were so glad he let us know that everything you read in the school pamphlet is not true."

John's voice had a stiffness to it, as though he held back rage, "That sounds interesting. What other boys did you meet?"

Araminta pushed it, "We met two guys named Ray and Malcolm. Malcolm is from a small town in Oklahoma, and he said there are never enough pretty girls in Oklahoma. He said Isabella and I was the prettiest girls he had ever seen. Malcolm has a math orientation with Isabella and an English orientation with me. Are the boys supposed to stare every time they see you? I know you watch me all the time, so it makes me wonder is that normal? I told Isabella it can't be normal, because you love me, and they don't know us, and they still stare. The boys are nice, but sometimes it's too many around at one time. I told Isabella it probably wasn't a good idea to leave our engagement rings home."

John interrupted, "You left your ring at home?"

Araminta said, "Yes, I thought it was wise to leave them so we don't lose them. When I tell the boys I am engaged for some reason they don't believe me. I don't understand why they keep talking as if I didn't say anything. This guy name Roy wants us to go to the movie for the freshmen tomorrow night. He said he has a buddy that would love to sit with Isabella, and he even has his own car."

The silence on the other end of the line was deafening.

"John, are you there?" The phone went dead. Araminta turned to Isabella and with a smile . "That's odd, we must have been disconnected."

I started laughing. "My great Aunt Araminta just clowned her beau."

Matilda reminded me. "Araminta was naïve. She wasn't a dullard or mean."

She just gave an account of a woman toying with a man. "And I still don't like your depiction of John."

She whispered, "Then you probably won't like what happened next."

Chapter 21

I begged Matilda. "Please do not tell me that boy went to the school the next day?"

"Wait until you pass judgment."

"Grandma, that's not a healthy relationship."

"He was her fiancé, and he couldn't trust her. He needed to get over there."

"Wait a minute. Don't tell me you and Grandpa Stanley knew he went?"

For the first time I saw a sheepish side to my great grandmother. "Yes, he came by and discussed it with us."

"And you let him go?" I was up in seat, confronting her.

"We did, but we insisted he take Jeff."

"Oh, well great, the other ram in the bush."

"It didn't turn out bad."

"Oh really? So I guess we should explore that visit then." I sat back and let her unwind this yarn."

John went to the Fleming house to get the blessing of Stanley. Matilda and Stanley gave it, but insisted he take Jeff. John agreed and stayed in the Fleming barn with Jeff that night. John packed a few things, but he insisted that they be allowed to search the girl's room for the rings.

"And you let them?" I was livid.

"Of course, they were gifts from them, gifts for life."

"Unbelievable."

"Let me explain."

"Carry on."

Matilda packed John and Jeff lunches for their stay, and told them to hurry back on Friday. John and Jeff kissed Matilda and told her they were going to leave around six in the morning, and would probably not see them till they returned on Friday.

John offered, "My dad said that if you needed to call Araminta or Isabella that you were welcome to come to our house to use our phone." John wrote the college number down. John and Jeff got a special kiss on the cheek for looking after their girls.

"You mean stalking them."

"I mean making sure they weren't taken advantage of."

I wanted to remind her that the girls were already being taken advantage of, but my great grandmother wouldn't have believed it.

While John and Jeff headed back to the barn to discuss what Araminta told John on the phone, Jeff became angry. Jeff was angry with Isabella agreeing with Araminta to leave her engagement ring at home. Jeff asked, "Who are all these boys all around them?"

John said, "I don't know, but I'm not surprise the boys are flocking about them. The day I hurt myself playing football and Araminta was walking by, and impulsively stopped and asked me was I alright, I was teased. I was teased by the guys in my class, 'John has the twin coming to him now.' What the guys were thinking about Araminta in school is probably what these guys at the college are thinking. Remember Jesse Tate said, 'Jeff is seeing one of the pretty Fleming twins.'"

Jeff said, "Yes I remember the teasing, Isabella use to tell me before she met me, how she and Araminta would always have guys ask them out, or can they come see them at their home. Isabella said the first time it happen it was one of the Fernando brothers. Isabella was thirteen, whenever Isabella and Araminta would get asked to go on a date or if the guy can come to their house, they would walk away and they never told their momma. Isabella said Momma always said all her daughters were beautiful, but that was Momma, she was obligated to say that. She said when a guy other than her father calls her beautiful, Araminta and Isabella would turn to stone. Isabella was scared, and would say thank you and walk away quickly. Isabella told me it wasn't until I started talking to her earlier this year that for the first time she felt comfortable enough to have a conversation with a boy. After that first day, we talked all the time, but she wouldn't take me home to meet the parents. Since Isabella and Araminta are the oldest children they had no experience in what to do. Jeff recalled that day in the barn when he met Matilda. I was glad Momma found us. I wasn't afraid, Isabella just didn't know how to ask her momma. I was so happy; I was ready to meet The Flemings."

Jeff said, "After my momma died three years ago and my dad a year before, I missed being in a home with my parents. I tell Isabella all the time how blessed she is to have parents. I was living with my brother Clifton for a *while, but I was getting in all kinds of trouble at school. I was hanging out with the wrong crowd. I had a friend that taught me how to do things, bad things to get what I needed. Many times I would go hungry, and Clifton wasn't used to checking on a child to make sure we was fed, homework done etc. I was fourteen, I had no money. My momma and daddy didn't have much. I remember that last Christmas with my momma, she told me to talk to that wonderful guidance counselor at my school to make sure I graduated. I didn't talk to him like Momma asked. I was angry, angry because she left, and I was alone. After I kept getting in trouble I knew the only thing I can do is do like my momma asked. I went into the guidance counselor's office and let him know everything I was going through and the last request my momma asked of me. Mr. Deyon is a Christian, and he talked to me on God's behalf. He knew I had to leave my brother Clifton's house because he wasn't capable of caring for me. I told him I had a sister in Pitt County and she attended In Gods Arms Methodist Church. He drove me down to her house, and she welcomed me into her family with open arms. Her husband Keith told me Adrianna and I talked about seeing if you could come live with us, but when it was written that your father stated in his will if any of his children are under eighteen, and he or his wife passed, the oldest male should take them in. My sister Shelby and I was under eighteen, but Shelby ran away to another County to stay with friends of Momma and Daddy. She knew Clifton wasn't going to search for her. Shelby had just turned seventeen, me on the other hand, I was fourteen and had to live with Clifton. I knew and understood why my father had his will written up that way. It was because when his father was young, he and his siblings was sent to an orphanage. His father died when he was ten, and his mother died in childbirth when he was eleven. There was no one to take them in. It was six children, all given to the state. My father would never talk about what happen to them. My father was ashamed. We did find out his sister Camille was raped and never recovered from that. She died in an insane asylum. They say a child was born, but no one knows where the child is today. My Dad has another sister born after Camille. Her name is Natalie, and she was born the year after Jeff's grandfather Addison Jordan died. The story we heard about Natalie's birth was when Natalie entered the world, the midwife stop tending to my grandmother and started cleaning and doing the prep work for the baby. Natalie was born in Grandma's bedroom."*

Jeff said his father was the fourth child and all he remembers was the screams. Jeff's oldest Aunt Lena was sixteen years old at the time her mother died and she was in the room when Natalie was born. Lena was wiping the sweat from her mother's forehead with a wet cloth. 'The midwife was my dad's Aunt Mabel. She never returned to Clifton's mother again. Clifton Sr. said we heard our momma cries are never to be heard again. Lena said she would scream to Auntie to help her momma, but her Aunt would only say, 'Let her sleep, she's just tired.' My grandmother never woke up again. Lena's Aunt Mabel Simon couldn't have children. Clifton Sr.'s mother's name was Rayelle Simon Jordan. Rayelle died in less than an hour. Lena said she bled to death. Aunt Mabel told Lena to call the church to have someone clean this up, and she left out the back door with Lena's baby sister Natalie Jordan. Mabel didn't attend Rayelle's funeral, she was heard laughing and playing with the baby on the day of the funeral. The state came knocking at her door to ask her could she ward all six children.

Mabel said she would only ward Natalie. She told the state to get the rest of them and never knock on her door again. Lena was only in the care of the state for six months. She saw a worker forcing this girl her age to come in a room with him. There were other workers down the hall hearing the girl's cries but they ignored the girl. The next day Lena snuck out through the laundry shute. Lena knew this place was no place for her and her siblings. Lena could get no one to help. She knew if her siblings waited until they turned eighteen no telling what may happen.

Three years later Camille became pregnant at the age of eleven by a worker. Clifton Sr., George, and James all escaped when the front door was left open while a worker whipped a boy in the next room. Clifton, George, and James never ran so fast in their lives. About a mile up the road was a swamp, and when they heard the dogs they stayed under until the coast was clear. After crawling out of the swamp, they rested on the ground to catch their breath. Clifton moved closer to George only to hear his last breath, George had died. Clifton and James refused to leave their brother on the ground. They carried him deep into the woods and used whatever they could find to dig a grave. The nightmare had both brothers letting the tears run its course. They were wet from the swamp, exhausted from running and grieving James death and Camille's pregnancy in that horrific place. They had no money, was starving and didn't know where Lena or Natalie were. They fell asleep a foot from the rode and was awaken by members of a church whose bus broke down. The members ask them were they alright. They told them no, and they listen to their story.

The pastor and the members heard Clifton and James story and the church fed them and had them to go on the bus to change their clothes. The church asked us if they would like to stay with them and live with their members of the church for as long as they wish. The church said they could go to school and join the church too. James and Clifton went to live with the church and was adopted by a wonderful couple that loved them very much. My dad met my momma at the church and married October thirtieth, 1884. They couldn't find anything on Camille. They heard she was sent to the insane asylum and eventually died. The baby Camille had was taken, and no news on where the baby was taken. We heard the baby name was Camille too.

My head spun. "Grandma, how do you know this in such detail?"

"Jeff told me the story."

"Sixty years ago?"

"That's right."

"And you remember it in such detail, right down to the names?"

"Is that unusual, child?"

"Uh, yeah. Yeah it is. It's downright astonishing."

Matilda smiled. "It is, isn't it?"

"Is that it?"

She shook her head. "There's more."

When Natalie was three years old, Aunt Mabel gave her to a neighbor to raise. Jeff heard Aunt Mabel started beating Natalie in the street and the neighbor who raised nine children of her own took Natalie in. The neighbor eventually died in her sleep after ten years of caring for Natalie. Natalie was thirteen when the neighbor died. Natalie married at fourteen, and her husband had to leave the county to find work. Natalie went with him and her husband's name was Crawford Billups. He was a mechanic. Jeff's dad was doing what he thought would be best for them by giving power of attorney to Clifton Jr., because of what happened to him.

Jeff couldn't fault him for trying. He believed they all would come together one day, and they would rejoice when that day came to pass. Mr. Deyon, Jeff, Keith, and Addrianna went to visit Clifton to get Clifton to give Keith and Addrianna power of attorney to care for Jeff full time. Clifton didn't have to sign the papers but he did it mainly because my sister Addrianna said if you don't want to visit Jeff in prison or in an insane asylum like their daddy's sister for the rest of his life, it would be advisable to sign the papers. They knew his hesitation was because of the check he received every month for Jeff and Shelby. Clifton Jordan Jr. signed over power of attorney to Keith and Addrianna Myles. Jeff owed his life to Mr. Deyon, Keith, and Addrianna.

I repeated. "Wow. That is an amazing recollection."

She eased into her chair. "Thank you."

Chapter 22

Even though the hour was late, I had to know what happened at that orientation. "I'm up if you are up. I want to know about what happened when they met up with the twins."

Matilda leaned in. "Well, as I remember Jeff telling it to John at the barn that night,"

"When I met Mrs. Fleming that day by the barn, I told the entire family my story. Mrs. Fleming had a right to ask me to tell my story because she didn't know me. It's amazing how I told her everything that happened to me, but she knew I left something out of my story, and then told me what it was. She said, 'You're practicing to be a preacher.' Isabella told me whatever I do don't lie because Momma may call you on it. Although I had no intentions of lying, it's just when you tell people you're practicing to be a minister, at my age, you're not taken seriously. I know I have a lot to learn but this is where God placed me.

"Another reason Isabella said she couldn't introduce me to her parents was because her father went to help his brother on his farm and had not made it back. Isabella said

her momma and the children had to help tend to that garden. I wanted to introduce myself to her momma then, as a matter of fact that's how we ended up in the barn that day, because she was trying to convince me, beg me even, pleading with me not to talk to her momma about us. Watching her and her siblings, four girls at that, pushing a tiller? I watched their momma do it along with Isabella and Araminta. Isabella and Araminta kept falling, and I couldn't watch anymore. I left, and wouldn't have come back until she was ready to let me meet the parents. I'm so grateful her mother accepted my offer. She made the children quit working the garden and tend to their regular chores. I love having someone check on me like my momma did. I didn't think I would miss that, but I did.

"I had started going to church with Keith and Addrianna and that's where I saw Isabella and Araminta. I knew they were in my class but they stayed up under their momma at church, I couldn't even say hi to them. I remember at school I saw them eating their lunch on the lawn, and I prayed so that I wouldn't get turned down, well at least not so bad. I decided to say hi. Isabella was the one I wanted. Araminta was so shy. Isabella was more assertive, I saw it that day. When I walked up to them, I said, 'Hello my name is Jefferson Jordan.' Araminta quickly left. She was walking fast into the school building. Isabella was still standing, very nervous, but she didn't run. I proceeded and said, 'I'm sorry if I disturbed you and your sister's lunch. As I said, I am Jefferson Jordan but everyone calls me Jeff. You attend In Gods Arms Church, don't you?' Isabella nodded. 'I attend there too with my sister and brother-in-law. You're Isabella?' Isabella nodded again and continued to stare at me. 'You don't have to be shy or nervous. I just wanted to say hi to a fellow In Gods Arms church goer. You know we have to stick together. I will leave so you can get to class. Thanks for letting me say hi.'

"As I walked away, Isabella said, 'how do you know my name?' I stopped walking, turned and walked slowly toward Isabella. I said, 'I thought everyone knew the prettiest girl's name in school.' Isabella's eyes were so big, she tried desperately to hide her smile but I said, 'Wait, what's that I see.' I ducked down and said, 'So you do know how to smile.' Isabella said in a whisper, 'It's you.' She looked away. I said very cautiously, because I didn't want to frighten her, 'What do you mean?' Isabella turned to me,

'It's you who made it easy to smile.' Isabella covered her mouth with her hand and looks down then lifted her eyes only to see my reaction. My smile was even bigger than Isabella's. 'It's a pleasure to be in your presence, Isabella.'"

Matilda concluded:

Isabella knew at that moment she couldn't be in the presence of Jeff without her knees knocking together. She always turned giddy nervous around Jeff, and her stomach felt like it tied in knots when she was with him.

I interrupted. "See, I like him. He's a nice boy."

Matilda laughed. "He's an eighty year old man. One thing Jeff knew about Isabella was that the soft, sweet, shy, sensitive side of her left when Araminta was around. She was so use to protecting Araminta but she never wanted Araminta to see the side that Jeff saw. I guess she liked to feel needed by her older sister.

I had not forgotten about John, sadly, I wanted to though. "What about the other boy?"

"John took it all in."

John waited to discuss his feeling for Araminta. When he had the time, he said, "After Araminta ask was I alright, the three guys on the football team came to me *after that and said, 'I'm going to ask her to the Barn Dance this Saturday night. One guy said, 'I'm going to talk to her father and see if I can court her,' and the last guy said, 'She is so pretty, you think she could be my wife someday?' I know some of them tried to talk to her because when I came to Araminta's birthday party and told her about the flowers I left on her desk, she had no idea who sent them. Jeff, she is so innocent, so sweet, if it wasn't for your fiancé, I probably wouldn't be talking to her now. Araminta kept telling me 'No' because of you and Isabella. I know if she kept telling me 'No,' she kept telling them no. Although Isabella was simply getting back at Araminta for answering her mother correctly about you being in the barn, Araminta wasn't trying to hurt Isabella."*

Jeff said, "I know, she does that sometimes because she has no one else to blame. I'm sure she blames me for some things, but the only thing I know she blames me for is when I helped you kidnap Araminta from her. Isabella is just as sensitive as Araminta. Did you know that?"

John said, "Yes, I know, but it's probably because she likes to feel like Araminta needs her, and Araminta makes Isabella feels like she is needed, that's one reason I know they both really love each other." John went on, "One thing I never told Araminta or her family is that when Araminta has to fight, she does, but for some reason when she is around her family members, like Isabella, and her momma, they baby and protect her like she needs it. I can't fault them too much because I enjoy babying her. I love it when she lets me have control and becomes my prey. I love when she tries to get out of a locked cage with me, and struggles to get free. It's when she succumbs and starts to feel helpless, and she will at that point let me have anything I want, to get what she wants, and what she wants, is nothing I can't handle. When that happens, I fall in love with her all over again."

"Are you hearing yourself, Grandma? Seriously did you just hear what you said?"

"It's water under the bridge, child."

I had to remember this was a story sixty years old. There was nothing I could do for a woman who was now in her eighties. "Keep going."

"Jeff laughed. 'It's amazing you say that because Isabella has been my prey since about a month after I moved here. She plays hard when you all are around, but

deep down she does the very same thing that Araminta does to you. She is shy when it's just the two of us. That tough girl façade fades and she becomes what I love; she becomes herself. I told Isabella about how she and Araminta are a lot alike during the time you got her back. I saw in her eyes that she knew what I was saying was true, but she didn't acknowledge it to me. It's a game that I love, and I'm sure you do too, John, because they are letting us be the men in their lives, and not trying to become one of us."

John smiled. "That's why I'm going tomorrow to fight whoever I have to, to get my prey back." They laughed themselves to sleep.

When John and Jeff left the next morning, John wasn't sure he could stay calm and not become angry. He told Jeff, "Jeff, if we were not going to be college students here with them for the next four years, I know I couldn't handle them being here alone without us. Jeff, can you see Araminta coming home one weekend with a guy who said he is just a friend?"

Jeff shook his head. "I can see them both doing it if we weren't there."

In the distance, they could make out the college, and the two young men prepared themselves for something that might change everything in their lives.

I couldn't help but hope that the twins had found new beaus, but something told me these two guys were in this story for the long haul.

Chapter 23

My thoughts lingered on the meeting, and even though the hour was late, I had to know more. "More, please."

Matilda had me hooked:

As John drove around the girl's dormitory, Jeff saw Araminta talking to a guy in front of the library. John slowed to a stop and got an eyeful. Jeff looked for Isabella but there was no sign of her. John got out of the car and Jeff measured his mood.

Jeff said, "Should we wait until we get to our rooming house so we can sit them down and have a heart to heart with them?"

John promised, "I'm calm."

However, Jeff begged to differ.

John noticed Jeff not moving. "What's the problem, Jeff?"

Jeff worried. "I just want you to calm down before you blow up and regret it."

John agreed, "Okay Jeff, do you want to pray over me?"

Jeff said, "Yes."

As Jeff prayed, John smiled as he said, 'Amen.' John saw Araminta still talking and laughing with some boy. They walked calmly over to the library, and Araminta caught sight of John.

Araminta shouted, "John, Jeff, oh my, where did you come from, it's not Friday."

John stepped forward, lifted her up and kissed her. Araminta stared at John. She knew why he did it.

Jeff watched the other boy's face as John handled his business.

The boy asked, "Who is this guy?"

John held out his hand. "I am Araminta's loving fiancé, please to meet you."

The boy looked at Araminta with shock across his face. He said, "You have a fiancé?"

"Araminta blushed. "Yes, I do."

John and Jeff smiled, and Jeff said under his breath, "One down, one to go." While they watched, the boy stomped down the library steps looking back at John in complete disgust. Jeff asked, "Where is Isabella?"

Araminta turned around and pointed. "Isabella is right there with Billy and George."

Jeff fumed and John messed with him, "Do we need to pray first?"

Jeff said, "Not now, John. Hug Araminta, and I will be right back."

John laughed and Araminta cautioned Jeff, "They are just talking."

John said, "It's not important. What is important is you. What's this I hear, you telling me about all these boys staring at you and Isabella?"

Araminta said, "Is there a problem with that?"

John watched five boys go by and stare at Araminta. As the boys passed by, two of them came back with John standing there. One of them asked Araminta if she was going to the dance that night. John grabbed Araminta and held her tightly before sealing her lips with a kiss. "She will be with her fiancé tonight."

The boys shrugged and moved on. Araminta felt stifled and pushed away. "Why did you have to be so forceful? They were only being friendly."

My question exactly. "Grandma, again, not liking this boy."

"Just wait." She picked up where she left off:

John took a step back. "Who am I if I can't hug my future?"

Araminta said, "You know that's not what I meant." Araminta whispered, "They didn't know I had a fiancé, but we don't have to shock them?"

John reached into his pocket. "I agree with you, we shouldn't shock them like that." He pulled Araminta's hand to him. "We should never have them wonder again." He placed Araminta's ring back on her finger.

Araminta sighed. "Okay, John." She accepted a kiss from John.

John asked, "Can we go to dinner off campus? I would like to talk to you."

Araminta said, "I will have to sign out with the resident assistant. Just in case Momma calls, they will know what to tell her."

John said, "Okay, let's go pick up Jeff and Isabella and sign you both out."

When John and Araminta reached Isabella and Jeff, Isabella held Jeff's hand and cried, "I love you too."

When Isabella saw John and Araminta, she straightened and let Jeff's hand go. She jumped up and hugged John. "Why didn't you tell Araminta you two were coming here today?"

John messed with Isabella, "If we did that we wouldn't have seen you with Billy and George."

Isabella frowned and Jeff's smile ended. Isabella said, "We were just talking, John. Araminta knew that."

Araminta said, "That's what I told him."

Jeff still looked mad. John passed Isabella's ring to Jeff and he slid it on Isabella's finger.

After dinner, Isabella and Araminta had three hours before they had to be back to the dorm. John and Jeff took them to a park. John and Araminta were a half mile down one end of the Park, and Jeff and Isabella were a half mile down the other end. Jeff and John needed to have moments alone with their women.

Jeff and Isabella found a wonderful picnic table in the park to sit and talk. Jeff needed to talk about boys and several other things. Jeff asked Isabella, "Do you know what engagement means?"

Isabella shrugged. "Why do you ask?"

Jeff said, "On Christmas day, when I declared my love for you, and ask you to be my wife, did you think that meant for you to remove the ring from your hand as soon as you leave town?"

Isabella reeled back. "Jeff I didn't want---"

Jeff cut her off, "If you won't be honest with yourself, how could I expect you to be honest with me?"

Jeff's harshness startled Isabella. "Jeff, I," she looked down.

Jeff said, "I didn't mean to sound harsh, but I have to be honest with you, I don't think you are ready to be engaged."

Isabella objected. Her mouth opened but said nothing.

Jeff said, "It's okay Isabella, you don't have to love me, or want me. We can end this today, and I will leave your parent's barn and move back in with Keith and Addrianna."

Isabella grabbed Jeff's arm. "No Jeff, please, I love you, I do, please don't move away from me, my family." Isabella broke down. The cold protective shell she relied on to hide the softness on the inside died.

Jeff held her and whispered, "Tell me the truth, why do you want me to stay?"

She lifted her head from his chest.

Jeff said, "I need to know right now."

Isabella gushed, "I love you, Jeff. I can't see my life without you. You were there to lift me out of my shyness. You taught me to think of more than myself, and to consider others."

Jeff heard what he needed.

Isabella whispered, "Please don't leave?"

Jeff said, "I have another question for you, and I want the truth."

Isabella said, "Ask me anything, Jeff. I will tell you the truth."

Jeff asked, "Why, when you were leaving to go to this orientation week, you let Araminta talk you into leaving your ring at home?" Jeff cautioned her, "Remember, I want the truth!"

Isabella's tears clouded her view. "I have to admit, I think I was taking you for granted. After everything you said to me, you made me reflect on everything I have done and said, and what I was feeling and I owe you an apology. I am so sorry for not showing you respect like you have always shown me. I guess it's true, you don't know what you've got until it's gone. You love me, and I know you do. The engagement rings at home was honestly because Araminta said it was awkward wearing jewelry and I agreed, and I figured since I would be away from you, I could get away without wearing it for a week without hurting you."

Jeff said, "I want you to know you broke my heart when you made that choice. I didn't think you were ready for this lifetime commitment with me." He changed the subject, "Then when John and I come here to the college, you are with two guys, only to jump up quickly when I surprised you. You looked so angry with me for spoiling your fun. Many times, I think you do things like this because you know I love you and will always be there for you."

Isabella watched Jeff as he explained his feelings. She cried and shook her head. "No, no, no."

Jeff said, "I wonder are you saying no now because your life may change in a minute and you're afraid to lose me?"

Isabella pleaded, "Please, let me talk."

Jeff nodded. "But please know, I want the truth."

Isabella nodded. "I meant no harm. I love my ring; it means everything to me. I'm sorry for removing the ring. I'm sorry I hurt you, I'm sorry I broke your heart. Jeff, I know you said you didn't think I was ready for this lifetime commitment, but I wanted to let you know I am ready for you. I have to admit you are my only boyfriend, and although this is new for you and me, you handle it with ease. This was a reality check, and I feel awful for what I have put you through."

Jeff interrupted, "Why do you only show affection in private with me and push me away in public?"

Isabella dropped her head and let tears fall. "I'm so sorry, please forgive me."

Jeff continued. "You didn't answer the question?"

Isabella had no tissue to wipe her eyes, and Jeff wasn't offering her any assistance. She wiped her eyes with her hands. "My sister Araminta's shyness was worst than mine. The protectiveness that John teases me about is something that makes me feel a little better about me. I am not as shy as Araminta, and Araminta would always hide behind me. It made it look like I was protecting her but I wasn't. I was just a little more brave. I can show affection easy in private, but if you remember many times I couldn't stare into your eyes, I would even then, turn away from you. Jeff I can't believe you wanted me."

Jeff's scoffed at her thinking that.

Isabella said, "That first day you spoke to me in the school yard, it's a wonder I didn't faint. I don't know if you noticed my knees were knocking, my lips kept shivering, and my voice trembled. Araminta and I would hear the pretty Fleming twins all the time, and that made the shyness worse. Jeff, you sounded so confident when you spoke, you were caring, and that pulled me out of the hole I was in, but it still doesn't excuse what I've done to you. I am sorry, and as much as I love you and would love to start over with you, I understand if you want to break up with me."

"Grandma, this seems pretty detailed. How much of this is truth, and how much is embellishment?"

"Child, I have second sight. I remember it as though I'm there."

"Yeah, okay. So did they recapture that moment?"

"Let me conclude:

Isabella stood. She turned and hurried away, trying not to let him see her bawling. She came to an oak tree. She held on to a limb and lowered herself only to be caught by Jeff into his lap. She tried to push away, but he held her tight.

He turned her around and wiped the tears.

Isabella resisted. "Let me go, Jeff."

Jeff grabbed her arms and pulled her close. Isabella felt helpless and didn't want to look at him. "Please."

He insisted, "Look at me."

Isabella had no fight left. She surrendered with nothing to offer. She couldn't forgive herself for what she had put him through.

Jeff wiped her eyes again, but the tears continued to fall like a waterfall. Jeff kissed the top of Isabella's head. "It hurts me to put you through that, and I will never do that again. I had to do it to see if you really wanted us. I'm not going anywhere Isabella, I'm here for the long haul and I need to know if you are too?"

Isabella nodded.

Jeff said, "During this talk, you broke down twice. Every guard you ever had up was broken and tossed to the floor, you didn't care that I saw you vulnerable, you wanted me, just as much as I want you."

Isabella rubbed his hand. "I love you." They kissed, kissed without regard to the outside world passing by. It felt right, and neither one doubted anything about each other. He held her and she held him. Everything dissolved into the passion that had always been there.

Jeff smiled. "We better get going, so you can get back to the dorm before the curfew. We promised your resident assistant, Toshia, we would have you back before then."

Isabella sniffed. "Thank you."

Jeff asked, "For what?"

Isabella smiled. "For you."

Jeff whispered, "I love you." They melded from the afternoon revelations in each other's arms, walking blissfully away.

I was less sold on Jeff than before. He started coming across as a slicker version of John, but I couldn't help wondering how much of Matilda's love for the boys grew from the years after these events. I had to keep digging forward to find out what happened after this. "I am really interested to find out more but I'm getting tired, Grandma."

She begged. "One more, I promise it will be off to bed for you after that one." She tilted her gaze at me. "Please?"

I couldn't refuse that. "Sure."

Chapter 24

Matilda switched to John:

At the other end of the park, John and Araminta walked hand in hand around a picnic table, John smiling at her. He stopped and lifted Araminta onto the table. He held her hand. "Araminta I want to talk to you about something."

Araminta said, "Sure John."

John said, "Do you know that some of the boys at the school were flirting with you and wanted more than they led you to believe."

Araminta played naïve, "Like what?"

John said, "The guy who wanted to go to a private room with you in the library, the guy that wanted to get you off campus, and told you not to believe the school pamphlet of the freshman rules. Do you understand what I'm saying?"

"Araminta shook her head with a convincing air of disbelief. "So they wasn't just being friendly, they wanted to harm us?"

John said, "I hope they didn't want to harm you, but they wanted you. Do you know what engagement means?"

Araminta said, "Yes, it's what we are, you and me and me with you."

John said, "Do you realize that those boys were flirting with you? You had no ring to show you belong to someone, and as pretty as the both of you are, they was tryin' to be more than a guy on campus. Did you enjoy the flirting and attention they gave you?"

Araminta hesitated. "It wasn't bad. It passed the time til Friday when I was supposed to see you."

John offered, "Araminta what if I told you two of the Hendricks sisters ask me out to a movie and dinner, and wanted me to take the other one shopping. How would you feel?"

Araminta smiled. "They are pretty girls. Did you go?"

John said, "No Araminta, how can you ask that? I was asking you what if I did?"

Araminta offered, "If you had, there isn't much I can say about it."

John shook his head. "I wanted you to see what you letting these guys flirt with you does to me."

Araminta winced. "John the boys flirting with me made you upset?"

John asked, "When did you think I was coming to the college?"

Araminta said, "Momma and Daddy were coming to pick us up."

John surmised, "So I wasn't supposed to be here, correct?"

Araminta agreed, "Correct."

John said, "The fact that you told me about the flirt Monday night, and you saw me Tuesday morning should answer your question about if I was upset."

Araminta half-heartedly apologized, "I'm sorry, John."

John said, "It's okay. Araminta I know you didn't viciously try to hurt me, and you know if we are going to flirt, we will flirt with each other, deal?"

Araminta rolled her eyes. "Very well." Araminta patted John's hand, but he wanted more and pulled her in for a kiss.

He swept her off the table and stood.

Araminta tried to remain light in the moment, "You are so strong."

John said, "I enjoy kissing you, let's do it some more."

Araminta diverted him. "Not here in public."

John had an idea. "Has your momma ever talked to you about sex?"

Araminta wanted to stop that idea. "John!"

John said, "What? We are engaged to be married, Araminta. Don't tell me you're too shy to discuss it with me?"

Araminta wiggled free and stood. "Let's not get ahead of ourselves."

John motioned for her to pay attention. "Look at me Araminta?"

Araminta sighed and sweat pulsated from her forehead. He was taking this to a level she wasn't ready to deal with.

John said, "Will you be this shy once we are married?"

Araminta wasn't shy, she had no real knowledge of sex, and she wasn't about to learn right then. "Momma told me and Isabella never to lie down with a boy, if you do, you're pregnant, and you don't ever want to be pregnant unless you're married to your husband."

John's eyes widened. "Your momma said that?"

Araminta said, "Yes, she told that to me and Isabella, but I think she was too nervous to tell us everything."

John said, "Everything? You mean that's all you know about sex?"

Araminta repeated, "John!"

John insisted, "Araminta, look at me, please. Here, sit with me. You know you don't have to be bashful about this conversation, but I have to know. Is this all you know about sex, about laying down you get pregnant?"

Araminta nodded, half in jest, half to end it. "Is there more?"

John's brows furrowed and he moved back to stare at her. "You know what a penis and a vagina is, don't you?"

Araminta jumped off the table. She'd had enough and started walking away.

John yelled, "Where are you going?"

Araminta said, "I'm getting away from you talking to me."

John stood and caught up to her. He scooped her up kicking and screaming, carrying her back to the picnic table.

Araminta fussed, "I don't want to talk about this, John."

John said, "Listen to me, Araminta. I will not have you ignorant. I want you to be open to talk to me about anything. Our first time talking about this should not be the night of our wedding."

Araminta twisted, uncomfortable with the subject, uncomfortable about the subject with him.

John held her. "We are going to have this conversation because we should."

Araminta said, "If that's what you want, go have it with Jeff."

John grabbed her held her in place. "No, I think I will have it with you." Against her will he opened up with, "You know I have a penis, and you have a vagina."

"Grandma, they did not really have this conversation. You are pulling my leg."

"Gospel truth, child."

Did Araminta know anything about sex? It sounded like this was playing with him."

"Not a lick. I avoided the birds and the bees. My mistake I suppose, but I so cherished their innocence."

I shook my head. "It's a wonder they didn't get pregnant at twelve."

"Why do you say that?"

"Because the less you know, the easy to trick. My father lives by that credo."

"Well, they didn't."

"And so tell me how John manipulated her."

"He didn't."

Let's hear more and see."

She went on:

Araminta closed her eyes and resisted listening

John patted her face. "Stay with me."

"John, please no more of that talk."

John said, 'I will make a deal with you, if you don't want to have the conversation with me, then you have to do option two."

"Araminta said, "John listen, I made a deal with you, and we are engaged, but I guess I forgot what all engagement entails, and the marriage that follows. I forgot about the sex. The kissing is fine, but I rather not have to deal with the sex until I'm ready, and right now I'm not ready. Momma never told us about the p word and the v word, and now I understand why. If you feel sick while hearing those words something is wrong, and my body tells me to let this go. I know I may be making a big mistake, but friendship is not a bad thing for us. I know you're ready for marriage, but maybe we can just become friends for now, or if you don't want to wait for me, I understand. You move on and find a woman who is ready for what you're ready for. I don't want to learn about sex, it's just too revealing to me. I'm just not ready. So, friends?" She held her hand out in a mock shake.

John objected, "Friends? No! Araminta that's not the way you do things. We talk, and if talking doesn't work, *you talk some more. You may be uncomfortable talking about this, but you don't give up on us."*

"Grandma, please tell me this is where their story ends? I so want him to not be my great uncle. Tell me they called it quits right there?"

"Sorry, that isn't how their story unfolds."

"I knew you would say that. Okay, spill it."

Matilda finished:

Araminta said, "I don't want to talk about sex, and you do. You want me to come around to your way of thinking, but I don't want to think about sex. Becoming friends is the only way I can guarantee I don't have to deal with this."

John insisted, "This is not over, Araminta."

Araminta said, "It is if I have to discuss sex. Let's not argue, John. Friendship is not a bad thing either."

John said, "Araminta if you think you are not going to be the love of my life anymore you have lost your mind. Don't be scared of learning about sex, embrace that you have a man that wants to teach you about sex. I will not let you go, Araminta, and if you try to break up with me for that reason, I will call a meeting with our parents and the church, and we will sit down and discuss this until you understand everything there is to know about sex."

I stared at Matilda. "This just gets more and more horrible, Grandma."

"Why?"

"Did you understand that conversation? First, he said there is no way she is breaking up with him, then he said if she tried he would bring in their parents and the church. You don't see how damaging that is to a woman?"

"The times, child, the times."

"The times or not, it's not right."

"How long have you been married?"

"Not one day yet."

"I was married for all my adult life until Stanley died, and I never wanted another, so it doesn't seem to be too bad a method."

"That's your argument, because it worked for you? We have fought for our rights for the last one hundred years. You of all people should be aware of what second class citizens women have been. This attitude is why."

"Do you want to hear about their lives or do you want to argue relationship in the 1920s?"

She was right. I had transferred my 1980 beliefs on how things were done back then. "Please, continue. I will promise to keep my mouth shut." I smiled, "Until the next time John irritates me."

Matilda grinned, "That means a few more interruptions."

"Great," I said with sarcasm.

"So, where was I?"

"Forcing her to talk about sex."

Araminta was frantic. "John, no, please. Please don't call my parents and the church and your parents. This subject isn't one I want to discuss, not the p word or the v word, okay? I may not know what sex really is, but kissing is about all I want to deal with, you seem to like it when you kiss me, right?"

John looked at Araminta. "If you think I'm going to marry the love of my life and just kiss her, you really have lost your mind, Araminta. When we marry I want to make love to my wife, not just her lips. Araminta you might as well get yourself in gear and get ready to learn what a penis is and a vagina."

Araminta put her foot down. "John, stop! We aren't going to go further with this."

John said, "I will let you think about this for five to ten minutes, and then I will ask you again."

John nibbled on a sandwich while Araminta brewed. John took in the scenery. He knew Araminta wouldn't want to be in a room with her parents, his parents, and the pastor discussing her fear of learning about sex.

John said, "Am I going to tell you about sex or will my parents?"

Araminta shot back, "I'll ask my momma, thank you."

John shook his head. "Araminta, your momma only told you not to lie down with a boy because you'll be pregnant. Me or my parents?"

Araminta said, "Wait a minute, John, My momma will tell me the truth if I ask her."

John shook his head. "Araminta we have been through that."

Araminta said, "I don't care what you want, I'll learn on my own time?"

John didn't give in. "I guess than it's the family and church way."

Araminta scowled, "How dare you."

John cornered her and made sure she realized who ultimately was in charge. "What did you say to me?" He waited but Araminta cowered. He went on, "That's what I thought. We'll get my momma to teach you, teach you good what sex is. Then you will like it and your husband will love you for being such a great wife. You won't have to worry, your sister and I will be sitting right next to you holding your hand while my momma tells you everything, and you won't leave until she finishes. Is that a deal?"

Araminta shrunk, she had no options. "Okay."

John's mood turned happy. "Okay, we better get to the dorm before you miss curfew."

"Grandma, the conditioning was done. He'd broken her down, and I'm sure he took her virginity."

"No talk like that."

I smiled, I suspected she still lived in the stifling age of not hearing anything about sex. "So how did the rest of that night go?"

Araminta told John that Isabella didn't know anything about sex either. John said he would have Isabella and Jeff in attendance with John's Mom and Araminta. He hugged Araminta. "Thank you."

Jeff and Isabella met up with them and agreed to leave the next day after a quick tour of the local hospital. Araminta and Isabella's career choices were health management with desires to go into nursing. Their counselors wanted the students to visit the hospital to meet with the nurses and nurse's aides, and have a walk-through of the facilities.

The counselors said John and Jeff were welcome to come with them to visit the hospital. When they got there, the administrator introduced them to their intern for the morning. Her name was Mrs. Bill. Mrs. Bill was nice. She showed them all around the hospital, a new experience for the girls, who had never been in a hospital. The twins had been born at home with the help of a midwife. As they took the tour, they entered the maternity ward and saw all the babies. Isabella and Araminta thought that babies were so little.

John grabbed Araminta's hand. "I want seven of those."

Araminta looked aghast. "Not here, John."

John rubbed Araminta's hand. "Okay, Araminta." He laughed, she didn't.

Mrs. Bill took them down the hall to the employee daycare. Jeff moved toward the bathroom, pulling John with him. When they got to the bathroom, John turned. "What's wrong, Jeff?" John worried. "Jeff, are you okay? You don't look too good. Why are you sweating?"

Jeff stared back. "John I think that intern, Mrs. Bill, is my Aunt. Remember I told you the story of my father's siblings had to go to the orphanage?"

I interrupted Grandma. "Wow, that's a major left turn."

"Life has many left turns. She continued:

John said, "Yes, and Camille died, right?"

Jeff said, "Yes, but remember I told you my grandmother was pregnant when my grandfather died and she was pregnant with my father's sister Natalie Jordan, and my grandmother's sister let my grandmother die?"

John said, "Wait a minute, what makes you think she is Natalie?"

Jeff said, "If you ever saw my Aunt Lena, you would know. Lena and Natalie are sisters."

John paused. "Okay, ask her what her first name is."

"Jeff said, "Okay."

John said, "You're going to have to control the shocked on your face."

Jeff said, "I will try."

John and Jeff rejoined the group. As they continued on the tour, Jeff couldn't help but stare at Mrs. Bill.

As they listen to Mrs. Bill discussing sanitizing, another intern got off the elevator. "Hey, Nat, you ready for lunch?"

Jeff pumped his fist. Isabella went to see what was wrong. Before John could respond, the intern said, "Do you want me to pick up Jefferson for you and have him ready."

Mrs. Bill said, "Yes, I should be finish in ten minutes."

Jeff hyperventilated, and Mrs. Bill offered a small conference room with two gurneys.

Mrs. Bill said, "Place him on the gurney, and let me look at him."

Isabella turned to John. "What's wrong with Jeff?"

John dismissed her. "You will find out in a minute, just let me handle this."

When Mrs. Bill checked Jeff, he started crying. Mrs. Bill turned to John. "Is his blood pressure usually steady or is it normally high or low?"

John said, "His blood pressure is usually high when he is in the presence of a blood relative."

Isabella interrupted, "What are you talking about John? Jeff doesn't have high blood pressure."

John looked at Isabella. "He does today." John stood on the opposite side of the gurney and faced Mrs. Bill. "Mrs. Bill, is your name Natalie Jordan?" Mrs. Bill looked at John. "That's my maiden name, and my married name is Billups, but here at the hospital they call me Mrs. Bill. Why?"

John said, "Well, did you have a brother named Clifton Jordan Sr.?" Natalie's stiffened. John said, 'Jeff's father was Clifton Jordan Sr. and you are his Aunt.' Mrs.

Bill staggered, and John caught her. He placed her on the second gurney and rolled it beside Jeff's.

Isabella and Araminta ran to get a nurse for Mrs. Bill and Jeff. Jeff and his new found aunt hyperventilated and cried. They reached out and grabbed hands and didn't let go. Araminta and Isabella rushed in with nurses who looked over Jeff and Mrs. Bill. After the nurses got them calmed down, one asked, "Is this your brother?"

John said, "Yes, yes he is." John looked over to Jeff and Jeff tried to smile but tears welled in his eyes. Isabella hugged Jeff.

Before the four left the hospital to head home, Mrs. Bill introduced them to her youngest son, Jefferson. More tears fell. No one minded because the joy that overcame two people, who were connected by blood but separate by hatred, made the twin's and the boy's spring break turn special, an emotion packed event. The ride home and the stories told to Stanley and Matilda were priceless. The generations would continue to grow when the entire family would meet that summer for the best family reunion in Pitt County's, Greenville Township history.

"Grandma, that's quite the story."

"Yes, remarkable things happen in some remarkable ways."

Nellie came into the room and tapped her watch. "It's late girls, are you two burning the midnight oil?"

I nodded. "I'm deciphering fables from facts."

Nellie offered, "Sometimes those fables are more fact and the facts are mere fables."

I stood and stretched. "And isn't that where the mystery lies?"

Matilda hadn't moved from her spot. Time didn't seem to register with her and I suspect she didn't want to end our session.

"Grandma, we need to get some rest. I know I'm tired, and if I'm tired, I would be surprised that you aren't."

She smiled. "I suppose you should get your rest. Rest is important, because we have many miles to go for you to understand where you belong in this family."

With that, I turned to the bedroom, sure we had many more conversations ahead.

Chapter 25

Sunday morning and like the day before, roasted coffee and breakfast woke me, luring me to the kitchen. Matilda was already seated and had on her Sunday best. Nellie had on a skirt but still hadn't put on a blouse, covered with a t-shirt that read, 'Are you really here?' on the back it read, 'Were you ever?'

I sat and held my cup up. "Ready." We had stayed up well past my usual hour, and I needed a fix of caffeine.

Nellie turned with a glass of orange juice. "You will get your coffee after you have something good for you."

"Coffee is good for me. You don't know what I'm like when I'm cranky."

She smiled. "Drink your juice."

I obliged and then requested coffee.

"Cream and sugar?"

"No I like it black."

Matilda found my delivery funny.

My arm hurt. "This doesn't feel good." I rubbed a patch of arm that had an unusual pain.

Nellie and Matilda shared a view that didn't go unnoticed by me. "What?"

Matilda suggested. We need to get you through more of the family history. After church we will continue, okay?"

I shrugged. "Well, it's why I came down here."

After I dressed, I offered to drive, but Nellie had that already called. We helped Matilda down the steps and into the car, but by the time I got there, I realized I was in as bad a shape as she was. My ankle and side hurt as well.

I offered, "Maybe I shouldn't go."

In unison, Nellie and Matilda objected. "No!"

"Well then, if you two are insisting so vehemently, who am I to argue?"

Matilda pulled me into the backseat with her. "Besides, I want you to meet Nellie's son, the preacher."

We made it to a beautiful church on a beautiful fall day in the Carolinas. My pain intensified, and Nellie took to aiding both Matilda and me. "I just don't know what happened. I guess I slept wrong."

Her stiff smile offered little relief. "Let's get you into the pews so you can rest."

The crowd noise disoriented me. Chatter buzzed, people made acquaintances with neighbors, and I focused on a beating that I couldn't place.

Matilda patted my knee. "We'll get you back to the house so we can get on with the twins."

For some reason that sounded reasonable. "I'd like that."

Matilda pointed to a striking young man taking the podium. "That's Nathan, Nellie's son."

He couldn't have been but maybe thirty; a swirl of auburn hair, big frame, and a booming baritone voice. "Congregation, what if life here is nothing more than a rest stop for a life we have yet to live?"

The next thing I remember was a pat on my cheek and a drink of water. I was in the pastor's office and that same voice hovered over me asking if I was okay.

I caught my bearings and sat up. "Yeah, I think the late night and early morning got the best of me."

He smiled. "My mother says you are Matilda's great granddaughter?"

"I am. Nellie tells me you are her son?"

He grinned. "I am." He continued. "I was worried my sermon was so bad that you fell asleep on me."

"I'm sure with the size of your church and the number of members I saw, you must be pretty good."

"Well, that's not for me to say. I just do what I'm called to do."

I was a bit scrambled and hoped my, "Yes, don't we all," didn't come across as dry and rude. I forced a limp laugh and he helped me stand. "Thank you."

"You're welcome."

My arm felt better but that ankle still felt tweaked. I put some pressure on it and knew I'd look like a cripple if I took a step. "Hmm." I tested it again. Nope, that wasn't going to support me.

Pastor Nathan turned away and grabbed a cane leaning against a wall. "Just so happens that I have this vintage cane. It might not be the most vogue, but I think it'll work as an extra wheel for you."

I accepted it without question. "You are a savior."

"No, I just bring word of the savior."

"Fair enough."

Nellie made her way into the office and checked up on me. "Are you okay?"

"Yeah, I seem to be better in some spots, and worse in others, but I'll live."

"Then let's get you back to the house."

I asked her son. "Can I use the phone here?"

"Absolutely." He assisted me to a phone on his desk. "Do you need privacy?"

"No, just checking in with my parents." I dialed the number and like before, I got a disconnection notice. I tried my fiancé and got the same result. "This is too weird." I turned to Nellie. "It would appear it's not your phone, but the entire state of North Carolina that is down."

Pastor Nathan gave his mother a kiss on the cheek and offered, "I'll come by and check up on you three ladies today."

Nellie and I made it out to the car where Matilda sat waiting.

"Are you feeling better, child?"

"Yes, Grandma, I am, but for some reason my ankle hurts."

Nellie sat in the front seat and turned to Matilda. "Tildy, you better hurry with your stories, I think she'll need to get home tomorrow."

Matilda nodded. "Yes, it was a pleasure having her here, and I'm sure she'll get back as soon as she can."

They carried on as if I wasn't there. "I'm in no hurry to leave; I can probably stay a few more days."

Matilda shook her head. "No, you have places to be, but I feel you'll be back, and in a better way next time."

I watched the countryside sprawl out around us as we drove out past the pastures and farms. We turned up the familiar road and when we got to the house, Nellie helped us out one at a time.

After we'd settled in, had a bite to eat, Nellie started a fire, and found my quilt. Matilda sat next to me and said, "Now, let's continue."

Chapter 26

Matilda said with a bold reference to our last reading, "I believe this story was headed into the territory of sex."

She surprised me. "I thought you were too ladylike to call that out?"

"Well, it is what happened."

"I can't wait to hear this."

She plowed in without introductions:

John said to Jeff, "Araminta and I had a wonderful conversation when we were in the park. I always wanted to know what she knew about sex." Jeff had no idea what was coming. John said, "I know this is a surprise, but I was talking to my mom and dad, and I asked them about sex two years ago. They told me everything, so I told Araminta about that conversation."

Jeff was subdued. "How did she take it?"

John said, "She never got comfortable. She pushed it off when I mentioned I have a penis and she has a vagina. It took me five minutes to get her to at least listen."

Jeff laughed. "I can imagine."

John continued, "This is my future wife and an important element in a marriage is sex. Araminta doesn't know where babies come from. I can't have my wife walking around ignorant. Araminta is fighting me on this, but I gave her a choice. I told her either I can teach her, or my mother and father can teach her."

Jeff asked. "Who did she pick?" John said, Araminta wants my momma only? I told her as long as I can be there holding her hand. Mind you, she don't want to deal with any of this, but she knows my foot is down and she has no choice."

Jeff asked, "What did she say?"

John admitted, "Araminta reluctantly said okay. I told Araminta maybe you want to have Isabella there for support. Araminta said she couldn't have her sister there looking at her while we had that talk."

Jeff said, "Can I offer a solution?"

John said, "Please."

Jeff said, "Can Isabella and I be in on this meeting?"

John said, "I wouldn't have the meeting without you. I knew you were going to be dealing with my issue. Isabella will not go along with this, will she?"

Jeff said, "Well, while you and Araminta were discussing sex in the park, Isabella and I was discussing breaking up."

John said, "What! Breaking up?"

Jeff said, "I had to have a heart to heart with her about how she was treating me. We finally decided we love each other enough to try and make this relationship work. The sex class may be hard on her, but I do believe she will make a go of it."

John said, "You guys must have had some deep conversations if she changed that much?"

Jeff said, "I had to break her, and it's not something I'm proud of, but she seems to appreciate the outcome. Isabella has changed a lot, and I'm proud of her for it."

My ankle may have hurt, but I had enough spunk to spit out, "Men!"

"What?"

"They can be so arrogant in their assumptions that we need to be 'trained,' as though we are a pet."

"I don't think that's what Jeff meant."

"But if the story goes as you have stated it, that's what he said, and that's what that means. He 'broke' her. Gee, can he put a saddle on her now?"

"I know you don't approve, but this was on them, and it was their lives."

I shook my head and waved her to carry on.

John said, "What do you mean you had to break her?"

Jeff explained, "Well, I threw everything at her that bothered me about our relationship, and allowed her to speak on it. Isabella broke down twice, crying and telling me she was sorry, and in the end, she got up and left the picnic table hopeless, helpless, feeling she lost me, and lost everything. I had to manhandle her to get her to finally stop pushing and pulling away from me. Each time Isabella tried to fight, I fought harder to the point where she had no other choice but to surrender. Isabella had nothing left to offer me but her limp body covered in tears. I spoke to her while I wipe her eyes, and told her it hurt me to put her through that, but I had to see if she really wanted me. I told her I will never do that again, and I'm not going anywhere, I'm here for the long haul. I finally saw Isabella vulnerable side and it's something I thought I wanted to see, but I was wrong, it was something that made me want to care for her, to bandage her sores, and kiss them away. I knew I needed her, and loved her, and wanted to take care of her for the rest of my life. I always knew she was like Araminta, I told her that before. Isabella would hide her soft side, especially around Araminta and her Mom. I saw through that, and knew there's something more to this girl. The park trip was the break I needed to see another side of her, and it was beautiful inside her soft treasures. Those treasures were clean, because she hardly used them. I still look at her and she blushes when she sees me looking. I'm not ashamed though, she knows I will look all day if I could. I'm so glad she is with me, I love her."

"Grandma, this isn't healthy. Women shouldn't be treated like that."

"You must keep listening. Things change, they always do."

I sighed.

Chapter 27

I wanted to know, "So who did the teaching of this Sex Ed, John?"

Matilda shook her head. "You are such a cynic."

"Then who?"

"John's mother."

"And she did it over you, why?"

"She was schooled in such things."

"I see. I can't wait to hear how this went."

"Well, on that day,"

Mrs. Whitney said, "I need Isabella and Araminta to sit on this side of the room, and John and Jeff be seated on that side of the room."

John said, "Momma, I told Araminta I would be here holding her hand."

Mrs. Whitney said, "I'm doing this because I want Araminta and Isabella to ask me any questions they may have." She turned to Jeff, "John knows everything I'm going to talk about, so Jeff, if you have any questions, let me know. John and Jeff, I need to speak to the girls first, so would you guys step outside, and I will come get you for us to begin."

John pleaded, "But Momma, I promised Araminta I wouldn't leave her, you already separated us from the sofas."

I had to intervene. "Grandma, that boy didn't promise her, he told her he was going to be there. He's making out that she wanted him there."

"Be that as it may, he did tell her that he would do it, and now his mother was contradicting that."

"And she should have raised that young man better." What patience my great grandmother had. She would take my outbursts without so much as a raised eyebrow.

"She did a fine job on that boy."

"Yes, it sounds like he was lovely." I steamed as only an independent woman could.

Matilda waited for me to finish. When I had sufficiently flamed out, she went on with the sex class:

Mrs. Whitney said, "John, there are things only women need to know. I understand you supporting

Araminta, but let Momma handle this part. Araminta and Isabella will be alright."

Unhappy, he and Jeff headed outside. Mrs. Whitney said, "Girls, I want to make sure you know there's nothing to be nervous about. I'm going to tell you things you will need to know now and when you marry. My first question is; do you know what a penis is?" Mrs. Whitney sat with her question hovering in the air. "Araminta, you can go first."

Araminta turned to Isabella, and Isabella couldn't look up.

Mrs. Whitney repeated, "Well Araminta?"

Araminta said, "Mrs. Whitney can I ask a question?"

Mrs. Whitney said, "Okay Araminta."

Araminta asked, "Can you tell me why I need to have this conversation when I'm not having sex with your son, and don't plan on it until we are married, which is several years from now? I just don't see the need to get into this right now."

Mrs. Whitney said, "Well, It's really about education, and I think that I should be the judge of when you should learn it. Learning about the human body isn't just about sex; it's about all sorts of things that will make you a mature woman. Since we will be covering the anatomy of sex, we might as well cover the nature of love and sex, and how they play a role in healthy relationships." She had dismissed Araminta, much as her son had done. She turned to Isabella. "You are ready to learn about the human body, yes?"

Isabella blushed. "I'll admit, I'm a little embarrassed."

Mrs. Whitney smiled. "Don't be. We will make this quick and painless. Let me ask some questions. Isabella, do you know what a penis is?"

Isabella looked up, knowing she had to participate. "Mrs. Whitney it's what he has."

Mrs. Whitney said, "Very good, but where is it located?"

Isabella said, "It's down at his private part."

Mrs. Whitney said, "Point to the general area of his private part for me."

Isabella motioned slowly to her private part with embarrassment.

Mrs. Whitney said, "It's nothing to be embarrassed about, this is reality, and I don't want you to be married and scared to make love to your husband, that's how problems start." Mrs. Whitney continued, "We will have sessions until you get this down."

Isabella and Araminta turned to each other, and Araminta asked, "You mean this isn't the first and last class?"

Mrs. Whitney shook her head. "Do you know what sex is?"

Araminta said, "No, and I didn't ask to take a course on it either."

Mrs. Whitney stopped her, "Then it looks like we have a lot to cover. I insist you take this course, and we won't let you stop until you know all the answers to all my questions on my list."

Araminta said, "Your list? What list?"

Mrs. Whitney said, "There are lots of sex related questions I need you girls to know before you marry. Now, Araminta, I'm going to put up a board and I want you to come up and draw a penis for me." She went about putting up a board and when she turned to Araminta, she was met with resistance. "Araminta?"

Araminta balked and crossed her arms.

Mrs. Whitney smiled. "Come, come, Araminta, I want to give Jeff and John good reports on participation, and eagerness to learn and retaining the information. You're not moving to the board, Araminta?" Mrs. Whitney picked up her book and wrote in it. She said, "Okay, Araminta that's not going to look too good on your report for the first day, but I can't make you, so Isabella, will you come to the board and draw a penis for me?"

Isabella didn't want to go to the board either; however, she took the chalk and drew a scrub bush, she had never seen a penis before but she did her best to show she wasn't going to make it difficult on her with Mrs. Whitney.

Mrs. Whitney clapped. "Very good, Isabella. You get a good report on participation and eagerness to learn. Keep up the good work."

Isabella smiled. Araminta shook her head. "Mrs. Whitney, do you mind if I speak to my sister alone for a minute?"

Mrs. Whitney said, "Now, now, Araminta, Isabella knows Jeff is counting on her doing well in this class for them and their marriage. Please don't say anything negative to Isabella about how good she is doing. Okay, Araminta?"

Araminta dismissed Mrs. Whitney's rebuke. "I just want to know why she is eager all of a sudden?"

Mrs. Whitney said, "I talked to John and Jeff when we were putting this class together, and I decided to grade the two of you, and they wanted to know the progress each week."

Araminta said, "Each week? Mrs. Whitney, I can't do this after today. I will talk to my momma and drag it out of her. It's not something I'm comfortable discussing at this time, and I want to know what changed my sister all of a sudden." Araminta's biggest fear is that her sister would suck her in to this by needing her there.

Isabella whispered, "Mrs. Whitney said I still have not finished the lesson for today."

Araminta didn't care and turned to Mrs. Whitney. "I've learned enough, and I better go. I will talk to you soon." Araminta motioned to her sister, "Come on, Isabella."

Mrs. Whitney said, "Let me get John."

Araminta stopped. "Mrs. Whitney, do what you must, but I ask that you don't get John. He will drag me back, and I will be miserable. Isabella and I will run out the back and stay over at our friend's house til morning, and John can go let my momma know." Araminta became agitated. "Come on, Isabella!"

Isabella turned on her sister and ran to find the boys. Araminta thought, 'traitor!'

John and Jeff came running back in the house as Araminta ran out the back. John followed with a lantern out to the road. Araminta had a hundred yard head start and ran with the energy of a horse. She made it to the country road, past the fields and flagged down a truck. Before John could make it to her, she was gone. She'd hitched a ride with Mr. Lee, one of her neighbors.

Mr. Lee asked, "What are you doing out here?"

Araminta said, "I was over at my friend's house, but I had to leave. I'm glad it was you I saw."

Mr. Lee said, "I'm glad to be of help."

When she made it to her house, she went and confronted her mother. Matilda saw a frantic look on

Araminta's face. "What's wrong, Araminta? Where is your sister?"

Araminta explained, "Momma, Isabella and Jeff are at John's house. John had a class for all four of us to teach us about sex."

Matilda drew a sigh.

Araminta said, "Momma. I don't want to go to that class, but John told me I had to go to make our future marriage better. Momma, I am fine where I am in my life, and I can wait. I'm not supposed to be married for another four years. So, I am not going to take that class anymore. Momma, please help me. John will be looking for me, and I need your help."

Matilda went in the kitchen and put some water on the stove for tea. Araminta followed her as she got the tea cups and placed tea in each one. Matilda said, "Have a seat at the table, Araminta."

Araminta sat. "Yes, ma'am."

As Matilda stirred her tea, she told Araminta to put honey in and fix her tea to taste.

As she did, a loud bang of the door was followed by John, Jeff, and Isabella. Araminta jumped up and ran behind her momma. Araminta begged, "Momma, please don't let them take me back to that class, please, Momma. I don't want to go back."

Matilda looked at the trio and directed them to have a seat.

Araminta said, "Momma!"

Matilda said, "Araminta, I'm not going to let anybody harm my children, have a seat and finish fixing your tea while I talk to John."

Araminta said, "Yes, Momma."

Matilda asked the three, "Would you all like some tea?"

John and Jeff nodded, but Isabella said, "No thank you, Momma."

Matilda asked, "So John, what is going on? My baby tells me you're making her take a sex class. Isn't that for a momma to teach her daughters when she feels they are ready? What you're teaching might be too much for my baby to learn. I don't want her mind corrupted with things she don't need." Matilda continued, "So go ahead and speak, and I will listen."

John stood. "Thank you, Mrs. Fleming. Mrs. Fleming, you know I am crazy about your daughter, and you know I wouldn't have my momma teach Araminta, Isabella, or Jeff anything that would hurt them, but help them."

Matilda cut in, "Your momma is teaching this class?"

John said, "Yes ma'am, my momma used to be a counselor at a high school, and she found this learning helps the students when they are first married, and helps them with any problems that may come up."

I cried out. "Please, Grandma, tell me you stood up for her. She was being blindsided by everyone. Tell me you were there for her?"

"I did what was right."

I sunk in my chair. I knew it wasn't what was good for my great aunt.

She went on:

Matilda said, "Araminta?"

Araminta sunk in her chair. "Yes, Momma?"

Matilda said, "Araminta, you didn't tell me John's momma was teaching this class. I know John's momma, and she is a good woman."

Araminta whispered, "Yes, Momma, she is."

Matilda asked John, "What is it Araminta needs to do in this class, John?"

John said, "She just needs to participate, learn about sex so she will know what to do when we marry, and my momma will answer any questions Araminta, Isabella, and Jeff may have."

Matilda said, "And Araminta has been disrupting the class?"

John said, "Mrs. Fleming, Araminta is just scared - embarrassed mostly."

Araminta gathered some of her strength. "I am not embarrassed. For the last time this isn't about embarrassment. This is about appropriateness."

Matilda didn't let Araminta's outburst untrack her. "John, I need the truth, has Araminta been disruptive?"

John looked down. "Well, yes ma'am."

Matilda told Araminta to stand in front of her.

Araminta stood. "Momma---"

Matilda shushed Araminta. "I didn't have anyone to tell me about sex before I married, I had to learn everything on my own, and that made it painful for me. I want my children to have the best, more than I could ever have. Can you do something for Momma?" Araminta slumped. "Anything for you, Momma."

Matilda said, 'Can you do what John is asking you to do? I want you and Isabella and Jeff to know all you should know." Matilda addressed John. "Is there a punishment that my daughter is supposed to get for running away, and don't sugar coat it."

John grinned. He had been so sure Matilda would not support punishment. He smiled and shared a capricious gaze with Araminta. "Yes, ma'am."

"Grandma, are you kidding me? You not only didn't support her, you threw her under the bus? Why?"

"She needed this."

I couldn't believe I was compelled to listen to more. I was swimming upstream and not very well.

"I didn't asked John what that punishment was, only that he had my blessing to inflict it upon her."

My jaw dropped.

"My exact words were,"

"If she doesn't pass the class, I will blame you John, okay?"

John said, "You can count on me, Mrs. Fleming."

Araminta said, "But Momma, John has one desire out of this class, and I don't share it. He has told me I'm going to receive punishment if I don't participate, and yet, I've never been given the option if I want to or not. I just don't want to take the class. It's not about embarrassment." She eyed John like he was a liar.

John interrupted, "Mrs. Fleming, may I speak?"

Matilda said, "Yes, John."

"Mrs. Fleming, I would never do anything to Araminta if she would just participate in the class. I know she is resisting, you can ask Isabella and Jeff about it, but I do believe it's about embarrassment, they can tell you. Araminta is not the only one."

Isabella said, "Yes, Momma. I hate the embarrassment part too, but once I left the class it felt pretty good learning something I didn't know before."

Jeff said, "Mrs. Fleming, Isabella is right about the embarrassment part, but it's a part of life. It's better to know it than not know what to do when you marry."

Araminta had had enough. "That's their issue. I don't care if they are embarrassed. However, that's not my concern. I just don't want to be there. Now, I'll go because of you," she pointed to her mother, "but no one is going to tell me why I don't want to go but me."

John said, "See, that's what I'm talking about. I will do all I can, but she has to try as well."

"Matilda turned to an angry Araminta. 'Smile baby, that man loves you. Everyone in this room loves you. Now, John, do you need for Araminta to go back to your house tonight to say sorry to your momma for messing up the class?"

John said, "Yes, Mrs. Fleming. That would be helpful."

Matilda said, "You have my permission, just be home before ten thirty. Now, scoot, I have to finish combing Addie's hair." Matilda turned to her daughter. "Araminta?"

Araminta nodded, "Yes, Momma?"

Matilda told her, "Hug John, and tell him you're sorry, baby."

Araminta shook her head. "I'll say I'm sorry, but no hugs."

"Matilda said, "Do like your momma said, baby."

Araminta waved her off. She walked over to John with her head held high, and whispered, 'I'm sorry, John,' but her words were cold.

"John tried to reach out for a hug, but Araminta backed away and held an open palm between them.

"You're going to have to give me plenty of kisses for this."

Araminta shook her head as though trapped. "Really? Is that what you think?"

He nodded as his glare never left his face.

The four walked out to the truck, and Araminta stopped before getting in. He ushered Jeff and Isabella to get in first. "Sorry, but I'm not sitting next to him."

John ordered her, "Get in, Araminta."

Jeff waited. "You heard him."

She smiled, "Fine." She pulled her coat closed and hopped in the bed of the truck. She patted the back window. "Go!"

John stepped out and started to reach in to get her. Matilda shouted from the porch, "Is there a problem?"

Araminta said, "If you touch me, I'll scream."

John looked at Matilda. "No ma'am. Just making sure Araminta is warm enough. She wants to ride back here."

Matilda shouted to Araminta, "Is that what you want?"

"Yes, Momma."

Matilda shrugged and went inside. The four of them went to John's.

"Ugh. That is the worst thing I've ever heard. Not only did you turn your back on her, but her boyfriend told her she had to make up for it?" I shook my head. "This is wrong in any era."

"Well, she did go to the lessons, so you might want to wait and see how they went."

My head toggled like a bobble head. "Yeah, I want to know."

Chapter 28

"So your daughter was trapped into having to do what John said. Forced against her will of free choice."

Matilda found me funny. "She turned out pretty good."

"And how did those lessons go?"

Matilda picked up where she left off:

When they got to John's house, John excused Jeff and Isabella. "I'll be in, in a second." He waited until they'd entered the house and he leaned over the bed of the truck. "What are you feeling, Araminta?"

Araminta resigned to a fate she didn't want. "Whatever my momma wants. It's not fair, and you think you have the right to punish me too."

John said, "I will only punish you if you get out of line in the class."

I bristled with each reference to male dominance that Grandma imposed on the story.

Araminta said, 'I hope you know I don't want to be here, doesn't that bother you?"

John said "No, not really. It doesn't bother me because you're the one that's going to suffer, and if you're suffering makes all of us suffer, then we will have to do something about that, and it may be drastic."

Araminta's laugh had irony in its tone. "John, John, John. So I guess I will face some sort of punishment for my beliefs. How fair is that?"

John offered, "Love isn't fair." He continued, "Are we going back to class and apologizing to Momma?"

Araminta sighed. She stood and John held a hand to lift her out. She opted to get out the other side, on her own. From across the bed she reminded him, "I have agreed to do so because of my mother, not you. So leave it at that."

John put his foot down. "It's not bad when you participate and do what the teacher says. Isabella didn't try to run away. Why can't you follow her lead?"

Araminta exploded. "Because I'm not Isabella, and you aren't Jeff?"

John insisted, "She just wants to help her future marriage. That's all."

Araminta penetrated his stare. "Yes, she does. That should tell you something."

John flamed in fury. "How dare you make some accusation about our love." He demanded. "Come here."

Araminta pushed off and walked inside, steps ahead of him.

John motioned for Araminta to sit down in their teaching room. Isabella, Jeff, and Mrs. Whitney entered. John said, "Isabella, I want to make this clear with you and Jeff, If my fiancé mentions anything to you about how she thinks this class is bad or doesn't show me her love, you let me know, and she will find out what is bad for her." He turned his rage on Araminta, "Araminta, I don't want to hear you talking about poor relationships. Otherwise, I will tie you down and tell you sex 101 myself, and you will listen to it, too. Do you hear me?'

Araminta kept her rage to herself. "Yes, John."

John leaned on his woman, "Do you have something you'd like to say to the class?" Araminta, deflated, defeated, and done trying, offered, "Mrs. Whitney, I'm sorry I disrupted your class. It will never happen again."

John added, "Don't you owe me an apology also?" Araminta gave a sympathetic look to John. "No, I don't."

He bristled. "You have made a claim I don't care about you."

"I didn't mean to imply that you didn't care about me. Forgive me if that's what you thought." She smiled. "No, it's more about my feelings you don't care about."

The room had a hush, not an eye left the two of them.

Mrs. Whitney said, "This too shall pass. The two of you stand." Both Araminta and John stood before her. "Now, turn to each other and give each other a hug." John grabbed her and gave her a hug she'd not soon forget. "Now, doesn't that feel better?" She smiled and Araminta took her seat. "We still have forty minutes left to class. Do all four of you want to make good use of the time?"

John said, "I think we should, and Momma, what is Araminta's progress thus far?"

Mrs. Whitney said, "Araminta wasn't trying to draw a penis like I asked, so I asked Isabella, and she received two stars for participation and eagerness to learn."

Jeff said, "Ah, that's great, baby. I'm so proud of you." Jeff kissed her and they both turned to Mrs. Whitney.

John stared at Araminta. Araminta eyed Isabella. Mrs. Whitney said, "Araminta, will you go to the board and draw a penis for me?"

Araminta looked at her future momma-in-law and said, "Isabella already did."

John broke in, "Hold up, Momma." He turned to Araminta. "When the teacher asks you to do something pertaining to the subject, don't you dare question it. Do you understand me?" He lorded over her, "I said, do you understand me?"

Araminta coward at John's anger. "Yes, John, I'm very sorry."

John taunted her, "The teacher is waiting?"

Araminta stared at John. "Sure." She stood, walked to the board, drew a circle and sat down.

"Thank you, Araminta" Mrs. Whitney said. "John can you draw an accurate picture of a penis for me?"

John said, "Yes, Momma." John drew a penis on the board, and Araminta shook her head.

John said, "I'm done, Momma."

Mrs. Whitney said, "Thank you, John." She again turned to Araminta. "Can you draw a vagina for me?"

Araminta hesitated, got up, hands shaking and drew a picture. Mrs. Whitney congratulated her, but Araminta went back to her seat without acknowledging anyone.

John said, "It's nothing to be embarrassed about, you're doing good."

Mrs. Whitney asked Jeff, "Can you draw what breasts look like?"

Jeff stiffened. He approached the board with hesitancy and drew breasts.

Isabella couldn't look, but Mrs. Whitney told Jeff to lift Isabella's head and explain to her what he drew.

Jeff said, "I drew my vision of breasts."

Mrs. Whitney said it was beautiful and looked like real breasts. She asked the class to complete an essay on the benefits of taking the class, and what would they like to get out of it. "I need five hundred words, and you have to convince me it's what you want to do. Also, I want you to tell me where you think babies come from." She smiled. "Class meets back on Friday night, and I look forward to spending time with you again."

She pulled the girls aside. "Araminta and Isabella did you enjoy the class?"

Araminta said. "Mrs. Whitney, I'll tell you the same thing I told John, if you really want to hear it. So, why don't you ask Isabella? I think her answer will be more to your liking."

Isabella did her best to break the tension. "Thank you, Mrs. Whitney."

Mrs. Whitney played the role of unaffected well. "You're welcome, Isabella. Next week, we will discuss how the penis gets in the vagina."

I couldn't move. "Wow. Did your daughters really go through that, or are you kidding me?" I really wondered if my hundred year old great grandmother might be the greatest prankster in the world.

"That's how it happened, child."

"And they continued with all the classes?"

"They did."

"I'm going to use the restroom, and then I want to know more about how your daughters faired with those men."

She seemed pleased with herself. "I'll be here waiting."

Chapter 29

My ankle had stiffened, and my arm hurt again. I didn't want to bring it up. The ladies had looks of concern when it sprang up on me earlier that morning, so I kept it to myself. Even sitting on the toilet was hard, my entire left side started to ache. I tried to put it aside, concentrate on my purpose of being there. I put myself in a good mood, thinking about the sharpness of my great grandmother. I concentrated on her and let it wash over me. If she didn't complain about sitting in a seat all afternoon discussing her children with a petulant great granddaughter, I certainly could endure my phantom pains.

When I made it back to the front room, I found tea waiting for me. I caught the backside of Nellie leaving the room. She passed along, "I thought you could use a little chamomile."

"Thank you, Nellie."

"She turned and smiled, an angel's smile. "You're welcome."

Matilda added. "She's a fantastic lady, no?"

"Yes, very much so. You are lucky, Grandma to have her."

"Yes I am."

We sat there, reloading I think. I had to gear myself for more of relationships I didn't fully understand. "Are you ready for more?"

Matilda laughed. "That was my question for you."

"Yeah, I'm ready. Tell me more about the twins."

Matilda had a knack for not mincing words, and her openings were usually without set up:

As John drove Araminta, Jeff, and Isabella back home, he noticed the silence. Jeff and Isabella hugged, caressing each other's fingers. Araminta looked out the window, distant. John reached over and held her hand, but she remained cold. John called her name.

Araminta spoke against the window, "Yes, John?" Her voice cracked, and he pulled her close. Tears fell from her face.

When the truck stopped, John asked her, "Please wait."

Jeff and Isabella bid goodnight. Isabella hopped off his lap and they piled out of the truck. "Goodnight, John, see you in the morning."

John pulled Araminta into a clutch against his chest. He took a tissue and wiped her eyes. "Araminta, look at me please."

Araminta turned.

John asked, "What's wrong, baby?"

Araminta said, "You really don't get it do you?"

John sighed. "I'm not talking about tonight. I'm talking about us. What has gone sour? I haven't stopped loving you from day one. I've never hit you, I've given you whatever I have. Why are you pulling away?"

She studied his face. He really didn't understand. "Tonight is the symptom John. "You say you are nice, and that you've never laid a hand on me, but you might as well as do it, because you're telling me what I can or can't do is just as bad. Now, I want to go in the house. I did what you ask me to do in class, John. Can't I react how I want now that class is over? I feel as though my choices are being made for me, so I am going to cry. Of course, that won't matter to you. You disappoint me, but I did what you asked.”

Her words created an echo, nothing stirred. Just two people eyeing futures that didn't seem to intersect.

John pleaded, 'What did you want me to do, let you destroy the class, knowing we need it? My momma took a lot of time developing that class for us, and all the interruptions were uncalled for. Now that class is over you're telling me you are mad at me for doing the right thing?”

“Araminta pushed back, “Unbelievable. You really don't listen. How about this then, I just want to feel what I'm feeling without you telling me how to feel.”

John said, “Okay, that's fair. Maybe tomorrow you will feel better,” John tried to kiss her lips, but she turned away. John took her chin and forced her to face him. He kissed again, but she pursed her lips.

Araminta pushed away and slid to the other end of the truck, opened the door and escaped. “Goodnight,” She slammed the door shut.

John had no idea how difficult it would be. He saw Jeff enter the barn so he parked and went in. Turns out Jeff wanted to talk too.

Jeff said, "I like the class."

John said, "So do I, but Araminta's mad at me because I forced her to take the class."

Jeff said, "We knew it would be hard on her."

John said, "It seems she will participate in class, but be mad at me afterwards. I will see how she treats me tomorrow, and you check with Isabella to see how she treats her, and we will do this all this week until we go back to class Friday."

Jeff said, "Your momma is a good teacher."

John agreed, "I know, she was a counselor at a high school in another county, and she will counsel all of us."

Jeff nodded. "That's great, man. I'm glad because we need all the help we can get."

John admitted, "You were right about Isabella. That talk you guys had must have been very helpful."

Jeff said, "It was, and I'm so proud of her for doing all she can even in the midst of feeling embarrassed. She is really making an effort, and I will look forward to this class every time we go. And John don't worry about Araminta, she will come around. She loves you, you know that."

John hesitated, "I know she does, but I'll be glad when she gets like Isabella and participates, and doesn't feel like it's pulling teeth."

Jeff laughed. "Let's get some rest tonight and see what tomorrow brings." John agreed. "See you in the morning, Jeff."

As the sun rose, a new day formed and Jeff walked Isabella and Araminta to class.

John was a few minutes behind them. "Good Morning."

Araminta ignored John.

Class began with an assignment. The bell rang for lunch and Araminta raced out of class, far away from the building to a mammoth stone rock and opened her book to read and eat her sandwich alone. Araminta wanted to have a peaceful lunch with no interruptions from John.

John, Jeff, and Isabella watched her sitting alone. John said, "I'm trying to be patient with her, but she is making it difficult."

Isabella said, "She loves you John, she's just upset."

John said, "I hope so."

Isabella said "You know she doesn't have the patience to stay mad, although this is long for her."

John said, "I know. I think I'm going to have to start being bold if she still doesn't want to talk to me."

Jeff said, "What do you mean bold?"

John said, "Watch." John walked up the hill and startled her. Araminta dropped her last piece of sandwich. John said, "I'm sorry I made you drop your sandwich, but you can have mine. I have two."

Araminta dismissed him, "No, thanks." She closed her book and was about to leave when John closed the gap between them and made her tremble.

John said, "Don't be frightened, Araminta, you're my woman, and I wanted to talk to you."

Araminta stepped away from John, but John blocked her. Araminta's fear and anger grew. She hyperventilated.

John said, "I'm trying to be patient with you Araminta, but you are trying my patience."

Araminta froze. "Please, I have to go back to class."

John countered, "But the bell hasn't rung."

Araminta insisted, "I need to talk to Mrs. Nelson."

John squinted. "You're lying, Araminta."

Araminta tried to walk away, but John grabbed her and tried to kiss her. Araminta pushed away. John forced his lips on her and she stopped resisting. She gave in. He'd broken her. She gave him what he wanted, and although she was terrified and mad, she stopped resisting.

John slowed the kiss and knew he could have anything he wanted. He cut the kiss off and grabbed his books. "Don't do that again. See you in class." John asserted his dominance over Araminta.

Araminta picked up her books and walked slowly to class. She decided to hold her ground.

John had the approval of her parents, of his parent, of her sister; he'd not take her insolence again. 'I will kiss her like that all the time now because she is trying to be brave.' Besides, her momma invited John to dinner. He was in with the family.

When class ended, John grabbed Araminta's hand to let her know he was driving Jeff and Isabella home, and he wanted to drive her home also. John didn't have to work that day.

Araminta told John, "I would rather walk."

John dragged Araminta by the arm to the side of the building and threw her books down. She tried to bend down to pick them up, but John grabbed her and kissed her again.

Araminta tried to fight it, but his strength overpowered her and giving in was the only way to not get hurt. John placed her arms behind her back and pinned her against the wall. She pretended it was consensual. John kept kissing.

One of John's hands left her wrists and held her head in the palm of his hand, and Araminta pulled away and used her head to try and push off his chest. He held her as though they were happy, yet his happiness seemed to be all that mattered. John journeyed his lips to her ear. "I miss you." John's hand went back to her wrists.

Araminta arms went limp, twisted behind her back, idle in place. "Are we done?"

John told her, "Not until I say so."

Araminta sighed. "I give up. If that's what you want, and that's what my family wants, I give."

John had what he wanted, and he relished the victory. "Come on, let's get you, Isabella, and Jeff home."

"While John drove, Isabella and Jeff hugged, and Araminta played the good girlfriend, sat close and let John fondle her fingers.

John asked, "Have you completed your homework assignment for sex education class for Friday night?"

Araminta's smile faded. "You have what you want, do you have to drag me through more things I don't want to do? I haven't started my paper; I have no plans to write it. I thought that kiss meant I didn't have to go back."

John knew he would have to use drastic measures to get Araminta to go to the sex education class. Since Araminta was trying to avoid it, he would have to have to break her more. It would hurt, but he loved her too much not to try. As John drove to the Fleming's house, he let slip, "Araminta, your mother invited me to dinner tonight, but I would like to talk to Jeff and Isabella for a minute, can you go on in and we will be in shortly?"

Araminta didn't want them having conversations about her. "What's wrong, why can't I stay?"

John tried not to show how angry he was. "There's nothing wrong baby, trust me, everything is fine, we will be in shortly." John dismissed her with a kiss her on the forehead.

Araminta reluctantly went in the house. Her self-worth diminished to a piece of property.

John said to Jeff and Isabella, "It comes down to what I didn't want to do Jeff. I'm going to have to break her. My momma and I have done all we can do, and Araminta is determined she cannot take this class because of the discomfort she is feeling. If I didn't know she loved me, I would let this go, but I know she loves me, and I love her, and if breaking her is what it will take then Friday night will be the night."

Isabella said, "You mean break her like Jeff broke me?" Jeff and John looked down. Isabella said, "It worked for Jeff and me, I didn't know why he was so hostile with me, but now I know he was trying to see if I really wanted us. It hurt a lot, but I understand why Jeff had to do it." Isabella turned to Jeff. "I'm so grateful he did because I couldn't see what I was doing to him."

Jeff kissed Isabella, and they looked into each other's eyes. Isabella turned to John. "How do you plan on doing it?"

John said, "Here's the plan, after dinner I want to call a meeting with Mr. and Mrs. Fleming, and you two. I need you two to take Mr. Fleming out to the barn to show him something about the Kerosene heater or anything so you can tell him what the plan is." John gave the two his elaborate plan, one that would force Araminta to give in.

Isabella said, "If this is for my sister's happiness, I can take anything she dishes out."

John said, "Good girl."

Jeff said, "I think we are ready." As John, Jeff, and Isabella entered the house, Jeff saw Stanley leaving out the back door and caught up to him. He took Stanley to the barn and told him the plan.

John went in the kitchen to hug his second momma and see what was cooking. Matilda let John taste the cornbread and a spoonful of vegetables.

Araminta came in and watched her momma and John.

Matilda said, "Araminta, you want to fix John his plate; I'm going to fix the other plates."

Matilda left the kitchen and John watched Araminta. "I love you."

Araminta didn't trust him. "What's going on, John?"

John shrugged. "Nothing is going on, everything that happens at this point is for our happiness, remember that."

Araminta squinted. "At this point? What do you mean, John?"

John said, "You know how you ignored me because you were so angry with me because of how I treated you in the class?"

Araminta nodded. "It's not about how you treat me in class, it's about how you treat me everywhere."

John said, "Well, I'm not going to ignore you, I won't use your method, I have a method of my own. You see, my method will stick, it will end all the interruptions, the ignoring me, the running away, the having lunch alone, hiding behind your momma, and any useless thoughts left in your head. My method will work, and I hate to have to go to this extreme, but you are worth it." John felt powerful. "Araminta, you must learn as well."

Araminta grabbed John's arm. "John, you won. Please don't do what you're going to do. I'm sorry, I just---"

John placed a finger to Araminta's mouth. "It's too late. This is what I need from you at this point, stop ignoring me."

Araminta nodded with the coldest of deliveries. "Yes, John, anything."

John smiled. "Anything?"

Araminta exhaled and gave in, "Anything you want, I'm sorry."

John cornered her. "So you're going to class Friday night, correct?"

Araminta had to answer him or else he would know she was lying. "Yes, I will go."

He smiled and thought, 'This will help my plan to break her because I won't have to drag her to class, she will come freely.' John said, "So it looks like you have more homework than you thought."

Araminta knew what John meant. She gave a pale smile. He reminded her, "Everything that happens at this point is for our happiness, remember that."

What could she do? "Oh, yes. I will get right on that paper, I want Mrs. Whitney to be proud of me."

Matilda called everyone to dinner. John saw Jeff and Stanley coming in the back door. He looked at Stanley and Jeff, and they nodded. John's plan was on. He knew why Araminta's tone changed. Araminta was on to them, and she knew her last hope was mercy.

After dinner, John said, "Dinner was delicious, Mrs. Fleming. These were the best cornbreads."

Matilda said, "Thank you, John."

Araminta added, "Yes, Momma, they get better every time."

Matilda nodded. "Thank you, Araminta."

John had noticed Araminta opening up.

Araminta said, "John would you like me to get you more cornbread from the kitchen?"

John said, "No thanks, Araminta. I'm fine."

Araminta asked, "Momma, would you like more ice tea?"

Matilda waved it off. "I'm good, baby, thanks"

Araminta told Isabella, "I will do the dishes tonight, I will start now."

"Isabella said, "Araminta, I will take care of them, it's fine."

Araminta insisted, "No it's okay, I have already started running the water."

Isabella shrugged. "Okay."

John looked at Isabella and winked. He was on to Araminta. She couldn't beat him. Did she really think she could?

Araminta came in with the peach cobbler. "Momma, shall I cut it for everyone?"

Matilda said, "Maybe later, baby. They are still eating dinner."

Araminta said, "Okay, Momma."

John followed Araminta to the kitchen. "Whats wrong, Araminta?" John cornered her.

Araminta said, "I'm fine, just overwhelmed, I guess."

John said, "Overwhelmed about what?"

Araminta confronted John. "Don't play that game. I know you have something planned for me."

John shrugged. "You know you've done wrong, correct?"

Araminta asked John, "Is it wrong to feel the class isn't good for me?" She stepped closer and showed her teeth. "Huh?"

John laughed. Her showing strength was a joke. "Araminta, yes, I chose this class because I love you, and I want to make sure we know everything we need to know before marriage. Baby, you don't know where babies come from. We need to know these things before we say 'I do.' Do you agree? Be honest?"

Araminta said, "I don't need to know yet, and if you push me, I might not need to know at all."

John held his ground. "Whatever happens, can't you admit that all people should know the facts?"

She had always prided herself on learning. "Okay, you have a point, but I want to feel the desire to learn, John. I mean, I'm not feeling the need right now. You know enough, that should be good enough."

John said, "Baby, that's why I'm in there with you. Whatever the teacher asks of me, I do as well, regardless of what I already know. I wanted to know about sex, that's why I asked my parents two years ago about it. I want you to know as well, so we both can be educated."

John approached Araminta, and she stood stone cold as he kissed her cheek.

Araminta shook her head. "So, I have done wrong because I guess I have wasted people's time, and I am with a man that did all this for me and my sister. I'm so lucky."

Her sarcasm irritated John. "Yep, Araminta, and that's why there are consequences, and you have had plenty of chances to correct the problem, but you chose not to do it."

Araminta raised her hands in mockery. "I promise I won't act up again. Is it really too late for me now?"

John found her insulting and had to show her that she couldn't defy him. He gave her the same dose of sarcasm. "Yes, it's too late, but I will remember this conversation and how you were trying. It may help a little. I will watch your progress and see what happens."

Araminta scoffed, "Thanks, John."

John tried to hold her but she tapped his arms away. He sighed. "I love you." He left the kitchen and called the meeting. John called Araminta to come back in and have a seat.

Araminta came in, ever the good little servant. "Yes, John."

Although John had to go through with his plan, he watched Araminta's reaction to his announcement. He stood. Araminta looked at John and nodded.

Stanley stood. "I need Joseph, Addie, Lillie, and Araminta to go to the barn."

Araminta played her role, "Can I get my notebook? I have a paper to write."

John nodded. "Yes."

After Araminta came back, Matilda said, "Araminta, cut some peach cobbler for the kids."

Araminta smiled. "Yes, Momma."

Araminta took Joseph's hand and told Addie and Lillie, "Let's go."

After they left, John said, "Araminta was very mad in the kitchen, but she knew I had to go on with my plan.

She is being very brave, but she doesn't know what the plan is, she only knows I'm going to do something to her."

Jeff said, "So tell them the plan."

John said, "Mr. and Mrs. Fleming, I'm going to have my dad pick you two up first and take you to our house. I will bring Jeff, Isabella, and Araminta to our house. The plan is for our parents to be in class when we get there. I will make sure I have Araminta enter the class last. I will have her get something for me from the kitchen before she enters, and instead of holding the door for her like she thinks I will, I will enter the class while she is in the kitchen. When Araminta enters the class she will remain standing and my momma will take over from there. Araminta will know this is part of the consequences for her actions, and if I know her like I think I do, she will accept her punishment, or she will break, either way what my parents have in store for her may just break her as well. If Araminta is still standing after my parents are done, my mother has a plan B, and that will be a surprise."

Stanley asked, "That's a punishment?"

John said, "It's enough to break Araminta and make her willingly take the class and go back to being sweet

Araminta again. Mrs. Fleming, when Araminta reacts, we will queue you and Mr. Fleming to leave instantly with my Dad. We don't want you to baby her. We want her to take the punishment and continue with the class."

Matilda said, 'Now I have a punishment too, to allow my baby to hurt, and I leave to go home? John I understand my baby. I can do this for you and Araminta."

John said, "Thank you, Mrs. Fleming."

I didn't interrupt Grandma once. I had gone beyond the pale. She had taken me to a place I didn't think possible, but in all the conversation, I discovered that my great aunt Araminta was discovering a backbone, and Matilda understood that. She wasn't testing me, she had been testing her.

Chapter 30

I had time before lunch, so I asked Matilda to finish up with the Sex Ed story. I didn't particularly care for how the family treated Araminta, but I had to know if she gained her footing and stood up for herself.

Matilda obliged my request to continue:

Friday evening and John got to the Fleming house early to bring Araminta into the barn so she couldn't see her parents leave with Mr. Whitney. Matilda told Araminta and Isabella they were going to visit with Mr. and Mrs. Lee.

Araminta told Lillie to lock the door behind them and to do their homework. "You hear me, Addie?"

Addie said, "I'm doing my homework, now."

Joseph played with his toys in the family room.

Araminta said, "Momma should be home in an hour, bye."

As they pulled in the Whitney's long rutted road Jeff, Isabella, and John nodded out their plan. When they got to the house, John asked Araminta to get his notebook off the kitchen table. Araminta walked to the entrance of the class. John forewarned her there were consequences to what she had done. Araminta nodded and stood before everyone - Jeff, John, Isabella, Momma, Daddy, Mr. Whitney, and Mrs. Whitney. She shook her head, so this was their punishment? To be subjected to everyone she knew and loved?

John was proud of himself. He couldn't help but feel this was necessary. The love he had for her made him want to teach her a lesson. A

Araminta stood before everyone. She needed to get it over with.

Mrs. Whitney said, "Araminta?"

Araminta responded, "Yes ma'am?"

Mrs. Whitney said, "Thank you for attending your second lesson of our sex education class. In this lesson we will do something different. My husband and I would like to speak with you concerning our son."

Matilda said, "Araminta?"

Again Araminta responded, "Yes, Momma?"

Matilda asked, 'Why are your eyes on the floor, don't you see Mr. and Mrs. Whitney before you?"

Araminta wanted it over with, "Yes, Momma."

Matilda said, "Pay attention."

Araminta swallowed and looked at the Whitneys, "Yes, Momma."

Mr. Whitney said, "Araminta we love you, and we know you love John, and John loves you. We brought it to John's attention that we will not allow him to marry anyone who does not want to complete the sex education course. We discussed your actions in the class and they were deplorable. If you love someone, you would do all you can for each other. For example, when Isabella and Jeff had to go to the board to draw pictures, they didn't like it but they did it. As for you, you informed my wife that your sister had already drawn that picture when she asked you to draw it."

Stanley stood. "Who are you to tell the teacher what to do?"

Araminta remained stoic. "I'm sorry, Mr. Whitney."

Stanley scolded her, "Did I ask you to speak yet?"

Araminta stayed calm. "No."

Her father continued, "We told John if you have an issue with the class maybe you don't love him as much as you said you do, because who wouldn't want the best for their marriage?"

Mr. Whitney followed up with a comment, "I'm sorry for everything I have done to you and John."

Araminta paused to catch her breath. "I told John earlier, I was willing to come back to class, and will do as I'm told, but he informed me then that it was too late." Araminta's eyes pierced John. "Mrs. Whitney. I completed my---" she hesitated, "five hundred word paper, but I know you don't need it now." Araminta's head toggled forward and backward. "John, it would be best to do as your parents want you to do and move on. Again, I'm sorry." Araminta exhaled.

John position swung. "No, that's not it. That's not how this is happening." he tugged Araminta and whispered, "I told you not to play games. I love you and you will love me back. Are we clear?"

Araminta smiled. "Well, I'm sure you can always punish me for my insolence."

Isabella approached, and the three of them were in a huddle. "Araminta, please don't do this. Just go along."

Araminta teared up. Her twin was the only one who could truly break her. She couldn't let her go this alone.

She sighed, and pulled Isabella away from John. She asked, "Do you really want to do this?"

Isabella offered, "I have to. You may not, but I want you to. I need you with me. Please."

Araminta approached John, who had tears in his eyes. "You don't have to cry anymore, you can move on like your father wants you to, I will leave you alone." Araminta looked at Isabella. "Isabella can you and Jeff take me home?"

John tried to wrap his arms around Araminta, but she pushed herself out of John's arms. "I will be alright, John, you can let me go now."

Isabella pleaded in whispers, "Araminta, I told you I need you."

Araminta was torn. She shook her head. "I can't."

John approached her. "Araminta, my dad was lying about me moving on."

Araminta dismissed the thought. "Your dad wouldn't lie to me."

John said, "Momma can you tell Araminta the truth."

Mrs. Whitney approached. "Araminta, my husband and I concocted that story for John so you can see how much we love you, and we don't want to lose you. We wanted you to go to the class willingly with John and not fight him on it."

Araminta narrowed her focus on Mrs. Whitney. "Mr. Whitney lied to me?"

Mrs. Whitney weakly smiled. "Yes, dear. We all did. We love you, and we wanted to teach you a lesson that you would never forget. John loves you more than ever. Now do you feel like having class with us?"

Araminta frowned. "Not really, Mrs. Whitney, but you have me over a barrel, because my sister wants me to take the class, and I want it understood, that I'm doing this for her, not for anyone else."

John teared up. "I'm sorry for being a jerk. I love you."

Araminta held her head up high. She knew that she was free, and taking this class would be on her terms. There would be no more coercion. That night would be the beginning of the education to becoming adults for four young people.

Chapter 31

Nellie interrupted our session. "You look like you could eat some lunch."

I wasn't sure if I could eat it or needed to sip it through a straw. With each passing moment, new pains cropped up. I hid that swallowing hurt, and walked without the cane, just so I didn't arouse concern from Matilda and Nellie.

As though she'd read my mind, Nellie had homemade chicken soup on tap, and I sat at the table and ate as much as she could give me.

Nellie sat across from me and didn't give her food much notice, just kept an eye on me. "She doesn't look good, Tildy."

Matilda didn't look up from her bowl. "Nope, Cassandra needs to get going by mornin'."

I split their conversation. "I'm fine, besides, I'm enjoying learning about all my relatives."

Nellie rebutted. "You aren't fine, and if you don't hurry home, you might become too familiar with all these relatives."

"Nel!" Matilda stopped Nellie. "Let's give the girl her due. I'll wrap up the twins, and we will send her on her way; get her safe and sound home by tomorrow afternoon."

"Fair enough." Nellie stood, and I noticed she had left her Sunday clothes behind, in favor of a new outfit, a t-shirt that had another slogan; What If, and on the back; Why Not.

I snickered.

Nellie smiled. "You like it?"

"Yeah."

"I'll send it home with you."

Matilda had a single focus. As though she worried if she didn't give me all this information it would be lost forever, she coaxed me. "I would like to continue. We don't have a lot of time left, and there are so many miles more I need to tell you about. If you don't mind, while you sit there and eat, I'd like to continue."

Nellie offered, "While you two sit here in the kitchen, I need to run to the store, so I won't be in your way."

I asked, "Nellie, can you get my pen and pad from the front room?"

Before she left, she had my supplies in front of me. While I used soup to ease some of the pain, Matilda went into another story of the girls:

In home economics class, Isabella and Araminta were making pants. They required the entire class to make three pair of pants for their final grade. All the girls were excited to make pants in all colors, and different lengths, with buttons, ribbons, and flowers.

The boys, however, found a problem with women wearing pants. The boys felt the girls should be girls and wear dresses and skirts.

For Araminta and Isabella, two boys in particular were having fits about the new change in their wardrobe, and they were not looking forward to dealing with them in the latest fashion. The girls were saved by a mother who believed in fashion for the girls, and Mrs. Whitney who believed girls could wear pants and still be young ladies."

I sighed relief. "Finally something progressive about you, Grandma."

She dismissed my remark:

Araminta left her home economics class with Isabella, all smiles over the new style. When they reached John's car, the boys frowned.

Araminta said, "John it's a graduation requirement that we not only make three pair of pants, but we must wear each of them at least once."

Isabella asked Jeff, "Why do you dislike the pants?"

Jeff said, "It's not lady like, and ladies are suppose to wear dresses, not pants."

Araminta asked, "Where is that written?"

Jeff hemmed, "I don't know, but it's just not right, we are so use to seeing you in dresses, not pants."

John offered, "Araminta can wear them for those three days, but after that, I want to have the pants to burn for my bonfire."

Araminta said, "John that's not nice, I love my pants, and I plan to make more for the summer to take to school this fall. Besides, I think we have an agreement about what I can and can't do." Araminta didn't have to remind him that their only real contact had been a class on sex that cost John any closeness he had to Araminta.

Isabella shook off Jeff. "So do I. Jeff they're cute, and different."

John had slowly reverted back to his dominance. "Araminta, my foot is down, and there's nothing else to say about this subject."

Araminta eyed John, "We aren't married, and my momma said Isabella and I can make them, and wear them, and if that's not good enough for you, perhaps there are boys out there who would appreciate them." Araminta was finished.

John admitted, 'You are right, we are not married yet, and I can't go against your momma, but we will see." His expression had contempt.

Araminta felt uneasy. "What do you mean, John? You won't be able to hurt me, so I'm not worried about it?"

John said, "Araminta, those pants could paint you in a very bad light, and if enough people started talking about them, you might find I'm the only one who will see your beauty for what it is. Just letting you know that."

Araminta looked at Jeff. "Jeff you hate the pants on Isabella too?"

Jeff offered, "It's just that I love a woman in a dress, that's all. It is a look I can't get out of my head."

Isabella countered, "But we are not saying we are not wearing dresses anymore, we are just adding something new to our wardrobe, that's all."

John stared at Araminta, and she turned away. "Can we get going? I have a lot of homework to do."

Isabella concurred, "Me too."

John didn't move. "Does this homework involve making pants?"

Araminta said, "Oh, I see. Back when you wanted to punish me for not doing that stupid Sex Ed class, it wasn't cool to not do the homework, but now that I have a school requirement, you want to sabotage it? We have to complete our requirement for graduation, John. Now take us home."

John gave Araminta a disapproving look. "Okay."

John pulled up to the Matilda and Stanley's home and as Araminta turned to get out, he caught her hand.

Araminta pulled away but John kept his grip. Araminta smiled, sad for John. She leaned in and gave him a lonely kiss on the cheek. "It's not as bad as you think, John. Momma said pants are a big hit at other high schools.

Momma said your momma told her that, and Momma said your momma likes the pants too. Your momma was thinking of getting your sister Ella a pair I made."

John said, "The only person I'm concerned about wearing pants is you."

Araminta pulled her hand away and studied John's face. "Are you sure that's all you are concerned about?"

John felt lost. His power had slipped. "You've changed."

Araminta smiled. "I have, and believe me, it's for the better." She slid back in and gave John another kiss, a sympathy kiss. The first one she'd given him in months.

His eyes widened. "What's that for?"

Araminta said, "In spite of your behavior, if you play your cards right, you might find I can love you, John Xavier Whitney."

John smiled, and tried to kiss Araminta on the lips. Araminta shook her head. "Uh, uh, uh. Only if you play your cards right."

John asked, "If I surprised you with something would you be willing?"

Araminta said, "Depends on what the surprise is."

John asked, "How would you like to go to a matinee at the picture house on Saturday?"

Araminta's face lit up like the Fourth of July. "I have never been to a picture show."

John laughed. "Then I want to be the first to take you to one."

Araminta wondered if there was still hope in John. "John, thank you."

John bowed his head. "You're welcome. Saturday at noon, I will pick you up."

Araminta gave John another cheek kiss. Two so close, after none so far apart. "I can't wait."

Saturday morning, John's momma went over to Matilda's house to prepare Araminta for her first picture show. Jeff and Isabella would have gone with them but Jeff had to work all day in the field.

John's momma curled Araminta's hair and placed a thin bow on top. Matilda ironed Araminta's new pants, and Araminta wore a ruffled blouse. Momma Marilyn bought Araminta a gift for the occasion.

Araminta asked, "Momma Marilyn what is this?"

Marilyn said, "It's for you, dear, to hold your lipstick and money as you go to the movie."

Araminta shrugged. "But I don't have any lipstick, and very little money."

Marilyn said, "Why don't you open the package, dear?"

Araminta opened her gift – a small purse with lipstick and $1.00. Araminta's heart fluttered. "I never had this much money in my life. Momma Marilyn, I can't take this, I don't need it."

Marilyn said, "Don't you dare give that back to me or anyone, that's your play money, you use it as you see fit. Give your momma-in-law-to-be a hug."

Araminta realized some of John's best qualities were who his parents were, if only he could act more like them. "Oh, Momma Marilyn." Araminta hugged her second momma.

"John pulled up in front of the house.

Araminta ran to the mirror to clean up while Momma Marilyn kept John occupied. Matilda helped Araminta get dressed. "As pretty as you look, John won't be watching the picture; he will be looking at you, baby."

Araminta kissed her momma on the cheek. "I love you, Momma."

Matilda clutched her heart and hugged her baby.

Araminta made her debut out of the bedroom. John's huge smile turned grim as she waltzed out in pants. John's Momma ran interference. "Isn't Araminta pretty, John?"

John kept his words in but anger flashed over his face. Araminta looked at John's momma for help, but she sighed. Araminta turned to her momma, and Matilda rubbed Araminta's back. "Just be patient."

There was no hope for John, and she was afraid to look up. When she did, he sneered. Araminta broke the ice. "Hello, John."

John stared.

Araminta continued. She wasn't going to let his behavior stop her from seeing the show. "What time does the picture show start?"

"John paused. "Why would you want to know what time the picture show starts? You're not going."

Araminta reminded him, "You asked me out to the matinee picture show today, Remember?"

John felt his strength return with his mother standing there. "We are not going anywhere until you change your clothes."

John's momma rebuked him. "John! What has gotten into you? Araminta is beautiful just the way she is; this is senseless, take her to the picture show house and have a wonderful time together."

Matilda added, "Araminta got all prettied up for you, John, she loves you."

John said, "I know she does, and I love her, but Araminta knows how I feel about pants."

John's Momma said, "I was the one who suggested Araminta wear the pants, John, not Araminta. So don't take this out on her."

John said, "I'm not taking anything out on Araminta, Momma. I only asked her to change her clothes so we can go."

Araminta looked at Momma Marilyn and Marilyn said, "It's up to you, you can tell my son you will not go, or you can go change your clothes."

Araminta looked at her momma, and Matilda said the same thing. Araminta set John straight, "John, I won't change my clothes."

John's agitation spewed forward. "If you think I'm taking you to the picture show with those pants on, think again!" John stormed out the front door, got in his car and sped off.

The three women stood there, wondering what just happened. Araminta shrugged. "Oh, well." She'd planned to make the best of it and wear her pants around the house when someone knocked on the front door. Araminta answered, half expecting it to be John. Instead a young man introduced himself as the new neighbor boy. The neighbor walked up the long rutted drive to the Fleming house and introduced himself to Araminta. Araminta stepped out with her new pants, her ruffled blouse, her long curled hair done by her momma-in-law to be, and her new little purse over her shoulder.

"Wow, nice pants." A tall young man marveled at her clothing. "That's really cool." He held his hand out. "My name is Alexander Hill."

I was giddy. "Grandma, the savior I've been waiting for!"

"Well, we will see about that."

"Either way, it's something to hold onto, and I want to know more."

Chapter 32

"Matilda, don't you dare stop. I want to know more about Mr. Hill."

Matilda challenged me. "You know that John won't be too pleased about this."

"Go away John, gone John, whatever."

"Very well."

He stated, "I just moved in about a mile down the road. I don't know anyone in the area." He kept his hands in his pockets. "I moved from Georgia, and I'm starting at the local high school tomorrow to finish up my senior year."

Araminta cooed, "Hello, Alexander. I'm Araminta, welcome to the neighborhood."

Matilda and Marilyn came to the door.

Araminta said, "Momma, Momma Marilyn, this is Alexander Hill, a new neighbor from up the road. Matilda and Momma Marilyn came out onto the porch. Their faces soured, and Marilyn said, "Araminta is my son John's fiancée, they are engaged to be married."

Alexander said, "Oh, congratulations, Araminta."

Araminta wasn't too happy with that revelation but presented a 'Thank you' anyway.

Matilda asked, "Who are your folks, Alexander?"

Alexander said, "Emmett and Millicent Hill."

Matilda didn't know the name, but asked, "What brings you down this way?"

Alexander returned, "I'm on my way to the store, but I wasn't quite sure of the direction."

Araminta said, "I can show you, where's your car?"

Alexander said, "I parked it up on the road. Someone roared out of here and I was afraid there might be more."

Araminta shook her head. "Oh, that was John. Never mind him." Araminta said, "Momma, Momma Marilyn, I will be right back."

Matilda tried to stop her daughter. "Araminta maybe you should let someone else take Alexander to the store, you're engaged, honey."

Araminta ignored her. "Alexander, give me a minute. Can I meet you at your car?"

Alexander hesitated, nodded, and headed back up the driveway to the road.

As Alexander made his way down the dirt path to the road, Araminta turned to the women. "John decided not to take me to the movies, remember?"

Matilda sighed, "But that doesn't make two wrongs a right."

Araminta waved her mother off. "I'm going to enjoy my Saturday, and a neighbor needs help. I'm going to help him." She turned and made her way to the road.

"Grandma, I'm seeing good and bad things coming."

She winked, "I don't think it takes second sight to figure that one out."

We both laughed. "So, what happened next?"

Jeff came running out, dressed in dungarees, to find Matilda and Marilyn on the porch watching the road. He ran up to the porch. "Where did Araminta go, and who was that guy?"

Matilda said, "That was Alexander Hill, a new neighbor, and Araminta is showing him where the store is."

Jeff asked, "As in like pointing it out, or going with him?" Matilda's look of concern gave Jeff the answer. "No! That guy likes her."

Marilyn nodded. "We know, we can tell by how he looked at her."

Jeff paced. "I tried telling John about that guy, how he has been walking by the road. He must have seen girls here and wondered about them. John was so preoccupied with Araminta's pants that he didn't pay too much attention."

Matilda's curiosity piqued, "Alexander walks down the road a lot?"

Jeff said, "Yeah, a guy can tell if another guy is girl watching, and he was girl watching. He probably saw John leave and decided to get bold and knock on the door."

Matilda stared at Jeff. "Why wasn't this brought to my attention?"

Jeff smiled, "If I brought to attention all the boys who have girl watched this house, you'd be on the front porch all day, every day."

Matilda grinned at the thought all her daughters were beauties. "I suppose."

Jeff shrugged. 'I better get to the fields. Just stay here and look out for Araminta to come back, and try not to worry."

Matilda stopped Jeff. "Why not worry?"

Jeff turned to John's mom. "No offense, but I actually talked to Alexander, and he's a pretty decent fellow." Jeff kissed gave the ladies a quick peck and headed out to the field to work.

Matilda told Jeff, "Don't work too hard, when you're done, come into the house, we may need you."

Jeff smiled. "Will do."

I smiled at Matilda, "The plot thickens."

Matilda sighed, "Yes, unfortunately, it did."

Chapter 33

Matilda didn't wait for me to ask for more:

Matilda and Marilyn headed into the house for coffee and discuss the talks both John and Araminta needed when either of them returned. Two hours later someone pounded on the door. Matilda caught her breath, and Marilyn got up from the table. Their eyes like deer in headlights as John's voice hollered to be let in.

When Matilda unlocked the door, John stared at them. "Let me talk to Araminta. I have something to say."

Marilyn said, "Joh, Joh, Joh, John, what are you doing back here?"

Matilda kept her composer and hugged him. "Come on in here, baby. Are you hungry? I got some chicken on the stove, fresh from the pan."

For a moment, she distracted him. "Yes, Momma, I would love some, thanks."

Matilda made John a plate of chicken and vegetables, and a tall glass of ice tea.

John kissed his momma on the cheek. "Where's Araminta? I need to talk to her."

Matilda hesitated. "John, come eat first."

John took his jacket off and sat. He stared at his momma and Matilda. He tossed a piece of chicken in his mouth. "If one of you don't tell me what's going on I'm going to start screaming."

Marilyn said, "Araminta is showing a new neighbor the store. She will be back."

John chowed down. "What new neighbor?"

Matilda and Marilyn looked at each other.

John stopped, half chewed chicken clinging to his lips. His demeaner changed. "Momma, and I mean both of you, where is Araminta?"

Matilda reminded John, "You decided that your feelings were more important than hers, so getting upset that she's not here, when you drove off is rather off putting, young man."

John nodded. "Yes, I suppose it is, but now, where is she?"

Matilda was about to refuse an answer when a car pulled up. The squeal of a brake, the rumble of an engine. Matilda went to the door and realized Araminta getting out of a young man's car wasn't going to go well if John saw it.

However, she couldn't stop John from pushing past her and catching the sight for himself.

John mumbled to the ladies. "And what do we have here?"

John's momma cautioned him. "Be respectful."

"Nothing but, Momma." He stepped off to the porch and headed to the passenger door of the car. "Hi, baby!"

Araminta held her hand up to stop him, continuing her conversation with Alexander. "Alex, thank you for the movie. It was the first one I've ever gone to, and I couldn't have had a finer gentleman take me than you."

John opened the door and assisted Araminta out with a speedy pull. He leaned in and eyed the driver. "Hello."

John kept a surface demeanor of cordiality to his smoldering anger. "This is the new neighbor? Well, come on. I have to shake this man's hand." John pulled Araminta along and circled the car.

Alexander got out and shook John's hand. They stood the same height, the same build.

John said, "Did Araminta show you where the store is?"

Alexander smiled. "Yes she did, thank you."

John took a good look. "And your name is?"

Alexander responded, "Alexander Hill, but my friends call me Alex."

John returned. "Well, I'll make sure I keep it Alexander then."

Alexander shrugged. 'I wasn't asking you to call me Alex."

John alternated his view between Araminta and Alexander. "So you took in a movie in those pants, huh?"

Alexander asked, "My pants, or hers?"

John disregarded his remark and focused on Araminta.

Araminta smiled. "Yes, and it was incredible." She rubbed in her disdain.

John smiled and let Alexander know. "We are engaged to be married; this is my fiancé that I love very much." John tried to kiss Araminta on the forehead, but she resisted the offer.

Alexander said, "That's wonderful. A woman like that would be a princess to have for a wife."

John asked, "Do you have a sweetheart?"

Alexander paused; he and Araminta stared briefly at each other. "Not yet."

John winked. "Well, there are plenty of available women around town, but this household has no available women. If you have to come back here, see Jeff in the barn, he will gladly help you."

Alexander etched a hollow frown on his face. "Sure."

Matilda offered from the porch, "Nice to meet you."

John said, "Thanks again, Alexander."

Alexander returned to his car. He gave a polite nod, and he and Araminta waved before he drove off.

John pulled Araminta up the steps, and plunked her down on a stump. Towering over her. "Can we all get in the house? I need to talk to Araminta."

Araminta glared. "What about?"

John lost patience. "Get in the house, Araminta, before my food gets cold. Momma. Araminta may be hungry too." He returned hover over Araminta. "I came back here to apologize to you, and your two mommas tried their best not to tell me you were with a strange man. Now tell me, why were you in the new neighbor's car?"

Araminta said, "Can I sit up, please? It's hard to talk with blood rushing to my head like this."

John said, "As long as you know it will be temporary."

Araminta pulled from his grasp, stood and went into the house. "The new neighbor came over to introduce himself, because he didn't know where the store was."

John asked, "And how did a movie come out of that?"

Araminta shrugged. "Seems to me that since you didn't want to take me, and I still wanted to go, and that since we were right down the street from it, why not go." She rubbed it in. "It was great, too."

John pitched back, "So a stranger is more important than me, Araminta?"

Araminta dug in. "No, being treated with respect is more important than you, John."

John said, "Alexander knew you were engaged, and he ask to take you to the movies anyway?"

Araminta corrected him. "He didn't ask me, I asked him."

John's anger quaked from his lips. "How dare you."

Marilyn said, "Araminta, please don't go anywhere near him again. He is no good. You are engaged to be married, and if that kind of man is willing to overlook that and knows you're engaged, he is not a good person to be around, sweetheart."

They made it into the kitchen and Araminta shook her head. "No offense, Mrs. Whitney, but I'll pass judgments on who is good and who is bad. Thank you for your concern though."

John's momma was taken aback. "I see."

John interrupted, "Jeff tried to warn me about him, but I was so caught up in Araminta's pants, I just didn't pay too much attention to what he was saying."

Matilda said, "Yes, Jeff told us that."

John stood and went around the table.

Araminta braced herself.

John leaned over and whispered in her ear. "I'm sorry for how I acted, now you show me the same respect."

Matilda asked John, "So you are okay with Araminta's pants then?"

John looked at his momma Matilda and rolled his eyes. "Momma, please don't bring that up, because

Araminta will not be wearing as many pants as she thinks. Remember Araminta, you said no to me because you had your two mommas on each side of you."

John's momma, still reeling from Araminta's forcefulness, said, "Araminta knows how to say no to you without us being present."

Araminta offered a response to Mrs. Whitney. "I'd say I can tell him no, but your son isn't very good at taking no when the two of you aren't around."

John shouted, "That's a lie."

Araminta went on. "It's the truth, and you know it."

She turned to her mother. "The person here who needs some lessons is John, and he needs lessons on how to treat his woman." She craned her neck to look John in the face. "Yeah, I still called myself your woman, but you are dangerously close to that not being true."

Mrs. Whitney turned to her son. "For the love of God, son, start treating Araminta with respect."

Jeff had come in the back door. "Hey, I see everyone is back home. You two go to the movie?"

John scowled. "No. I'm going to listen to you a lot better now; you were right about that new neighbor."

Araminta stood. "Momma, I'm not very hungry, and I'm starting to get a stomach ache. Would it be okay if I went and lay down?" She caught John staring, "Alone?"

Matilda nodded. "I'll come check on you before dinner. Go lay down."

I was like a schoolgirl. "Oh Grandma, I like Alex!"

Matilda continued with the growth of Araminta:

After the Whitneys had left and Jeff had retired to the barn, the house was empty except for mother and daughter. The other kids were visiting relatives and Araminta made her way out to the kitchen. Araminta stopped her mother, motioned for her to take a seat.

Matilda hugged her. "What is it baby?"

Araminta cried. "Momma, my breasts hurt."

Matilda cupped one of Araminta's breast in her hand. "Did they just start hurting?"

Araminta said, "They were sore this morning, but it's worse now, and I'm bleeding worse than I've ever bled before."

Matilda said, "Let me get my special miracle cream, I just made a new batch last night. My miracle cream will take care of this in time. When Isabella got home Sunday evening, she was going through the same thing. I used the special miracle cream on Isabella too."

Araminta asked, "What is it, Momma?"

Matilda smiled. "It's a lady issue, hon."

Araminta went on, "What did you do for Isabella?"

Matilda smiled. "Well, for starters, I told Jeff, he'd have to stay away for a little while."

Araminta frowned. "How did he take that?"

Matilda laughed. "Not well."

Chapter 34

I hadn't lost track of Isabella, but my thoughts were so strong on Araminta. Her growth during that senior year was phenomenal. However, I had wondered about how twins viewed things, both independently and together.

"Grandma, what was Isabella doing during this time?"

"Well, she went through the same things Araminta did, and her lady issues affected her relationship with Jeff."

"How so?"

As I recall:

Jeff's face was in pain wanting to see Isabella, to touch and hold her. He knew there was no way he could go a week without seeing Isabella. They had gotten so close. Jeff had a piece of him missing, and he needed to get that piece back. He had no idea what was wrong with Isabella. He just wished he could see her. He knew while Isabella was sleeping through her pain, he wouldn't be able to sleep at all. All that evening when Jeff left Matilda, he sat in that barn attaching all of Isabella's hurt that she slept away to his persona. He remembered when they knew they were meant for one another. When they got home from orientation week, things were different for them. He knew she was his life from that day forward, and nothing would separate them again. Jeff asked God how could he be without Isabella for a week or more, knowing she was ailing. He prayed God heal Isabella and Araminta, because they both were connected.

Jeff needed God's help. For Jeff, this wasn't a small matter. To him, this was his future, the woman he talked to everyday. The woman he had learned to kiss softly, and smell the soap on her neck, and brush his lips across the fragments of soap particles remaining, placing his fingers through her thick long ocean breeze hair. This was the woman he had learned to stare at and know what she thought. A woman who blushed when she saw him, allowed him to know she felt something. He did something to her that she wouldn't openly admit because the truth was embedded in her.

Jeff knew it would be Isabella who wouldn't want to stay away from him for more than a week. He knew her attachment was just as great as his. Where he wouldn't rush her, she would make the attempt, even if her body was still not willing. Her heart would make the effort for his sake, and he would be patient enough to at least hear what she needed of him. Selfishness was nowhere to be found with those two, their bond was thicker than themselves. Their hearts were invested, and that kind of investment involved more than pure title, it involved commitment. The ring was for the world, the heart was for each other. Jeff knew Isabella was his soul mate.

The next morning, Jeff felt better but missed that piece of his soul. He got ready for school and headed up to the house to see Matilda for breakfast and a quick hello. Matilda was in the kitchen cooking breakfast.

Jeff said, "Good morning, Momma." Jeff kissed Matilda on the cheek. He sat at the table and looked at Isabella's bedroom door.

Matilda said, "Jeff, Isabella asked me to give you this." It was a note, a beautiful note from Jeff's girl.

Jeff jumped up. "Thanks, Momma," and hugged her.

Matilda said, "You're welcome, baby. Now eat up before your eggs get cold." She handed Jeff and a lunch, along with a second note, one for John from Araminta.

Jeff said, "I'm not sure I should be the one to give John this note."

Matilda pushed it to him. "Whatever she's written to him is between them. If it's bad, it's not your fault."

He sighed. "Okay."

He left the house and when he made it to the road, he opened his note and read it:

Dear Jeff,

First, I love you and I know you are worried, but I am fine. It's just something so personal that we made Momma promise not to tell you or John. We will tell you ourselves when we are able. Momma told me you were very concerned about me, I knew you would be and I wanted to make you smile even if I wasn't there with you. When I wake, you're on my mind, when I'm trying to sleep, you're on my mind. This came on so suddenly we didn't have time to tell you or John and now we can't see you. I appreciate that I can write to you and tell you, you are the bright lights of my heart, how can I blush unless you're there? It's going to be complicated explaining this to you, but I know you're going to want to know what is going on. It's very personal and I never heard of it before, but I'm a living witness that it did happen to a set of twins at the same time. Jeff can you write me back, and I will write you back. I'm sure your letters will make me smile. I'm use to kissing you every day now, you spoiled me. We will have *a lot of making up to do when this is over, so clear your calendar and write in Isabella Maggie Annie Fleming has a meeting with you.....ASAP.. Love you....****Bella***

Jeff was five minutes from school when John pulled up. He had a huge frown on his face. Jeff was so happy with his note he forgot the reason he got the note in the first place.

He handed John his note. "This is from Araminta."

There was apprehension on John's face. "What is it?"

Jeff said, "It's about why they are both sick."

John scoffed. "Sick? Yeah, right. She is just trying to avoid me. Probably with that Alexander guy."

Jeff disputed that. "I doubt that since it's both girls."

John huffed. "Whatever." He asked, "How long are they supposed to be out of school?"

Jeff checked his note. "A week."

John said, "What do you mean they are out of school for this whole week? What is wrong with them? I want answers, Jeff!"

Jeff shrugged. "They won't tell me, or you. Mrs. Fleming said it's a secret she couldn't tell."

John stopped walking. "Jeff, do you think because Mrs. Fleming said for me to stay off the property for a week that I will stay off Fleming land?"

Jeff said, "Araminta hoped you would because Araminta can't see you now."

John would have none of it. "When we are let out for lunch, we are taking a trip to see Mrs. Fleming, so be ready."

Jeff said, "John we really shouldn't. Why do you think Araminta gave your ring back to you? If you aren't careful, there won't be a marriage. Mrs. Fleming has so much on her plate with tending to Isabella and Araminta and getting the other kids off to school and the cooking and cleaning and then her new sons."

John said, "Jeff that woman lying in that house supposedly sick is my fiancé, and right now I need to fix

315

her attitude, so if you think I'm going to turn my back on that house for a week you don't really know me."

Jeff said, "Oh I know you, as a matter of fact, Mrs. Fleming and I were talking about this very subject yesterday. We knew you would ignore Mrs. Fleming's wants about coming on the property."

John said, "Mrs Fleming's wants or Araminta's?"

Jeff countered, "Does it matter?"

John thought about it. "Yeah, it does. Because I think Araminta isn't giving me a fair chance to show her that I'm her fiancé."

Jeff tried to reason with him. "John, are you listening to yourself? Think about it. Both women are home, it's something they both have. Araminta isn't avoiding you."

John said, "Now Jeff, What is wrong with them?"

Jeff said, "Honestly, I have no idea. Mrs. Fleming said it's nothing I can do. They sleep to alleviate the pain. I was eating dinner yesterday at the dining room table, and Isabella started screaming so loud, and I watched Mrs. Fleming run from the kitchen to their bedroom to care for her. I wanted to help, but all I could do was sit back. When *she left the bedroom, I asked if everything was alright, and she said fine, just something they had to rest over."*

As if John heard nothing, he reiterated, "Let's head on in the school building, we have a field trip to take at lunch time."

I broke in. "See, Grandma, that young man wasn't right in the head."

"He was a ram, child."

"Oh, he was something alright, but I think it's a disservice to rams everywhere to call him that."

Matilda recalled more:

As John sat at his desk, he pulled out his history book to hide reading Araminta's letter. The letter confirmed what Jeff had stated:

> *Dear John,*
>
> *Hello John, Sorry for how Saturday turned out, and I had hoped we could discuss some of the things we need to talk about, however, something else has come up and I need to ask of you to be understanding. It's a personal issue I*

don't think I will be able to tell you about at this time.

Listen to me John Xavier Whitney.....I WANT YOU TO STAY OFF THE PROPERTY FOR THIS ENTIRE WEEK. I know Momma or Jeff has told you, and I know you will try and do what you always do, which is whatever you want, but it's really nothing you can do. Momma is doing everything, and you can't help her at all. You are free to ask Momma if she needs anything, because I know you will ignore my wanting you to stay away. I will deal with you on that later. If you want to salvage our relationship, you will listen to me. However, I'm not sure you are capable of that. I guess we will see if you will get punished for not listening.

Yours.....................Araminta Jolinda Debbra Fleming

Minta~

John wondered about the cryptic 'yours' response. No, 'I love you,' just a meaningless, 'yours.'

When the teacher let them out for lunch, John raced to his car with Jeff tagging along. John hauled over to the Flemings and as they pulled up to the house, a quiet calm surrounded the place. John walked up the stairs and knocked on the door.

Matilda opened the door. "John, Jeff, what are you two doing here at this time?"

John gave Matilda a kiss and a hug. "I'm here to see my baby, Araminta. Jeff told me she was ill, but I need to check on her. Is it alright?"

Matilda turned to Jeff. "Jeff, I expect this sort of behavior from him, but not you. Did you tell John what Araminta said about John coming on the property?"

Jeff said, "Yes ma'am, I did, but Momma, you know John wouldn't listen to that."

She stayed on Jeff, "And why did you come with him?"

Jeff shrugged. "Figured I could keep him out of trouble if he starts up."

Matilda looked at John. "John, the girls can't see anyone, not this week. They are in pain and sleep mostly."

John said, "Momma, I need to know what is wrong with her? Is it our argument on Saturday?"

Matilda offered, "John, as serious as this illness is, it isn't nearly the wound that you inflicted on her on Saturday. Yet, I assure this has nothing to do with that. It's female troubles, nothing to concern you about."

John said, "Female trouble? What kind of female trouble?"

Matilda said, "Araminta and Isabella don't want you to know unless they tell you. They won't be able to do that til next week."

John stared down Matilda. "Momma, I won't be able to wait til next week to see my Araminta. That's too long."

Matilda said, "Too bad, John. That's how it's going to be. And the last time I checked, this is still my house, those are still my daughters, and these are still my rules. She is too sick to see you this week, that's why Araminta told you to stay away. It will be over soon, and they will be in school next week."

John went on, "Momma, if you won't let me see her, can you please tell us what is wrong?"

Matilda questioned, "Is guilt eating you up, John? Because if it is, it serves you right, but sadly, this has nothing to do with Saturday. Understand?"

Jeff sat back, amused watching Momma crucify John.

John attempted to step around Matilda, but Jeff jumped up and took a stand. "John, stop it."

John turned. "If you want a ride back to school, you better stay up with me." Jeff followed John out of the house and they drove off.

John told Jeff, "You know I will be there every day until I can see her?"

Jeff shook his head. "Let me out."

John sneered. "What?"

Jeff said it again. "Let me out. Schools only a little ways further. I don't need to listen to your nonsense. You don't listen to anyone but yourself. Now let me out."

John refused. "I will do no such thing. We are best friends and that's never going to change."

Jeff realized something. "That's how you are with Araminta, isn't it? Anytime anyone disagrees with you, you dismiss as their fault."

John argued, "You are wrong."

Jeff laughed. "See, that's it." They pulled into the parking lot and Jeff hopped out. "Think about what I've said, definitely think about what Mrs. Fleming has said."

Of course John didn't think about what Matilda said, because he came to the house every day that week, and every day that week he was turned away. Monday morning of the second week, the girls made it back to school. John was parked out front to take Jeff, Araminta, and Isabella to school, but there was a catch. Isabella and Araminta told Matilda to tell John and Jeff to go on to school without them. They would rather walk alone.

John was just happy to see they were coming, so he agreed. "Okay, Momma. We will see them at school."

As the girls walked to school, they were covered up with jackets, with their notebooks in front, covering their chests. Isabella and Araminta were nervous seeing John and Jeff, and hoped they wouldn't have to explain what happened to them. As they turned the last corner to school, John and Jeff came out of the bushes.

Isabella looked down, and Araminta turned around and started walking toward home dragging Isabella.

Jeff said, "Isabella, please don't leave."

Isabella stopped and turned around.

Jeff said, "Would it be okay if we talked a minute?"

Isabella hesitated, nervous, she stuttered, "Would, would, would, it be okay if we talked at lunch time? Would that be okay?"

Jeff said, "That would be perfect. Thank you."

Isabella looked at Jeff. "Thank you, Jeff."

Araminta still held onto Isabella's arm. John stared at Araminta like he wanted to shake answers from her. Jeff turn for the school, and John followed, grumbling as he did.

Isabella and Araminta walked twenty feet behind. Inside the class, Isabella switched seats with Araminta so John wouldn't be behind her.

When Mrs. Nelson stepped out of the class for a few minutes, John asked Isabella, "Can you switch seats with Araminta? I really need to talk to her."

Isabella said, "I wouldn't mind, John, it's just she ask me to switch with her. She said she just wasn't ready to talk to you yet."

John stood and stooped beside Araminta. "Can I have lunch with you today?"

Araminta stared ahead. "I have to meet with Mrs. Nelson at lunch time today, sorry."

Mrs. Nelson entered and asked everyone to pull out their history books. John went back to his seat, a cauldron of anger brewing. Araminta let out an exhale as john went back to his seat. She knew when lunch was called, she had to go sit beside Mrs. Nelson's desk and be ready to duck John. She realized the time away had not made the heart grow fonder. She wasn't ready to deal with John; she wasn't prepared to tell the truth about her feelings, or about lying to protect his.

When lunchtime came Jeff and Isabella had something to discuss. Jeff didn't care if he got in trouble for disrupting class, he missed her, and he wanted to see her. He wanted her to know how much he missed her. Ms. Nelson stepped out and Jeff held his hand out toward Isabella and stared in her eyes.

Isabella said, *"Jeff, Ms. Nelson will be right back."*

Jeff kept his hand out until Isabella grabbed it, and when she did, he gently squeezed it.

Isabella was embarrassed, but Jeff showed her what he missed without her. Isabella missed him too. The hour hit noon and the kids stood to make their way outside for lunch. Jeff was the first one to jump up and walk to Isabella's desk to help her stand.

Isabella placed her hand in his hand.

Jeff said, "Just push down on my hand and stand."

Isabella tried to take her hand back after Jeff helped her, but he wouldn't let go until they got to their space for lunch. Jeff had one of Matilda's quilts in a bag with a small pillow in case she needed it. He laid the quilt out next to one of the mammoth rocks in case Isabella needed to rest her back against something. He held both her hands as she sat down on the quilt. He had a single wild flower, and after he sat down next to Isabella, he placed it in her hair. The first tear fell from her cheek as she saw how much this man missed her. Isabella reached for Jeff, and he placed her head on his chest. "I love you, Isabella Fleming."

Isabella said, "I'm so sorry I couldn't see you."

Jeff said, "It's not your fault. Am I hurting you, holding you this way?"

Isabella said, "No, I'm right where I want to be."

Jeff knew the Fleming women shed plenty of tears, so he had enough tissues in his pocket. He wanted to make sure Isabella ate lunch before it was over. "After you eat, you can begin to tell me what happened."

Isabella nodded.

After they ate, Isabella asked Jeff if he could hold her while she told the story.

Jeff said, "I always love to hold you, Isabella, but why?"

Isabella said, "Because the story is somewhat embarrassing."

Jeff said, "Sure, whatever makes you comfortable, I'm just so happy to have you here with me."

Jeff held her and Isabella told the story of what they went through. She could see Jeff's mouth open wide as she did.

After Isabella finished, Jeff said, "Is that why you're wearing a Jacket?"

Isabella nodded.

Jeff said, "So you have to wear the jacket every day or just today?"

Isabella frowned. "I'm not used to them, so I'd rather hide them."

Jeff said, "You have something else hiding them too?"

Isabella looked down.

Jeff lifted her chin. "Tell me."

Isabella said, "It's a piece of sheet."

Jeff asked, "Why?"

Isabella said, "It presses them and makes them look smaller." Isabella dropped her head.

Jeff saw how difficult a talk it was. "What makes you unhappy about removing the sheet?"

Isabella said, "It holds them in place, makes them smaller looking. I don't want to remove the sheet."

Jeff said, "Are you experiencing pain with that sheet?"

Isabella nodded.

Jeff reached for Isabella's chin. He stared into her eyes. "I know you don't want to deal with any of this, but I won't feel right if you are having pain when it's not *necessary. I worried last week when your momma said you were having pain. Isabella could you do something for me?"*

Isabella said in a rush, "But Jeff, it's just temporary. It won't last long."

Jeff said, "Isabella, I know you're saying this because it covers you, but you have to look at long term. What if it damages you? How could I live with myself knowing I could have stopped it? I love you too much to let you hurt yourself."

Isabella grabbed Jeff's hand. "Jeff, I know you love and care for me, but I'm not use to them, I'm so uncomfortable with them, maybe in time the sheets can go away?"

Jeff implored, "Isabella look at me, and tell me the truth, are you in pain when the sheet is squeezing your breasts to a smaller size?"

She knew Jeff had her best interest at heart, she also knew she wouldn't be able to hide anymore, but she loved him and was ready to let it go. She said, "Yes, I am in pain from the sheet squeezing me."

Jeff said, "Isabella, could you throw the sheets away, please?" Jeff told her everything was going to be fine. The end of lunch came, and they packed up. Jeff still held Isabella's hand going back to class.

Lunch time was over and Araminta went back to Isabella's seat and waited til the class came in. She pulled out her English book and pretended to read. She knew John would pass by, but she hoped Isabella could beat John to his desk.

John came first and looked furious. He stopped in front of Araminta and placed his hand on her desk. "Araminta. I understand I must be gentle with you, but my patience has run out. I need to talk to you. I know what you're doing. You're trying to stay away from me because you're afraid to tell me what happened to you. Baby, I waited a week and now I can't wait any longer. I need to talk to you. When school is over will you tell your mother I'm taking you to the park, and ask if I can come to dinner tonight? You and I will be home by six. I'm your fiancé. I'm not a boyfriend."

"You don't get it, John, this isn't about what happened to me this week. That's not why I'm avoiding you. This is about us."

Before he could protest, Mrs. Nelson entered and John simply uttered, "Okay." He waited for anything else, but she treated him as though he didn't exist.

Isabella saw Araminta's expression, and saw John's frown.

Araminta passed Isabella a secret note:

> *Isabella, John is trying to force me to go to the park with him after school. I know he wants me to explain everything, but I don't want to, and I'm afraid he will physically force me. I'm going to get a hall pass and head for the bathroom. When I do, I'm going to get a head start and get home before class is over. Please stall him for me. Can you get my books and stuff off my desk and bring them home with you. Will you do this for me?*

Minta~

Isabella sent Araminta a return note:

> *Although I don't want to get in the middle of you and John, I have to agree with you sometimes. Walk as fast as you can and lock yourself in the bedroom. You know he is coming. You know he isn't giving up that easy. He sees the engagement as binding. So BEWARE, because you know he will get you at some point, you know his mind is calculating. Be careful.*
>
> *I love you sis, now GET READY>>>>>>>>>>>>>>GO.......see you at home.*
>
> *Bella~*

Araminta left the school building and hurried home. She went to her room and locked the door. Matilda said she would keep John away and tell him she still wasn't feeling well.

Araminta unlocked her door. "You will tell him no such thing. Just tell him I don't want to see him, and that my lady issue has nothing to do with it."

Matilda frowned, "You don't mean that."

Araminta closed the door and locked it. She shouted through the door, "Yes, Momma, I do."

Matilda, like Isabella, was worried that John would reach Araminta soon, and Araminta might have to tell John everything that she wasn't ready to say.

As she suspected, John showed up soon after. Matilda told John Araminta had eaten and went to bed. Matilda told John Araminta needed time and that his best action should be to give it to her.

John said, "Momma, you are on my side right? You can see how unreasonable Araminta is being? Shoot, Jeff and I are both wonderful men, and we have done nothing but right by your daughters. Can I trust you to talk to her?"

Matilda had a cross to bear. She had to do what was right by her daughter, whether her daughter was right or wrong. "John, absence makes the heart grow fonder."

John agreed, "And my heart is mighty missin' her right now." He gave Matilda a day. "Do what you have to do to talk to her, after tomorrow, I'll do what I have to do. Okay?"

Matilda said, "I know you love her, John, and in her own way, I'm sure she loves you, but I'm not about to have you tell me that I have any amount of time to do your bidding. Now you may talk to your mother that way, but I can assure you that this is the last time you will ever talk to me that way. Are we clear?"

John kept his poker face. "I'm sure you'll work your momma magic."

Matilda said, "Just love her, and if it's meant to be, she will be in your arms soon enough."

John said, "Yes, Momma."

"Okay, Grandma, I know you are against that boy now."

"Child, I told you before, there are as many twists as a pig's tail. I might be against him at that point, but later things might change. You just need to keep an open mind."

"My mind has been open all along." I chuckled. "I'm open to the fact that I didn't like him from the first time you described him."

She changed the subject. "How are you feeling?"

I'd nearly forgotten my whole left side had gone numb. I guess a good story could do that. I lied. "I'm feeling great."

She shook her head. "That's still not enough to keep you from being sent home tomorrow."

I understood. I hadn't been able to reach my parents or fiancé and I really did need to get back up there. "I promise you, I'm coming back."

"Come back complete, promise me that."

I didn't know how to answer that. I wasn't aware I was incomplete. "Of course."

Matilda smiled. "I'm holding you to that."

Chapter 35

"So did John come over that night?"

"No, we didn't have any more incidents that night."

"What about the next day?"

Grandma winked:

Araminta and Isabella left for school an hour early. They knew John would make some sort of scene, so they did everything different that morning. Mrs. Nelson was usually in class early, and Matilda approved a note excusing them for taking the bathroom pass.

"Mrs. Nelson understood, and Araminta asked her to make time at lunch to work with her on a research paper. Isabella told Jeff she would have to help her sister, and that she hoped he would keep John from interfering.

However, nothing prepared them for the new student. When John arrived and saw that Araminta had already been there for quite some time, he waited patiently for her to separate from the teacher, but she seemed determined to stay close to Mrs. Nelson. The clock neared class time, and he knew she'd have to take her seat, and then he could speak to her. Just before the bell rang, a young man entered and asked if that was Mrs. Nelson's class. It was Alexander.

Mrs. Nelson asked, "What is your name?"

He bowed his head, "Alexander Hill."

Araminta felt the vapors. "Alex, so good to see you again."

He smiled. "The pleasure is all mine."

Whether Mrs. Nelson was oblivious to the issues with Araminta and John, or if she was very aware of them, she did something unusual. "Well, Araminta, since you seem to know this young man, and since I should break up that team of four you all have over there in your corner, I'm going to move you to that corner," she pointed to an opposite side of the room. "And Alexander, you can sit next to her in that other vacant seat."

John raised his hand, "Mrs. Nelson, Alexander can have my seat. I'll move with Araminta."

Mrs. Nelson turned him down. "No, you stay where you are."

John stood. "No, I'm moving."

Mrs. Nelson stood. "Excuse me?"

John repeated himself. "Araminta and I are engaged and I'm not leaving her side."

Araminta whispered something to Mrs. Nelson, and she pointed to John. "John, I need you to go to the principal's office, please."

John looked around. He had the students' attention. They waited for what he would do. "Why?"

Mrs. Nelson said, "For not following the teacher's rules."

Araminta couldn't help but find irony in the situation John was in. She wondered how it felt when someone accused him of not following a teacher's orders. Mrs. Nelson snapped her fingers. "Today, Mr. Whitney."

John picked up his books and came forward. He passed Alexander and gave him the eye. When he passed Araminta, he whispered, "I'll be at the house tonight, with my parents for a meeting."

He exited, and she realized that was only a short reprieve. He'd be back. She took her new seat, and Alexander sat next to her. "Are you okay, Araminta?"

She smiled. "I am now. Thank you."

He offered, "Do you need a ride home, today?"

Her eyes lit up. "Could you?"

He grinned. "Of course."

When lunch came, Araminta was aware the principal was letting John come back so she kept her plans with Mrs. Nelson. Before she went to her desk, she warned Alexander. "Alex, please be careful. John and I aren't on speaking terms right now and he might take it out on you."

Alexander didn't seem to be too worried. "I'll be fine."

As she worked on her paper with Mrs. Nelson, she couldn't help but notice that Alexander had joined the rest of the boys, minus John, in a football game. Alexander was a star. He was fast and could tackle like a professional.

Mrs. Nelson caught her attention. "You do know that a young lady engaged shouldn't be desirin' another man?"

Araminta sighed. "You saw that?"

She winked. "I think the whole class saw it."

She confided in Mrs. Nelson. "Can I ask you a question?"

Mrs. Nelson nodded.

"What do you do when you realize that two people might not be suited for each other?"

Her teacher exhaled. "You put yourself in this position. You might have to suffer the consequences."

Araminta put a hand to her chest. "You mean I may have to go through with it?"

Mrs. Nelson shook her head. "Not necessarily, but you do owe him a chance to prove himself."

Araminta protested. "Haven't I already done that?"

Her teacher shrugged. "I don't know, have you?"

Araminta chewed on Mrs. Nelson's words for the rest of the day. She excused herself early, and Alexander did the same. Before John had realized what she had done, he was well behind them when he ran out of the classroom. Alexander and Araminta were already on the road by the time everyone else had left the school. She knew better than to offer a visit to Alexander. She got out at the corner of their long dirt driveway and waved goodbye as he drove off. As she walked up the path, she heard a noise. A loud screeching exploded through the silence. It's got louder. She wondered what could that be? Dust and sand picked up on the other side of the trees. Someone had turned down the driveway in a hurry. She knew who it was. She dropped her books and started running toward the house. John's truck sped down the path. It stopped in front of her and John jumped out and walked toward her.

Araminta screamed "Oh, no!" She turned and yelled, "Momma!" She could see the house and nothing stirred. Araminta turned back to John. John stared with frustration. She put her hands on her hips. "What do you want?"

John continued to stare at her, eyes filled with anger. "What do I want? You seriously are asking me that? Araminta Jolinda Debbra Fleming, you have evaded me for the last time. Because your momma told me I have to be gentle with you is the only reason I have had more patience this week than I have ever had. It's been two weeks, and you haven't given me so much as a friendly wink."

"John I---"

John cut her off, "Don't you dare say one word now."

Araminta frowned.

John continued, "I am so angry with you. Will you let me take you to dinner? I'd like to talk to my fiancé."

Araminta had no idea how to tell John how she felt, but she knew she couldn't do it alone. "I can't have dinner with you tonight, but I would be able to on Sunday."

John backed away. "You want me to wait two more days? After two weeks?"

She offered, "It's either that, or not at all." Araminta had learned to control him. What she hoped is that he would tire of that and not want her, but instead he agreed.

"Very well. I'll be here Sunday at five."

Araminta had bought herself two days. She headed back to her things and discovered her sister and Jeff coming up the path with her books. "Thanks." She took the books from Jeff.

Jeff said, "I saw John peeling out of here, I'm surprised you're okay. He left like he wanted to tear into somebody."

Araminta shrugged. "Yeah, I was able to soothe the beast."

Jeff asked, "What are your plans, Araminta?"

She shook her head. "I don't know, but telling you probably isn't the best decision I could make. You will just run and tell him."

He promised. "Well, we are best friends, but I wouldn't tell him anything you tell me in confidence."

Araminta disagreed. "I don't know, Jeff. He's pretty good at forcing people to tell him things."

Jeff laughed, "Yeah, he is, but I'm not too worried."

Araminta rubbed the stress from her temples. "Like I said, I don't rightfully know what I'm going to do. I'll cross that bridge when Sunday rolls around."

Chapter 36

"Grandma, how did that Sunday go? I want to know before we break for lunch, is that okay?"

"Well first, child, I need to tell you how the cat got out of the bag for the girls ailment."

"Okay."

That Saturday, Jeff had some errands to run for Stanley and then he was going to meet up with John. He'd stopped at a Chinese restaurant for lunch and ran into Alexander. Alexander had no idea who Jeff was, but Jeff knew him. They started up a conversation and when Jeff reminded him that he was Araminta's sister's fiancé, Alexander asked how the girls were feeling. Turns out he worked at the fabric barn, and one afternoon Matilda was in there getting fabric and started discussing the twins feeling unwell, and having a burst of female growing. Jeff already knew about the breasts growing, but not the other part. So when Jeff met up with John, he gave him a rare glimpse into the struggles of women.

I had to ask, even though I knew the answer, "Did that mellow him any?"

"I guess you'll have to hear my next story."

"I thought you would never ask." I grinned.

Matilda welcomed John and his parents on Sunday for Dinner. Araminta thought it would just be John, but she could see he was bringing in the big guns to try and persuade her that she wasn't treating their son with the respect he deserved.

John had flowers, and he wore a suit. "It's lovely to see you, Araminta. You look very pretty tonight." John gave her the flowers.

Araminta took them and handed them to her momma. "Flowers from John."

Matilda beamed. "John, that is so thoughtful of you."

John bowed to Matilda. "Thank you, Mrs. Fleming."

Matilda stopped. "Why not, Momma?"

John's face deflated. "I'm not sure that Araminta wishes for me to see you as my momma."

Matilda stopped him. "Of course she does. This is how relationships sometimes go. You take the good with the bad."

John smiled. "Thank you, Momma Fleming."

Matilda called everyone to the table. Araminta was placed next to John. Jeff said grace, and the meal went on with no speeches, no talk of marriages; just two families getting reacquainted. When they were done, John politely asked Araminta if he could talk to her on the porch. He promised to keep his distance. He just wanted to find out how she was.

When they made it to the porch, they sat next to each other and Araminta started. "So you wanted to have this dinner, so what's on your mind, John."

John had been coached on his behavior. His momma had given him strict instructions on how to act, but his overriding question had nothing to do with her ailment. He wanted to know about the neighbor. He bit his tongue. "So are you feeling better?"

She smiled. "Yes I am."

He continued. "Do you want to tell me what you had?"

She frowned. "It's kind of embarrassing, so I would like to not discuss it."

John pressed, "If you can't trust me on something like this, how will you ever be able to tell me secrets."

She shrugged. 'I don't know that I ever will be. Perhaps it's best that we don't pursue each other."

John's temper surfaced. "You can't tell me your breasts have been growing and your female parts have been acting up?"

Araminta stood. "Doesn't sound like you need me to tell you anything. Sounds like you already know?"

John continued, "Yeah I knew, and why didn't you tell me?"

She looked at him. "You just don't get it, John. You knew. You could have said, I heard about what happened and I'm sorry. Instead, you want to drag it out of me, even if it's uncomfortable."

John back pedaled. "Araminta, I'm sorry. I'm trying here. I really am. This isn't going to be easy for me. Please give me a chance to grow the way you have." Tears surfaced. "I'm really trying."

Araminta put her hands up. "I need to think about this, John. Just give me time, without pressuring me. I will agree to date you, but I'm calling off the engagement for right now."

John was shocked.

Before he could say something she was going to get mad over, she stepped back inside the house and went to her room. A few minutes later, Isabella entered the room. "You okay?"

Araminta rolled over and faced her sister. "Yeah, I'm fine."

Isabella scooted Araminta over and lay down with her. "John said you unengaged him."

Araminta nodded. "If he didn't act so bossy, I'd be fine, but it's not getting better, Bella."

Isabella hugged her sister, "I understand. So does Jeff." She continued, "You want Jeff to talk to him?"

Araminta shrugged. "I don't think it will do any good. I don't think he's capable of changing."

Her sister agreed. "Yeah, I think you may be right."

They spent the rest of the night talking, unaware that the Whitneys stayed around until nine, talking about how to get the young pair back together, and unaware that John and Jeff were out in the barn doing the same thing.

I turned to Grandma. "I hope they didn't succeed."

"You'll just have to wait and see."

Nellie entered the room. "Hey, you two. It's time for lunch, and I don't want it to get cold, so cut your story where you are and join me in the kitchen.

Chapter 37

Nellie asked me. "How are you feeling?"

The room felt cold. My joints were stiff, and the pains weren't getting better. "I'm fine." I tried to dismiss it. I had to know what would become of my Araminta and her sister.

Matilda interrupted. "We will hurry with the lunch. Get our stories in, and get you home before you know it. Then when you feel better, you can come back and I will start in on the rest of the family."

I was losing my appetite, but Nellie managed to get some more soup in me. When we finished, I needed help getting to the front room, and I asked if we could sit on the couch instead of the chairs. They placed me on one corner and covered me with my quilt. Matilda sat next to me, her hand on my knee and soldiered on:

That Monday was a holiday, and much to Matilda's surprise, the young neighbor came to the home to speak with Araminta. Matilda was about to send him away when Araminta heard his voice.

"Alex!" She ran from her room and met Matilda and Alexander at the door. "How are you?"

He smiled, teeth so white they shined against his chocolate skin. "I just wondered if you'd like to perhaps take in a picnic with me." He held his hand up to Matilda. "Nothing romantic, just a chance to talk."

Araminta turned to her momma. "I want to go, please tell me I can."

Matilda relented but called in Lillie.

Lillie peeked from the hallway. "Again?" She knew she was chaperoning another outing.

Her momma nodded. "Get your coat, you are going for a ride."

Matilda asked, "Do I need me to send food with you?"

Alexander smiled. "No, my mother made a nice basket up already."

Araminta teased him. "Pretty sure I was going to say yes, huh?"

He apologized. "Well, if you had said no, I would have eaten it all by myself, alone!"

When they drove off, Lillie twisted back and waved to her momma. "Where are we going?" Her mousy voice kicked out to her sister.

"I don't know, but I hope it's not in town. I don't need to try and explain this to my ex fiancé."

Alexander turned, surprised. "Ex?"

Araminta felt at ease for the first time in a year. "Yep."

They decided to drive to the coast. Only an hour away, they found a quiet shoreline to put a blanket down. Lillie made herself comfortable and Alexander opened a basket with food. "Lillie, you can have whatever you want."

She rifled through the food, and picked out a big fat pickle. Alexander laughed. "Good choice."

Alexander stood and asked, "Do you want to take a walk?" He looked back at Lillie. "I promise we won't go out of her sight."

Araminta rubbed her breasts, she was too sore to do too much walking.

Alexander said, "I heard, accidentally by the way, what you went through, so if you can't walk, I totally understand."

Araminta blushed. "Oh my goodness. You know?"

Alexander bowed his head. "I work at the Fabric Barn and your mother wasn't very quiet one day when she was talking to my boss. I'm sorry I know, but I figured you should know I know."

She smiled. "Thank you for telling me you knew."

He asked her. "Your mother said she was making bindings. That can't be very comfortable?"

Araminta admitted. "No, it's not. I'd prefer to take it off."

Alexander shrugged. "Then do."

Araminta said, "I'm kind of embarrassed."

Alexander tilted his head. "Why?"

She said, "My body is changing so fast."

Alexander offered. "It happens, I suppose. Can't much fight it though."

Araminta smiled. "You're right." She reached under her sweater and undid the clip and let the wrap loosen. She uncoiled it round and round until she could slip it out from under her sweater.

Alexander offered, "Honesty, with your sweater, you can't even tell."

She laughed. "Feels better too." They stood in silence and watched the birds swarm down onto the water to get fish. They saw boats passing, they watched the water splash up on massive rocks, and finally they watched the rocking of the waves with the extreme deep color of London blue, confessing such a peaceful sound. Araminta leaned in and laid her head against Alexander's shoulder.

Alexander put his arm around her and rubbed her shoulder. "Thanks for coming with me."

She returned, "Thanks for asking me."

Alexander spoke his mind. "Can I ask you a question?"

She lifted her head and studied Alexander's features. "Sure."

They started back toward Lillie. "Why did you break off your engagement?"

She crossed her arms and walked side by side, no pressure to do what anyone said. "Because of moments like this."

Alexander didn't understand and expressed confusion.

Araminta went on. "This conversation with John would have been one where he would have forced me to take off the binding and then accused me of trying to hide it from him. Everything is about him. If I were to resist, he would have taken it off himself. He'd claim they are his and he has the right to do it."

Alexander asked, "So how has he taken the break-up?"

Araminta's eyes widened. "Don't know. It just happened last night."

Alexander lifted a branch that hovered over the picnic area. "So is it over?"

She fretted. "I don't know. I still have a birthday party I pledged to go to, and everyone in my family wants me to make it work."

Alexander stared at Araminta. "What do you want?"

She smiled. "I'm kind of happy right now."

Alexander agreed. "Yeah, I have to agree with you."

They sat down and had lunch, and Alexander was true to his word. It was pleasant, and pressures of kisses and hugs didn't exist, even if Araminta had wished they did.

When they made it home, Araminta told her mother about the Fabric Barn, and Matilda was horrified that the young man knew, but was surprised how well behaved he'd been around her daughter. "He sounds like a gentleman, but please remember that you have to give John a fair chance to win your heart back."

Araminta shook her head. Would her momma ever get it? "He's had plenty of chances, and he had my heart. He just chose to toss it away."

Matilda stopped her. "Sometimes men just don't fully understand women. He'll get better I promise."

Araminta didn't want to think about John. She wanted to bask in the afternoon she'd just had. She went to her room to see if she could interest her sister in how her day went. Although telling her anything ran the risk of it getting back to John, and somehow she knew that John had more things up his sleeve to get her back. Instead, she just sat on the porch and enjoyed a spring afternoon.

Chapter 38

My body was slowly hurting more and more. Nelly and Matilda were right, I needed to get home, but I worried that the next day I wouldn't be able to drive. That's how sore I was becoming. If that was the case, I'd have to find a doctor down in North Carolina. I didn't let on that I was hurting, and since I was no longer mad at the way the story was evolving, keeping quiet was easier and easier.

Matilda knew my side was hurting, she had reached over and gently rubbed it. Her touch was near magical, and I could have cried it felt so soothing.

"So shall we get the kids to the next event?"

I nodded. "Please."

As day broke, a new wave of activities arose with coolness in the morning and a playfulness that could only enlighten the teenagers before the day's end. Araminta awoke to a wonderful possibility. It was six in the morning, a Tuesday and a school day. Araminta made a cup of tea for her momma and herself. Matilda was in the kitchen baking biscuits. Araminta asked if she could talk to her on the porch.

They sat there, taking in a Carolina day. "You know I have to go to John's birthday party, right?"

Matilda nodded. "It should be fun, and getting to know his family will be a highlight of your relationship."

Araminta realized her momma hadn't given up on John. "Well, I just want you to know that I'll give him a chance. I told Alex, as much as I like him, that I owe John for all he's done. But I also want you to know that I won't put up with his shenanigans ever again."

Matilda resigned herself. "I understand, but please don't just go through the motions, give him a real shot."

Araminta paused. Thought about what a real shot was. "I will."

As they sat there, Alexander pulled up. Matilda turned to Araminta. "Are you expecting that young man?"

Araminta shook her head. "No."

He exited his car with a handful of items. Matilda greeted him, and Alexander greeted her back. "Although it's mighty fine to see your daughter looking so lovely this morning, my visit is actually for you, Mrs. Fleming."

Matilda put her hand to her chest. "Me?"

"Yes, Ms. Ladonya at the Fabrics, Yarn, and Quilting Outlet wanted me to bring you this box of supplies. Since I have to get to school, I really don't have a chance to do so any other time of day. Sorry, if it's too early to receive visitors."

Matilda asked, "What are the supplies for, Alexander? I have enough cream for my daughters."

Alexander said, "Well, Ms. Ladonya was so impressed with the sample miracle cream you made for her, and the batches of cream you made for your daughters, Ms. Ladonya sent this note to you to see if you can make her ten jars of cream for fifty cents a jar a week. Ms. Ladonya sent enough supplies for Matilda to make twelve weeks worth of supplies, and when this runs out she will send more. Ms. Ladonya used the jar you gave her when Araminta and Isabella were sick, and now it appears the jar of cream worked wonders."

Matilda beamed. "You tell Ms. Ladonya I accept and will come to see her at the end of the week."

Alexander thanked Matilda, nodded to Araminta and left as quick as he arrived. That was a good thing, because as he pulled out onto the street, in came John, *there to pick up Jeff and Isabella. He pulled in behind the barn, aware that Araminta didn't want to see him.*

Matilda paid no attention to John pulling in, too happy over her newest endeavor. She said, "I need a name for this miracle cream. It appears to have done wonders for Araminta and Isabella, and Ms. Ladonya. I will call it Matilda's Miracle Cream."

Araminta kept her attention on the barn. "That's beautiful, Momma."

Matilda went in the house to tell Stanley, and to get ready for her next batch. She was so excited. Isabella was in the kitchen and all smiles about the news.

"I'll go tell Jeff."

Matilda told her, "John is here. I don't care if Araminta objects, if those boys want breakfast, bring them up to the house."

Isabella smiled. "Sure thing, Momma." She kissed her mother on the cheek as she passed her on the way to the barn.

The three of them returned to the house for breakfast, and Araminta made herself scarce. Isabella shouted throughout the house. "Araminta?"

Araminta popped her head out of the bedroom. "What do you want, Isabella?"

Isabella asked, "Will you go to the picture show with us tonight?" Isabella motioned to John, "Please."

Matilda made her way over to the two girls. "Remember, you are going to give him a chance."

Araminta sighed. "Okay, but I pay my own way."

Isabella stiffened. "Why?"

Araminta responded, "Because I don't want any strings attached."

Jeff's hearing was too good. He cheered and said, "Five o'clock."

Araminta said, "I will be ready." She added, "In pants!"

John had resigned himself that Araminta's respect and love had to be earned. Sitting clear across the room at school, next to the new kid didn't help matters, but being next to Jeff and Isabella encouraging him to be a gentleman did. He made it through the day without once, badgering Araminta.

Araminta asked Alexander for a ride. "Alex, will you give me a ride home?"

He smiled. "You didn't have to ask."

John remained calm as he watched his former fiancé drive off. It was okay, he was taking her to a movie that night.

John showed up at five, and Jeff joined him at the door to get the girls. Matilda let them in, and as John and Jeff stood at the front door waiting, Matilda called the twins. They came out of the bedroom in their pants, and John and Jeff looked at each other while Isabella jogged out the back door yelling for Momma to stop Jeff. Jeff knew Araminta was going to wear pants but not his Isabella. He'd already teased John about it, and now he had to face it as well.

Isabella screamed, "Momma, I may need some of Matilda's Miracle Cream before it's all over with."

Jeff caught Isabella and started to pretend to strangle her as he tickled her.

Isabella said, "Jeff, it tickles." She lay on the grass until Jeff pulled her in his lap for a long kiss. John and Araminta stood uncomfortably mismatched in the front room. Isabella continued to yell, "Momma, I need some more of Matilda's Miracle Cream, please." Jeff tickled Isabella beyond laughter.

Isabella, Araminta, Jeff, and John made it to the movie house. Not having the pressure of John lording over her, Araminta had a good time. The same couldn't be true for John. He had a hard time concentrating on the movie, wondering what Araminta was thinking. Jeff and Isabella talked about the movie all the way home, and thanks to Matilda and her miracle cream that saved the day for the girls to be completely healed. Jeff gave up on the idea of Isabella never wearing pants. Jeff looked at her in pants verses being in her room sick for a week. Isabella told him she would always wear her dresses because she loved them and the dresses were something her fiancé loved seeing. Who knew, the next year's style could be something worse, and all the unnecessary anxiety would have been for nothing. Isabella knew Jeff wouldn't fight her on the pants, he went with the flow.

Chapter 39

I turned to Grandma. "You got any of that Miracle Cream?" I coughed. "I think I might need some." My neck hurt. "If it's okay with you, I'm going to lie down and listen to the next story, Grandma."

She smiled. "As a matter of fact I do." She pulled a little satchel up and removed a jar. "You can put your head on my lap and I'll rub your shoulder for you."

I didn't want to make my hundred year old great grandmother do more work than she had to. "It's okay."

"Just put your head here and let Matilda do her magic." She began to rub a warm cream onto my neck, the soothing feel ran down my body and brought a sense of peace.

I listened to her story of John's birthday:

John Xavier Whitney would be turning eighteen years old a few weeks later. It was hard to believe John was that young. John was three months older than Araminta, but acted as if he had been there in another lifetime. It may have had something to do with John being the oldest of five children, but Araminta was the oldest of five children too.

John told his parents about Araminta the day after Araminta and Isabella's birthday party. John told his parents he met his wife, but in truth, Araminta had been his only girlfriend.

John's father and mother knew he found her, they wanted to meet the future Mrs. Whitney. What they hadn't told John's grandparents is that the young lady wasn't as sure of the relationship anymore.

Before Araminta's birthday party the year before, John had a long talk with his dad about the difficulty he had trying to secure the young lady's hand as his girlfriend. John's father told John to be persistent, let her know he was interested at all times. It was advice that John had taken too seriously.

John's father asked, "John, who is the young lady that you desire?"

John said, "Her name is Araminta Fleming, and Dad, she is not only beautiful, but she has the biggest heart of any woman I know."

Mr. Whitney said, "Does she feel the same way you do?"

John said, "She is shy, but she talks to me at school when I initiate it, but she won't let me come to her house. Araminta said with her twin sister seeing a guy at school, and that was more than her parents can handle."

Mr. Whitney said, "Do you believe that?"

John said, "Of course not, Dad. I know the reason she didn't let me come to her house. It's because of her shyness. When I was invited to Araminta's house by her twin sister, Isabella, I was going to do everything I could to secure Araminta's hand as my girlfriend before I left that day."

Mr. Whitney said, "You picked a gem there, John. She cares for you as you do for her, she loves you."

John said, "I know she does, Dad, and I want to make sure I do all I can to care for her for the rest of her life."

John's father met Araminta first at the quilting contest for Araminta's mother, Matilda, and Araminta met John's mother not too much longer after that. John's parents still believed John made the right choice choosing Araminta, even after she gave him back his ring. They were sure all of the problems were with her, and not with their son.

John said, "Dad, my aggressive personality scares her, she used to go along with it, but now she throws it in my face."

Mr. Whitney said, "You need to reevaluate how you treat her."

John said, "Well, her mother babies her, and her twin sister protects her. Maybe babying her is what I should start doing more of."

Mr. Whitney said, "Then that's right up your alley, you can turn all the lemons into lemonade."

John didn't have a problem telling anyone what was on his mind. John had learned to express his feelings from his momma and father, but he hadn't been taught to give, only to take.

John's father, Maddison Whitney, was twenty three when he married Marilyn Carston. Marilyn was twenty. Maddison and Marilyn met when they were in there last year of college. They both attended a two year college. Maddison fell in love with Marilyn's future plans to teach and raise a family that would make a difference in this *world. Marilyn fell in love with Maddison, wanting nothing but the best for her family. Maddison told Marilyn he wanted lots of sons. Marilyn was all for it, she gave birth to four sons, and then prayed to God for a daughter with the last pregnancy. God sent Marilyn Ella. Maddison and Marilyn's first born son, John Xavier Whitney, would prove to be incredible, smart, a good son with a huge heart. John taught his siblings a lot and knew his family would always be there for him. John's maternal grandmother, Ella Carston, used to watch John as a toddler. John learned as a boy, his grandma lived for hugs and kisses on the cheek. John loved to provide that for his grandma. Ms. Ella and John had something in common. They were born on the same day. They had always celebrated together. John had a superstition that if he could get Araminta to attend, that she would fall back in love with him. He wanted to make the moment special for him and Araminta.*

John's Grandfather was born in 1830. His name was Buford Carston. Ella was born in 1845. Buford and Ella Carston had fourteen children. Buford Carston was Marilyn Carston Whitney's father. The difference between Ella and Buford was Ella was a slave, but Buford was not, also

Buford was fifteen years older than Ella. John never liked that his Grandmother was a slave. John's Grandfather Buford was a Jr. In 1860, Buford Sr. died, and Buford Jr. was his only male heir. Buford Jr. had two sisters, but they only received a little, Buford Jr. received ninety-five percent of his father's inheritance. Ella's first child was born in 1859, by the time slavery ended Buford and Ella had four children. Ella used to live in a one room wood shack, but after slavery ended the home she shared with Buford and the children was a five room Rambler-style home. Ella felt good knowing she could start a garden and tend to her own garden for her family. By 1884, Ella and Buford had their last child, a girl name Marilyn Carston. Yes, John's Momma was the last of fourteen children. Buford and Ella had ten sons, and four girls, but only eight lived to adulthood. Three died at birth and the other three died from disease. Buford sent all that wanted to go to college to get their degree. Five went to college, and the other three became farmers. By the time Marilyn got married in 1904, her father wasn't able to walk her down the aisle. Marilyn had five older brothers, and the oldest, Forest, was given the honor. Marilyn's father paid a photographer to take pictures of the wedding. By September of 1904, Marilyn was pregnant with John Xavier Whitney. After John's birth, everyone noticed a remarkable resemblance between John and his grandfather. Babies change so everyone overlooked the resemblance. By 1911, Buford Jr. wasn't doing well, the doctors gave him less than two weeks.

Buford's three daughters kissed him and said, "Thank you for looking after our momma."

Buford said, "I love your momma." Buford's sons thanked their father for teaching them everything they knew. All his sons said they would look after Momma once he was gone.

Buford said, "Please do." Buford died four weeks later, on a cold January morning, surrounded by his family. Buford was eighty years old. The reading of Buford's will was different from the reading of Buford's father's will. Buford didn't slight his daughters like his father slighted his sisters. Buford gave all eight of his children the same. The children got seventy percent, and Ella got thirty percent. Ella was able to keep the house and the car and truck for someone to carry her whenever she needed to go.

John was at the funeral, and a few more babies that Marilyn had before 1911. Relatives stared at John once again because of the resemblance to his Grandfather.

With John about to turn eighteen, the hate he carried as a child, was the hate of a grown man. Three days before John's birthday, a letter came in the mail from Grandma Ella. It was a note card inviting John and his entire family to Grandma Ella's house on Sunday June 3, 1923.

When John opened the card and read it, the first thing he thought was, "So Grandma don't want us to have our special birthdays anymore?"

Marilyn said, "Maybe Momma figures you're a grown man now and wanted to do something different."

John said, "Momma you know nothing about this?"

Marilyn said, "No baby, I don't. This is all your Grandma's doing."

John said, 'You think she wouldn't mind if Araminta, Jeff, and Isabella come?' Marilyn said, 'Of course they can come, Momma wouldn't mine.' They all went to Grandma Ella's house.

John introduced Araminta to his Grandmother. He said, "Grandma this is Araminta, the future Mrs. Whitney."

Araminta bristled. She whispered, "John, don't tell people that."

He reminded her. "Most my family thinks we are engaged. A lot of them won't be around forever, so just go along with it."

Araminta shook her head. "This is stupid."

He begged, "Please."

She shook her head. "I'm going to regret this, but whatever."

"Thanks." He tried to kiss her but she turned away.

Araminta whispered to Ella, "Very nice to meet you, Ms. Ella."

Ms Ella said, "Give Momma some suga', Minta. You goin' to be my baby boy's wife, mmm?" Ms. Ella turned to John. "John, she is precious, make sure you take good care of her."

John stared at Araminta as she engaged with his grandma. John was so proud. "That's the plan, Grandma, and yes, she is precious. More than you know."

Araminta rolled her eyes. Living this lie was going to be insufferable.

John pulled Araminta to him, and Grandma Ella said, "Go ahead, baby, kiss Minta, don't be ashamed."

John said, "Grandma, you know I'm not ashamed to kiss Araminta."

Araminta warned him, "John, don't you dare."

John pulled Araminta to his chest, and in front of John's momma, Grandma Ella, Mr. Whitney, John's siblings, Isabella, Jeff, and Momma Whitney's two sisters, Madaline and Claira, John laid a kiss on Araminta that even embarrassed Isabella. No one said a word, and John had no shame in how long the kiss went on.

Araminta tried to push away but the John who treated Araminta like property, came out and pulled her closer. He knew his family and didn't care. When John finally let Araminta up for air, everyone gave them a round of applause.

Araminta was livid and wiped her lips on his shirt.

Isabella looked at Jeff. "Please don't do that to me, that is so embarrassing."

Jeff said, "I would never put you through that, but if you want we could go outside and---"

Isabella cut Jeff off, "Not in that yard, it's too spooky."

Jeff laughed, "I agree, but when we get back home can I have a date with you on the side of the barn?"

"Is that a date?" Isabella asked.

"Try and stop me." Jeff smiled.

John's Grandma asked everyone to have a seat. Mrs. Ella stood and asked John to come up with her. John went up to the front. "Grandma, no speeches please."

Grandma Ella said, "What I have for you is not a speech, as a matter of fact it's not from me. It's something given to me twelve years ago when you were six years old."

John frowned.

Ella said, "What's in this envelope was left for you from your Grandfather Buford Carston. He wrote this for you to open on your eighteenth birthday."

John said, 'For me?'

Grandma Ella said, "Yes, for you, baby, will you open it, and read it to us?" Grandma Ella sat.

John was nervous. "Here goes."

~~~~~~

Dear John;

I know you are only six years old, but I felt before I leave this earth, I better explain some things to you for your 18th birthday. I know you don't understand why people stare at you. I'm sure when you get older you will hear how they say you look like me. Well, it's no reason you shouldn't favor me, I am your Grandfather. I know you will grow up and wonder why you have the only pair of eyes like mines. I'm here to tell you it's in the blood. I hope you are not ashamed of your Grey eyes. I know I am a White man and you're a Black man, but our eyes are beautiful in any
~~~~~~

complexion. As you get older and see your surroundings where your Grandma lives, please don't hate me. Yes it's a Plantation, that's paid for and it was the law before 1865. I inherited this from my father Buford Carston Sr. I never harmed your Grandma throughout Slavery and after Slavery. I love your Grandma very much, and I hope one day you will be proud of me as you are your Grandma Ella. You can call me Grandpapa if you like, I would love to know that you did. John's tears wells up in his eyes, Araminta sees them about to fall. John tries not to move to keep the tears from falling in front of his family. Buford said, "Anyone of my children or Grandchildren could have been born with my eyes, but God chose you." Too late John's tears are falling hard and strong, John could barely see what he is reading now. I tried to do right by all my children. I write to you because you have something of mines that you cannot get rid of. I ask your Grandma to hold this letter for you until you turn eighteen, and hopefully you will love me, as I have always loved you. John can't see anymore, Araminta will hold John and finish the letter. Araminta reads: Enclosed is something else for you to be proud of about Mr. Buford Carston:

<u>Marriage License for the</u>

<u>State of North Carolina</u>

<u>for</u>

Buford Carston Jr.

Ella Carston

April 11, 1861

John looked at his Grandma, wiped his tears. "Grandma you were married to Grandpapa?" He looked to the heavens. "I love you, Grandpapa." John smiled and realized all these years he was angry for nothing. His grandfather loved them, really loved them. He carried anger around for no reason. He couldn't help he was a son of a slave master. He married John's grandmother and took care of her. He couldn't say anything bad about this man. Then on top of all that, he took the time to write John a letter on his sick bed, so his six year old grandson wouldn't grow up confused.

Jeff went up and gave John more tissue. Araminta felt compassion for her old boyfriend, but it was far more of an event for him than her. All she wanted to do was get out of there.

Jeff said, "This is a clean tissue I was saving for Isabella."

John said, "I have plenty in the car, trust me, I know."

Marilyn and her two sisters, Madaline and Claira, caught their breath.

Marilyn said, "Momma, you and Daddy were married and you are just telling us?"

Ella said, "I didn't tell you, your father told John. We got married on April 11, 1861, the day before the Civil War started."

Marilyn said, "But Momma, why didn't you or Daddy ever tell us?"

Ella said, "Your Father felt it was safe if only he and I knew, in case outsiders found out and tried to harm his family. I know my children was ashamed of us, thinking we wasn't married, but Buford couldn't marry me before slavery, although technically, he did. We got married before the Civil War, and we never told a soul. I knew about John's letter, but I promised Buford I wouldn't read the letter before John."

Ella asked her three daughters, "Now that you know we were married, can you love your father even in death?"

Marilyn said with a tearful voice, "Momma, we loved Daddy, it's just we knew why he didn't marry you because they may have hurt us, but we still hoped that he would have tried to marry you. We didn't want you to live alone all these years. I wished we would have known. I have so much respect for both of you. You both did the right thing and kept the secret."

John said, "This was the best birthday ever, Grandma."

Grandma Ella said, "Yes, It was baby, now can I get my hugs and kisses? It's my birthday too, you know."

The front door opened with a huge pink and blue birthday cake for Grandma Ella and John.

John cried again. Grandma Ella held her chest, and her daughters helped her to sit down. Araminta put John in a chair next to his Grandma. she placed her arms around John's neck as he sat next to her and continued wiping John's tears while singing;

Happy Birthday, Momma and John, Happy Birthday to you...

John tried to kiss Araminta as she sang to him, but the tears kept falling, which was a good thing, because she was done with his kisses.

When the party ended the four teenagers hopped in John's car and headed home.

Jeff asked, "What were all those cabins on your Grandma Ella's property?"

John frowned. "They were slave cabins. Two hundred of them, and those shackles on the porch were the binds that kept the slaves from fleeing. Of course you know what the noose hanging from the tree was for."

As they rode back home from John's big eighteenth birthday party, John gave the history of all the slave quarters, still sitting on the property. They saw more than two hundred slave cabins on the property. Also all the remnants of slavery were still there - shackles laying on the porches, and the center yard with a hanging noose. It was hard to believe John's grandmother could live in a five bedroom house in the middle of where she was once a slave. For twelve years, Ella Carston lived on the Carston

Plantation as a slave, and became the heir of the property. It was amazing that a slave herself owned the very property in which she was the slave. John's angry thoughts of his Grandfather were no more. He smiled thinking of him.

Araminta said, "I often wondered where you got your eyes, John, your momma and father's eyes are brown, but I didn't want to ask."

Jeff said, "I knew what it could have been, but I didn't need to know. I know I have a brother who is my complexion but has grey eyes."

Matilda was stroking my hair. "That's why John had gray eyes."

I countered, "And I thought it was because he was jealous." I snickered and Matilda shushed me.

Chapter 40

I felt like I sat through a lot of nothing. None of what Matilda told me was going to make me like John, and I didn't gather it made Araminta like him either. "That's it? That's what he did to try and win her over?"

Matilda reminded me, "Don't forget, they still have graduation, and then they are going to college together."

My dread rose. "Okay, give it to me. I want to know what is going to happen."

It seemed to please Matilda that she had a willing ear, and that I had to have more:

As John, Jeff, Isabella, and Araminta drove back from John's birthday party, John asked Jeff, "Can I go back to the barn and get the summary that Mrs. Nelson had for us concerning World War I for our history final?"

Jeff said, "No. sorry, can't do that tonight, I will bring it tomorrow to class. I have a date with a certain young lady on the side of the barn tonight." Jeff blushed watching Isabella blush.

Isabella noticed his blush. "You blushed Jeff, I saw it."

Jeff blushed again. Jeff kissed her on the cheek. "I'm running to our spot, I will see you in a minute. See you later, John, Araminta." Jeff was gone.

Isabella said, "I guess I better go start blushing again, see you guys later."

Araminta and John shared an uncomfortable moment seeing her sister and Jeff so happy.

John said, "Since people are going for some sugar, how about we try to stoke that fire again?"

Araminta shook her head. "Not hardly." She started to exit the truck.

John backed off. "Okay, how about a conversation on the porch?"

Araminta kept running her mother's words of giving him a chance through her head. "Okay."

While they headed to the porch, Isabella made it to the side of the barn. Jeff gazed in Isabella's eyes under the full moon. Isabella blushed and looked away. Jeff called Isabella's name.

Isabella looked up. "Jeff you know what your gazing is doing to me, don't you?"

Jeff said, "Yes, look at me."

Isabella looked at Jeff and couldn't stop blushing.

Jeff loved to watch her blush. "Isabella, is it too much to ask? Let me just look at your eyes, and you look at mine."

Isabella agreed.

Jeff stepped a little closer and eased down Isabella's face, from her forehead capturing her lips. "I see you can't stop blushing when I watch your eyes, so I thought I better play capture your lips before you pass out."

Isabella laughed. "How do you do it?"

Jeff said, "Do what?"

Isabella said, "How do you watch my eyes and never blush?"

Jeff said, "Isabella when I gaze into your eyes, I see how blessed I am to have you. I do not take that lightly. I love you so much."

Isabella said, "I am so glad you love me, because I'm sure in love with you."

Jeff reached for Isabella head and pushed her lips to his, and her eyes were no longer gazing, they were finally closed.

While Jeff took care of business on the side of the barn, John was on the porch, grateful Araminta was able to meet his Grandma.

Araminta kept it platonic. "What a wonderful birthday present your grandma gave everyone after all these years."

John said, "I know, I don't think it all sunk in yet." He looked at Araminta. "I am so glad you came with me. Can I please show you how grateful I am."

Araminta shook her head. "John, don't try so hard. Just let us become friends again."

John whined, "I've always been your friend."

Araminta worried he'd never get it. "That's your problem. You don't see that you were not my friend. You thought being my boss was being my friend. When you learn that lesson, there might be hope for us." Araminta relived the irritation of the kiss in front of his family. "John. What you did at the party was inexcusable. I told you no, not here, and you totally ignored me. You not only *humiliated me in front of your family, but you did something you had no right to do."*

He smiled. "What if I did it one more time?"A

raminta cautioned John. "You don't want to know."

John smiled at Araminta. "Araminta you might as well get use to it, because it will happen again. Whether it's with me or someone else, it's what guys do."

Araminta started shaking her head. "No, John. Not all guys are like that."

John said, "I want to know what will happen when I do it, because I will do it again."

Araminta said, "Well, I will tell your parents on you."

John said, "Hmm, considering my parents were in the same room when it happened before and didn't stop it, what makes you so sure they will stop it?"

Araminta rationalized with him, "John why do you do this to me?"

John said, "Do you really want to know?"

Araminta said, "Yes, because this is wrong."

John said, "What is wrong?"

Araminta said, "The way you have your way with me, and others too."

John scoffed, "I have my way with you?"

Araminta stared at John. "How can you ask that question, John? You had your way all the time."

John said, "Really?"

Araminta said, "Yes."

John said, "Hmm, well let me ask you a question and answer truthfully. Who gives me my way?"

Araminta frowned. "You take it."

He responded, "You give me my way the same way you can't tell me no."

Araminta said, "But I have told you no before."

John stared in Araminta's eyes. "Araminta if you're talking about those pants, I gave you that one, but I tell you what. If you think you can stop giving me my way, and telling me no, I dare you to try it."

Araminta said, "What? Is this your attempt to get me back? I will not give you your way anymore, and I will tell you no, too."

John said, "We are going back to the way it was. I let you have too much, and that's why I lost you. I had a *conversation with my dad, and it dawned on me that I was too understanding." John laughed.*

Araminta said, "You need to leave, John."

He asked, "When, before or after I kiss you?"

She fumed. "Now! Good night, John."

Araminta walked to the front door, and John grabbed her hand. "We have not kissed goodnight yet."

Araminta said, "But I said goodnight to you, just not on the lips. I told you, you're not getting your way."

Araminta opened the front door, turned to John and watched the shocked expression. Araminta shut the door and left John standing on the porch with a bewildered expression.

John walked down the porch stairs bruised, remembering Jeff had a date with Isabella on the side of the barn. He walked up on those two. John cleared his throat, and they still didn't hear him. He cleared his throat a second time and they jumped. They didn't want to let go of each other. Jeff and Isabella stood and looked into each other eyes.

John said, "I'm sorry Jeff, Isabella. Jeff can I talk to you, I'm really sorry."

Isabella said, "It's okay, John."

Jeff said, "Let me walk Isabella to the back door, and I will be right back, meet me in the barn."

John nodded and went in the barn.

Jeff and Isabella walked to the back door. Jeff grabbed hold of her one last time. "The things you do to me, I dare not say, can I have another date next Friday night after the Prom?"

Isabella said, "Of course." She kissed him on the cheek. "Go see John. I will see you in the morning, goodnight."

Jeff said, "Night, baby."

Jeff waited until Isabella locked the door and ran to the barn.

When he got there he asked, "What's wrong, John?"

John said, "Araminta took me up on a challenge. I challenged her to try and not give me my way, and I also dared her to tell me no."

Jeff said, "You did what? Why did you do that? You two are broken up. Are you insane?"

John said, "I was trying to prove to her that she always gives me my way and never tells me no."

Jeff said, "She's proved that for the last month."

John said, "Yes, well she proved it again tonight by not letting me kiss her goodnight."

Jeff said, "You just can't play your cards right, John."

John snapped at Jeff, "I've not had a romantic moment with her in over a month. It's pretty easy to play it cool if you are getting kisses every day, but kind of hard when you haven't."

Jeff asked, "And whose fault is that?"

John concluded, "Araminta's."

Jeff shook his head. "No, it's your fault."

Jeff continued, "Just apologize to her, be a gentleman and everything will turn out fine."

John said, "Apologize?"

Jeff said, "Yes, for acting like you own her."

John said, "Jeff, Araminta has always given me my way, and never tells me no, why should I apologize for something she always did?"

Jeff said, "You need to realize she is a person as well, and she has feelings just as important as you, and you want to keep the peace, that's why. We don't want this to get bigger than it is."

John was confident he didn't have to apologize for anything. John told Jeff, "I will see you in school tomorrow morning."

Jeff thought, 'Oh boy, I might have to spend some time watching after John, hopefully he will do the right thing.'

The next day, as Araminta, Isabella, and Jeff walked to school, John pulled up beside them in his truck and offered to take them to school. Isabella and Jeff looked at Araminta.

Araminta said, "No thank you." She kept walking. Araminta didn't look at John.

John was shocked.

Jeff and Isabella said, "We will walk with her, John, thanks."

John drove off.

When Isabella, Jeff, and Araminta walked into class, there was no John. Araminta sat next to Alexander. Araminta asked Alexander about his weekend and didn't see John come in the class from the back door.

As he sat next to Isabella, he handed her a note for Araminta.

Alexander whispered, "What's that all about?"

Araminta answered, "John isn't ready to give up and thinks he can win, but not this time, this time he will learn a lesson."

Isabella stood and walked the note to Araminta. It read:

So you're going to teach me

a lesson, Araminta?

I will accept that challenge,

teach me a lesson.

Mrs. Nelson entered. "If you like to purchase tickets for the prom, see me a few minutes before class ends today." The prom was coming the next Friday. John couldn't see Araminta's face when Mrs. Nelson mentioned the prom, but Jeff could. Jeff saw Araminta turn to Alexander and say something. He also saw Alexander smile.

Jeff looked away, he knew this had trouble written all over it.

Mrs. Nelson said finals would be Monday and Tuesday and graduation would be Thursday of the next week. Araminta took a moment to give Isabella a note:

Go to lunch with Jeff, I will go on the other side of the building and study on the picnic table, I will be fine. PLEASE GO WITH JEFF…PLEASE!

When lunch rolled around, Araminta practically ran out the class. Jeff looked at Isabella and pulled out a tissue and told her to stop crying and go have lunch with your sister, I want to talk to John. Isabella nodded, and Jeff said everything will be alright.

Isabella ran out and found Araminta having a conversation with Alexander.

Araminta turned to her sister. "I told you to go have lunch with Jeff. If John followed you, this isn't going to be a good thing."

Isabella introduced herself to Alexander. "As you have probably guessed, I'm Araminta's twin. My name is Isabella."

Alexander bowed his head. "Yes, your sister has talked about you a lot. It's so good to finally meet you." He continued. "I'd have introduced myself, but your boyfriend seems to be a pretty good friend with John, and I don't think John likes me too well."

Isabella nodded. "That's probably an understatement."

Araminta said, "Maybe you should go back to Jeff."

Isabella said, "Jeff told me to have lunch with you. He's talking with John."

Alexander moved over, "Here, you can sit next to your sister, and I have a lot in my lunch sack if you would like something."

Isabella shared one of Alexander's sandwiches with Araminta. As they ate, and as the conversation made its way to the prom, Isabella said, "Momma will be finished with our prom dresses tonight, are you still going?"

Araminta shared a momentary stare with Alexander, then said, "No I have two books I have been meaning to read, and I think Friday night will be the perfect time to start."

Isabella said, "Araminta you don't mean that, do you?"

Araminta said, "Yes I do, and Isabella, I want you to not worry about me. I want you to enjoy your prom. I will ask Momma if Friday night I can spend the weekend with Grandma Lucy so I can study."

Isabella cried, "Araminta, no!" she motioned, "you-know-who will be heartbroken if you miss this dance."

Araminta laughed, "John? Isabella please don't worry about John, and don't worry about me, I just want you to have a wonderful time with the man you love and have memories to tell your grandchildren."

Isabella asked, "And what will you tell your Grandchildren?"

Araminta smiled and glanced at Alexander. "That the night of my prom, I was right where I wanted to be."

Isabella said, "Let me tell you something, Araminta, you are making a mistake."

Araminta shook her head. "I'll be fine."

Isabella frowned. "I love you, we are twins; we share a great bond together. Do you know there are twins who have died at birth, in house fires, and no telling what else? God has blessed us to live a wonderful life with Momma, Dad, Lillie, Addie and Joseph. We share things, and I want to share this. Even if you don't go with John, can you at least go with Jeff and me?"

Araminta waved her hand. "You and Jeff would have it conveniently arranged for John to be there. Sorry, Isabella, but I'm done being told what to do, and not having any say in what I want to do." Araminta smiled. "Thanks for being a wonderful sis, and I love you."

Isabella asked, "When are you going to tell Momma you're not going?"

Araminta shrugged. "Uh, I haven't thought about that."

Isabella scolded her. "All the time Momma put into both our Prom and Graduation dresses will devastate Momma."

Araminta said, "You're getting just like Momma, you want it to always be my fault. Don't worry about the prom dress, I think I can do something with it on Friday night."

Isabella tilted her head in confusion. "What's that supposed to mean?"

Araminta laughed. "Don't worry."

Alexander urged the girls. "Let's go, kids are moving back into the classroom. They headed back to the front of the building and saw John and Jeff coming their way.

Araminta told Isabella, "Go occupy them while we slip in the building."

Isabella tried to slow the boys down, but they fell into line twenty yards behind Araminta and Alexander. At the pace the boys were walking they were going to catch up to Araminta before she got to the classroom, and she didn't want trouble, so as they passed the principal's office, Araminta stated, "Alex, let's see about your transcripts," and ducked into the office.

John and Jeff continued on, knowing that the principal wouldn't have approved of a confrontation in his office.

The afternoon went by slow but just before class was over, Mrs. Nelson asks the class if anyone wanted to purchase prom tickets to do so. Araminta watched John and Jeff go up to Mrs. Nelson's desk to purchase tickets. Araminta saw John take two tickets. As she looked up, John stared at her.

When class ended, Araminta walked out, escorted by Alexander. Alexander opens his door for Araminta, and she thanked him for his politeness. On the drive home, he asked, "So you'd rather go to a movie than your prom?"

Araminta turned to Alexander, "It's not that, Alex. I would rather go to a movie with you, than to the prom with John."

He nodded, but pointed out. "You saw what I saw, he bought two tickets."

She coldly smiled. "He'll have to get a refund."

Alexander smiled. "You want a soda?"

Araminta shrugged. "Sure."

They detoured into town and Alexander bought her a soda. After they finished he took her home. She asked to be let off at the road, worried that John was at the barn.

Alexander offered, "I can take you all the way to the house. I'm not worried about John. I think when push comes to shove, he doesn't really want to fight me."

She sighed. "You don't know John."

Alexander accepted her request. "It's your wish." He stopped the car, and she got out before he could open the door. He bowed his head. "Thanks again for spending the time with me."

She smiled. "The pleasure was all mine."

Araminta waved as Alexander drove off, and when she stepped onto the path, she ran into John waiting for her.

Araminta caught her breath. "What do you want?"

John grabbed her and puts his hands around her waist from behind and locked them in place.

Araminta's hands shook as she tried to remove his, but he held her tight.

John moved his head to Araminta's right cheek and rubbed his lips against her cheek several times as if he was eating food.

Araminta yelled, "Why are you doing this to me?"

John released Araminta, and she ran the rest of the way home. Jeff and Isabella were on the porch watching her catch her breath, wiping her cheek of John's kisses. Araminta saw Jeff and Isabella look at each other. When

Araminta reached Jeff and Isabella, Araminta asked, "I know you know why he keeps doing things to me, please tell me."

Araminta tried to catch her breath as Jeff said, "You will find out Friday when school is out, but in the meantime show him love."

Araminta's eyes grew huge; she couldn't believe Jeff was on his side. She shouted, "Show him love? He just attacked me at the entrance to our property. He held me while he rubbed his lips against my cheek, then he let me go. Was he showing me love?"

Jeff and Isabella looked at each other, and Jeff said, "Why were you wiping his affection off your face?"

Araminta couldn't believe what she heard. "Jeff, you are as bad as he is. John was sucking my right cheek, as if he was trying to take it with him. Please tell me what is going on? Tell me you aren't encouraging him?"

Jeff said, "He told me to tell you, not to tell anyone what he is doing, or he will do more of it, he said you have been warned."

Araminta said, "If he keeps it up, I will tell someone, I will tell the principal. Let him know, he has been warned."

Jeff sighed. "Don't start a war with him, Araminta. He'll win." Jeff turned to Isabella and kissed her. "I will see you at dinner, baby." Jeff walked to the barn.

Isabella looked at Araminta.

Araminta asked, "Isabella, what's going on?"

Isabella whispered, "He's convinced you are coming back to him."

Araminta couldn't cry because she wasn't sad. She was mad. Araminta sat on the porch steps and watched an ant carry a piece of crumb, ten times its size into the grass. She spoke to the little creature. "Your task is easier than mine."

I worried for Araminta. "Grandma, tell me nothing bad happened to my great aunt Araminta, please?"

Ever the poker player, she didn't say yea or nay, just smiled. "You'll have to listen on."

Chapter 41

Matilda suggested, "Why don't we get a little food in you before we continue? It's pert near lunch."

I felt too sore to get up, comfortable lying there on the couch. "Can we just continue?"

Nellie had come into the front room, her head shaking. "Matilda, you're going to have to wrap things up. She might need to go home tonight." She stepped closer and bent down. She placed a hand on my forehead. "She a bit feverish."

Matilda asked, "Nel, bring her some warm tea and bring me some snaps. "We'll do the best we can from here."

Nellie smiled and went back to the kitchen.

"Please, Grandma, continue."

She smiled and slipped herself back into the past:

Matilda came to the door and said, "Araminta what are you doing baby?"

Araminta smiled and stood. "Nothing, Momma. I was trying to figure a problem for my science final next week."

Isabella stood behind Matilda nodding.

"Girls, come and try your prom dresses on so I can see if I need to make any changes." Matilda waved them inside. A tension arose between the sisters as Isabella wondered if her sister would come clean.

Araminta smiled. "Sure, Momma." Araminta stood and followed Matilda in.

Isabella's eyes widened wondering what her sister was up to.

Araminta tried the dress on and gushed over how wonderful it looked, never once mentioning that her plans to go to the prom had changed.

The next morning Araminta got ready for school and planned to leave early so she wouldn't have to deal with John and his unwelcomed surprises. She had to avoid Isabella and Jeff too. She told her momma, "Got to get to school early today to study some more for the finals."

Matilda said, "You're not going to wait for Isabella and Jeff?"

Araminta smiled. "No Momma, I have to talk with Mrs. Nelson." She picked up her lunch and kissed her momma goodbye. Araminta ran out the house and hurried to school. She was so happy. A peacefulness settled in, no

John, just a sense of freedom. Araminta still didn't know how she would tell her momma she wouldn't be going to the prom, but Momma would have to understand that the relationship with John wasn't working out, and Araminta ultimately had the say.

When she got to class, Mrs. Nelson welcomed her in and the two talked about her situation. "Mrs. Nelson, thank you for moving me to the other corner."

Mrs. Nelson smiled. "Well it does appear to have helped your focus." They went over the end of year assignments and her upcoming college. Their morning had just about gone off without a hitch until the door opened and in came John, Jeff, and Isabella - early.

They appeared to want to talk to Araminta, but Mrs. Nelson ran interference. "Please take a seat, Araminta and I are working on something."

John glared at Araminta and turned to Jeff. "Let's hang out in the schoolyard until the bell rings."

The two of them left while Isabella took her seat.

Mrs. Nelson whispered, "You know, Araminta, at some point you're going to have to talk to John. Would it help if I sat in while you two discussed things?"

Araminta shook her head. "It wouldn't matter. What I have to say, he won't listen to, and what he has to say, I don't care to hear."

Mrs. Nelson raised her eyebrows. "Well, the offer is there if you want it."

Araminta gave an exhausted smile. "Thank you for the offer."

Isabella caught her sister's attention. Araminta asked her teacher, "Mrs. Nelson, give me a minute. Let me find out what my sister has to say."

Mrs. Nelson nodded. Araminta approached her sister, hoping she wasn't going to try and persuade her to do something she didn't want to do. "Yes?"

Isabella lowered her voice. "At least talk to Jeff."

Araminta lifted her shoulders. "Why?"

Isabella implored her sister to lower her volume and keep the conversation away from Mrs. Nelson.

Araminta shook her head. "Anything you have tell me, Mrs. Nelson has already heard."

Isabella's eyes widened. "You told Mrs. Nelson what's going on?"

Araminta rolled her eyes. "I don't think it was a big surprise, she sees what goes on."

Isabella continued. "Still, will you hear Jeff out, please?"

Araminta crossed her arms. "Very well, but my mind is made up."

Isabella frowned. "Thank you, Sis." Isabella had one more request, "Can we do it away from Mrs. Nelson?"

Araminta turned to her teacher, who'd heard everything. "Is that okay, Mrs. Nelson?"

Mrs. Nelson smiled. "I will be back in a few. I'll go get some supplies from the other classroom."

Isabella left and brought back Jeff. Jeff, Isabella, and Araminta sat and Jeff said, "I see you left for school early today, Araminta."

Araminta said, "I wanted to walk in peace without having to deal with attacks from John."

Jeff guffawed. "Attacks?"

Araminta nodded. "Yes, attacks. Anyone who just grabs a person and kisses them without consent is attacking them, and I won't tolerate it anymore."

Jeff said, "Really? If I remember correctly John used to 'Attack' you all the time, and you didn't make a stand then. So now his behavior is attacking?"

Araminta couldn't believe Jeff took John's side. "It is when I don't want it anymore."

Jeff countered. "Well, for the rest of this week I want you to walk to school with us."

Araminta wasn't going to do that. "No. plain and simple. I'm not going to. I like walking alone, and there's nothing wrong with that."

Jeff said, "Araminta, I guess there's something I need to tell you now instead of waiting till Friday."

Araminta stopped him, "It doesn't matter what you have to say, Jeff, we have three more days of school, and I'm walking alone and that's all that needs to be said."

Jeff pleaded, "I am not talking to you as your brother-in-law, I am talking to you as a minister, and when I tell you something, I need you to take heed. You will find out the rest on Friday after school. You choose to not listen and there will be consequences to every action you make."

Araminta shrugged. 'There are consequences no matter what we do, Jeff. It doesn't take a minister to know *that. We'll see what consequences come on Friday, because all the consequences up to now have been because of John's behavior."*

Araminta had never seen Jeff take such a stand, and it surprised her when he blurted out, "Since your mouth is so smart, you have no second chances, you must get it right with John, and if he tries to become affectionate with you, you better accept it."

Araminta lost respect for Jeff. "I'm really sorry for you. It sounds like John has done the same thing to you."

Jeff responded, "Your smart mouth is going to undo you."

Araminta agreed. "Maybe."

Jeff gave an appeal to the past. "Just remember what it used to be like. John hasn't changed from that man."

Araminta laid her hand open to Jeff. "Exactly, he hasn't changed. That's my point. If he hasn't changed, I'm never going back." Araminta leaned in and whispered, "Maybe when we are all in college, and he sees that I'm a person just like him, he'll respect me and we can get back together, but for now, he needs to let me have my space."

They were at an impasse. Mrs. Nelson came back and asked, "I hope that gave you enough time?"

Araminta stood. "More than enough time, thank you, Mrs. Nelson."

The clock hit the top of the hour and Araminta took her seat across the room. The other students filed in, and Araminta watched John huddle with her sister and Jeff. From the expression on his face, he didn't like what they told him.

Alexander came in, sat next to Araminta. "How are you this morning?"

Araminta sat up. "I'm great, how are you?" She rested her chin on her palm and listened while he gave a detailed account of working before coming to school. She stared. "That sounds lovely."

Alexander eyed her with amusement. "It's just work."

Mrs. Nelson called the class to order and they opened their books to start the day.

Araminta didn't think she could use her sister to run interference for her, so she counted on Mrs. Nelson. With the end of class coming, Mrs. Nelson handed a note for Alexander to go to the office, and then asked Araminta to go to the office to pick up a supply.

When Araminta got to the office, Alexander waited. "Mrs. Nelson said I was to give you a ride."

Araminta asked, "What about my books?"

"She said she would bring them by your house."

For one day, she'd figured out how to get past John and home before he could surprise her with some sick action again. Alexander dropped her off at the doorstep and she sat on the porch as he drove off.

A half hour later, John dropped off Jeff and her sister, and Araminta went in before she was forced to have a conversation.

She passed her momma. "I'll be in my room until John leaves."

Matilda frowned but understood her daughter needed the space.

From her window, Araminta could see Jeff take Isabella to their spot to get their lips exercised and rejuvenated. She envied that they were in love. It was nice to be in love.

I mustered up enough energy to echo, 'Stay strong, Araminta."

Matilda chuckled. "Do you still have enough energy to keep listening?"

I nodded. "I'm still following you, Grandma."

Chapter 42

"Grandma, you seemed to know everything that took place. You mean to tell me you didn't know she didn't plan on going to the prom?"

Matilda patted my shoulder. "Of course I knew, but I had told John when he asked me to interfere that I wouldn't unless she asked me. She never did, so I decided to let her figure it out for herself."

"I'm glad you didn't say anything."

"Well, that Friday, things went a little sideways."

"Oh? What happened?"

John chomped at the bit. He was so sure Araminta was going to come to her senses, but he also knew he had to force her hand. He showed up that Friday morning at the Fleming house before anyone was up and waited out in his truck for any sign of life. When Matilda got up to sweep the porch, he jumped out of the truck and demanded to see Araminta.

"John, demanding something to me isn't going to make your situation better. I would suggest you request things in a more pleasant tone."

John bowed his head. "Sorry, Momma, may I please see Araminta? Today is Friday and she hasn't spoken to me all week, and the prom is tonight. I want to make sure that she is aware that we will be going to it."

Matilda studied his face. "I haven't heard anything about her not going. She hasn't mentioned anything, but she has tried on the dress, so I am guessing she is going."

John shook his head. "Are you sure? She told Isabella she doesn't want to go."

Matilda continued sweeping. "Not wanting to go, and going, are two different things."

Matilda looked down at me, and wiped a wayward strand from my face. "Well, as you can suspect, things didn't go as John nor Matilda had envisioned."

That morning, the last day of the school year, the day of the prom, Mrs. Nelson brought three dozen donuts, and the twins delivered Mrs. Nelson one of Matilda's quilts as a present for the fine job she did in teaching them. Matilda had stitched 'Thank you' across the throw.

John still didn't know what to expect from that night, and as badly as he wanted to pin Araminta down and prove his love, she never left her friend Alexander's side. He had to ask Jeff to nail down what Araminta's plans were.

Jeff and Isabella approached Araminta at lunch, and Alexander excused himself to let them talk.

Jeff said, "You know the other day when I changed my coat from future brother-in-law to minister, I did so because I needed you to understand the authority of the Lord."

Araminta shrugged. "I was unaware that you have an open channel with what the Lord says I should do, because I've been doin' a little prayin' myself and he's tellin' me something different."

Jeff started in on Araminta. "Well, what the good book says is that women should obey their men, and since you were upsetting your sister's big day, and you were upsetting your man, I can tell you on good word, that whatever you think the good Lord is telling you, you are deceived."

Araminta didn't say a word. She just let Jeff keep going.

"I had to do something. Araminta, John told me about what he done to you, and I told him it was wrong, and I told him to apologize to you the next day. He refused, and then Isabella told me how John heard you say you were going to teach John a lesson that John overheard. I told Isabella to go to lunch with you, and I was going to lunch with John. When I met with John, I informed him of what he needed to do to fix this mess because this was upsetting Isabella. Isabella is upset because Araminta is upset, and it all started because of his arrogance. I told John since he couldn't find it in himself to understand how he has pushed you away, he had to do what I tell him from now on until this is fixed. I told him my title has changed from brother

to minister, and he must show affection to you. Araminta you are making it hard because you won't give him a chance to change. You have given back the ring and are keeping company with another man, which is against God's law. You have been spoken for. I have told him, even if you keep resisting, John must try harder to catch you and to try every day until I say different."

Araminta stopped Jeff. "Well, I'm telling you to stop telling him that. Please, have him stop trying to catch me."

Jeff inhaled. "I can't do that, Araminta. It is my job to see you two back together." Jeff pleaded, "John has learned so much. He is a changed man."

Araminta found it delightfully funny that John had changed so quickly from just a few days before. "You mean like when he grabbed me the other day and started kissing me when I asked him to stop."

Jeff agreed. "I know that was wrong and we have discussed that. He will never do that again."

Araminta nodded back. "I know he won't, because he'll never have the chance, Jeff."

Isabella broke in, "So what about tonight? Will you at least go to the prom with him as a date?"

Araminta shook her head. "I have other plans."

Isabella packed up her lunch and hugged her sister. "I disagree with your decision, but I love you."

Jeff was less forgiving. "You need to think about what you are doing to this family we are making."

Araminta smiled but had no words. It was a family that they were making out to be wonderful, because for them it was wonderful. She returned her sister's gesture. "I love you too."

Jeff tried one more time. "What you don't realize is that John is going to make this night very special. His father has a friend with a Model 40 Sedan. You will be taken to the prom in luxury."

Araminta smiled. "You will be so lucky."

Jeff drew his ire at Araminta. "You are being selfish. John went to all this trouble as a prom gift for you."

Nothing was going to sway Araminta. She'd gone down this road before. It was John's way of seizing the upper hand on her. "Please, have a great time and let John know that I need time."

Jeff warned her, "There may not be time, you might be blowing this."

Araminta agreed. "If that's the case, then it was never meant to be."

Jeff turned in disgust and pulled Isabella with him. "Let's go."

Isabella made one last turn to plead with an expression of want.

Araminta felt the weight of letting her sister down. She knew that this would create another round of arguments, maybe more. She knew John wouldn't let it go, and she was sure her momma would have something to say as well. Yet, she owed John something, something far deeper than a relationship. She owed him her strength. He woke up the person she was meant to be.

I felt my pain lift for a moment. "Oh Grandma, she's the best."

A glistening in my great grandmother's eyes formed tears. I didn't know if she was proud of the daughter she'd become or if it was something else. "Are you okay?"

She smiled, weak and distant, as though she'd remember something painful. "Yeah, I'm okay. I'm so glad you are here listening to me."

"Tell me more!" I waited for her to tell me about what happened that night.

Chapter 43

Araminta was surprised her momma came to her defense. With Isabella complaining that Araminta would ruin the night, Matilda stood fast. She'd seen the determination in her daughter's eyes and knew she was a special kind of woman, one who was a leader. The once shy daughter had become a woman who knew what she wanted, and being treated like an equal was important to her, after all, her example had been there all her life, a twin. Equal was something she identified with. "Are you sure you want to go?"

Araminta said, "Yes, this is what I should do."

Matilda said, "And you want to wear the dress?"

Araminta smiled. "You made it, of course I'll want to wear it."

Matilda helped her into the burgundy gown. It was form fitting at the waist, and from the bottom of the neck down to the elbows there was lace, and lace to the top of the breast. A flare came out on the left side of the waist.

More fabric came out on that side and Matilda placed a silk piece that Araminta could hold or just let fall down the gown as a train. Matilda pulled the top of her hair up and it all fell back with millions of spirals going down her back. Matilda pinned her hair with a comb that lifted on the right side.

Matilda held back a tear. "Oh, child, you are such a beautiful young woman."

Araminta kissed her momma on the cheek. "Thank you, you are the best momma in the world."

Someone knocked at the door. "You better go, your ride is here." She grabbed her hand purse and hurried out.

A while later another knock echoed through the house. Matilda had answered the door to a determined John Whitney, whose parents stood behind their son. "Momma, I want you to get that dress on Araminta and get her out here. I am not going to take this disrespectin' any longer."

Matilda Bowed to Mr. and Mrs. Whitney and invited them in. She sighed. "I wish I could serve you up Araminta, but she left here about an hour ago."

It was hard for Matilda to look Marilyn in the eyes, but Marilyn came to Matilda and put her arms around her. "Everything will work out. Araminta just needs to grow up a little. She wasn't used to a man in her life. She's still a little girl."

Matilda didn't have the heart to tell her daughter's ex fiancé's parents that quite the opposite had happened. Matilda could hope that college might grow up John enough for Araminta to accept him back. "Yes, perhaps she will come around to her senses." Matilda continued. "I understand if you don't want to chaperone with me Marilyn."

Marilyn smiled. "I think John should go, just in case Araminta has a change of heart, and besides, we borrowed such a beautiful car, and with three such beautiful young adults it would be a waste not to let them enjoy the night."

Matilda thanked Marilyn and asked if she would like to see Isabella in her dress. Isabella's gown was a tight fitting and flared out about three inches above the knees, and had a slight train. It accented her top, and with the silk see-through jacket that stopped right below the breast, really brought the gown out. Teal in color, Matilda pulled the top of her hair up and it fell back with millions of spirals going down her back. Isabella had a hair comb that pinned the left side of her hair. Sadly, her sister had one that matched.

Marilyn put her hands to her lips and shed a tear. "She looks stunning."

Jeff and John wore suits, and Jeff presented Isabella a music box that Isabella always wanted. It played beautiful music, and inside the box was a necklace.

John had gotten Araminta a gold necklace and a music box as well. He turned to Matilda and handed it to her. "Please, even if Araminta doesn't want it, I want this family to have it."

Matilda hugged John and whispered, "Give it time."

He handed her Araminta's corsage. "Take this too."

Matilda's heart sank for the young man. Jeff pinned his corsage on Isabella, a matching flower for her dress.

The party of three, an odd number, gathered on the porch, and Stanley thanked Mr. Whitney for his generosity. Matilda followed the three, along with the Whitneys. They loaded into the sedan and waved to Stanley and the kids.

I broke into Matilda's story. "Oh, no she didn't. Tell me that Araminta went with that nice young man to the prom?"

Matilda looked down to me. "No, they didn't go to the prom."

My heart beat like a drummer. "Where then, Grandma?"

She continued:

Araminta and Alexander pulled into a restaurant parking lot. A new silent movie had just come out, and Alexander promised his week's salary on dinner and a movie. He dressed up in a suit, and to anyone in town, they looked like two kids coming from the prom.

Alexander asked, "Are you sure you don't want to go to the prom with John?"

Araminta took his arm. "No, I'm fine."

As they made their way into a swanky restaurant, and told the maitre d, a table for two, he wanted to know, "Just tell me that you aren't using me to make him jealous, or that I'm responsible for breaking you two up."

Araminta thought about it. "No and no. When I met John, I'd never dated anyone, and I thought he was charming, but before I knew it, I was engaged and I was his property. He made me go to a sex class that his mother taught."

Alexander stopped her. "A sex class?"

She waved him off. "Long story, anyway, he began to demand I do everything he told me to do, and as I saw it, that wasn't who I was."

Alexander nodded. "I see."

They ate a fine meal, and they saw a wonderful movie. Alexander presented no pressure. She liked that. When they got in the car, Araminta admitted, "I had the best night tonight. Thank you for being such a gentleman." She leaned across the seat and gave him a kiss on the cheek.

Alexander didn't know what to say. He just sat there.

"Are you okay, Alex."

He grinned. "Yeah, I'm great." He sighed, "But you have to do something you won't like, and you don't have to worry, I won't leave you alone."

Araminta tilted her head. "What are you talking about?"

He exhaled, "You spent a lot of energy this year on a relationship, good or bad, and you owe it to him to give him a dance."

Araminta was confused. "What?"

Alexander looked at his watch and continued, "As I see it, the dance ends in twenty minutes. If we hurry, you can get in there and give John the last dance."

Araminta objected, "But I don't want to."

Alexander told Araminta a story. "I had a girlfriend I had to leave. I knew we wouldn't see each other again, and I regretted not thanking her for the time we had together. That's all I'm suggesting. That guy spent nearly a year thinking he was marrying you. Maybe one dance is owed to him. Don't you think?"

Araminta sighed. "I guess."

Alexander promised. "I'll be out here in the car waiting. If you don't come back, I'll understand, but I'll be here."

She looked at him, "Promise?"

He nodded. "Absolutely."

They drove to the school and Araminta stepped out. "Stay here, please."

Alexander laughed. "I should be more worried than you." He winked.

Araminta made her way into the school. She heard the school principal yell over the crowd, last dance, and a Victrola started to spin a soft song. Araminta looked around and saw her momma, Mr. and Mrs. Whitney, and John sitting in a corner. She approached John and tapped him on the shoulder. When he turned, she asked, "Can I have this dance?"

John's eyes lit up and he stood without hesitation. As they made their way to the dance floor she whispered in his ear. *"I don't know what the future holds, and I'm not getting back together with you, but I was told that I owed you this for all that you've put into this last year, and for all the dreams you hoped for."*

John pulled away and looked into Araminta's eyes. "Did my momma tell you that?"

She shook her head. "No, Alex did."

John pulled her close and whispered back, "Tell him thank you."

They danced until the echo of the last note had died away. The lights slowly came on and Araminta excused herself. "I'm going to go, John."

John frowned, "So soon?"

She touched his cheek and turned. With that, she left as quickly as she came, and true to his word, Alexander waited for her.

By the time her mother and sister made it home, after a late night dinner, Araminta was fast asleep in her own bed.

I stared up at Grandma and cried.

Chapter 44

Sunrise was beautiful. Araminta and Isabella had tea with Matilda on the porch. Matilda was proud of both her girls. She turned to Araminta, "So how come you came to the dance? Did you get a change of heart?"

Araminta sipped on her tea. "No, Momma, Alex insisted that I owed John that dance for all he'd meant to us over the last year."

Matilda considered that a pretty mature thing to do. "Tell him that I thank him for that."

Araminta considered what a selfish gesture that was. "He's a really nice boy, Momma."

Isabella was indifferent, even a little cold about what her sister had done, but she was too happy about how the night went for her. "I'm just glad that John had something to talk about." She went on, "And boy did he talk about that last dance."

Matilda chuckled. "Yeah, he didn't stop talking all the way home."

Araminta hoped she hadn't led John on. "I hope Jeff talked about his night." She smiled at her sister.

Jeff came up from the barn. "I heard that, and yes, I talked about the night as well."

Isabella craned her neck and reached over her head to take Jeff's fingers. He sat next to her and asked. "Do I get a cup too?"

Matilda called Lillie and asked for her to bring Jeff a glass.

Isabella discussed some of the evening, "I forgot we didn't know how to dance."

Jeff said, "No big deal, we two stepped our way through the music and watched each other eyes, it was beautiful."

Matilda laughed. "I watched Jeff when you came out of the bedroom and his breath had stopped, I think.

That was the kind of night I wanted for you two. God has bless both of you and Jeff, and you both are growing up to be fine young adults, and that makes momma proud. It makes me sad to think my two girls will graduate and be gone next year."

Araminta looked at her momma. "Momma, what are you thinking about?"

Matilda grimaced. "I went to the time when I was your age and had to work and couldn't go to school." Matilda thought long, "I was straightening your rooms one day and came across one of your lesson books. I opened the book and tried to read it, but I didn't understand it, so I closed the book. I wasn't a slave, and neither was your dad, but there was no option for him to go to school," Matilda lamented, "but we made it through, and we always said our children would have an education."

Araminta felt the weight of her mother; how much she gave to make sure the girls had what they needed.

Jeff said, "Thank you for raising such a wonderful family, Momma."

Isabella speculated, "Momma, we can teach you and Dad to read?"

Araminta agreed, "Yes, Momma, let us teach you; you taught us by sending us to school, so let us teach you now.

Jeff said, "That's the best idea."

Araminta said, "By the time we leave for the college, Momma and Dad will be ready to read our letters from school."

Matilda smiled. "Will I be able to read the Bible?"

Jeff said, "You better be able to. I want to know my mother-in-law can follow one of my sermons when I have my own church."

Matilda asked, "You think you can teach someone my age to read?"

Araminta promised. "I know we can."

Matilda smiled. "Deal."

Jeff went about working on the farm, and the girls got up and helped their momma clean up the kitchen. When they finished, they had to put in the time for finals.

On Sunday, Jeff and the rest of the family went to church. John and his family were there too. It was awkward for Araminta. John wanted to sit next to her, but Araminta waved him off. "Remember what I said, John. Give it time." She moved between the younger kids while Jeff and Isabella sat together, with John and his parents on one side, and Matilda and Stanley on the other.

The rest of the day was spent studying. The girls quizzed each other, sure their grades were secured. Jeff pulled Isabella away from Araminta around four, and Araminta had a surprise visit from Alex.

Araminta told her mother, "Alex and I are going to go to the park to study, momma."

Matilda came out of the kitchen and blurted, "Hold on a minute." Her voice belied her temperament.

Araminta stopped, afraid what she was mad. "What?"

Matilda put her dish rag over her shoulder and came up to Alexander. She put her arms on his shoulders and felt for power, stood him up and looked him in the eye. "Araminta tells me you are a fine gentleman. Is that true?"

Alexander swallowed. "Yes, ma'am."

Matilda studied his face. "Had the opportunity to speak to your momma the other day. She seems like a fine woman too."

Alex repeated himself. "Yes ma'am."

Matilda said, "If you are a good man in my baby's eyes, you are a good man in mine. Make sure you stay that way."

Alexander echoed one more time, "Yes ma'am."

She squinted, "You say anything other than 'yes ma'am?'"

He hesitated and grinned. "Yes ma'am."

They laughed.

"What park are you taking Araminta to?"

He said, "To the Dewayne Lake Park."

Matilda liked that. "That's a good park, lots of people."

He said, "I'll have her home early. We need to study math."

Matilda pulled her towel from her shoulder and swiped it at the two. "Go on then, shoo. Times a wastin'."

Araminta and Alexander hurried out the door and drove off. As they left the property, Araminta could see John's truck tucked away behind the barn. She hoped he wasn't in the mood to follow her.

I coughed, a moist pressure on my chest, my eyes were heavy and more of me hurt. Still, I had to know more. "Grandma, this isn't going to turn out bad is it?"

She comforted me. "Child, we are almost there and then you can go home."

I didn't know how that was going to be possible. I didn't see myself driving back the five hundred miles I'd come. "Okay, then let's continue."

Chapter 45

Finals week had gone well for the twins. They had put their time in throughout the year and proved they were college ready. Araminta had done well, better than Isabella, but she put it to the fact that she had no distractions when it came to study time. Still, the two did themselves proud, and in the small class of less than thirty kids, they both were in the top ten, Araminta had the third highest grade point in the class. The highest grade, and Valedictorian was Cydra Jackson, and Salutatorian went to Richard Wilson, but Richie was shy and begged the principal to not make him give a speech, so it fell on Araminta. All week long, she tapped Mrs. Nelson on her ideas, and slowly formed what she would say, waiting for that moment before even her parents would hear it.

On Thursday, after a morning graduation, the Fleming house would give way to a graduation party for the girls. Matilda had to make a decision. To invite John would alienate her own daughter, but to not invite him would be devastating to the Whitneys, who had been like extended family for the last year.

On Wednesday night, Araminta came to Matilda. "Momma, I know you have that wonderful party set up for us tomorrow, and I would never disrespect you and ask you to un-invite a guest."

Matilda knew where her daughter was going. "It's been on my mind for the better half the week, baby. What would you like me to do?"

Araminta studied the room, all the family pitching in to cut streamers and blow up balloons. Food cooked on the stove, and Stanley and Joseph had raided a hive up on the hill for honey. Matilda had a batch of buttermilk biscuits baking. "All week long, as happy as I was taking tests so I could finish high school, I was worried about tomorrow."

Matilda reached out and pulled her oldest daughter close. She held her tight and whispered. "I don't want you to feel unwelcomed in your own home."

Araminta pulled away. "That's not my worry. I know I'm loved, and I know I'm welcomed. I'm more worried about you. I don't want you to feel pressured if I ask to not be here. I don't want you to feel guilty."

Matilda held her hands out. "Araminta, this party is for you."

Araminta shook her head. "That's not entirely true, Momma, it's for four of us. And if I force you to pick sides, I know you will pick me, and that would be unfair to a lot of people. I made a mistake when I agreed to get engaged without really being courted. We got lucky that Isabella and Jeff are so well matched. It's truly a blessing, but I am responsible for a lot of people being unhappy."

Matilda admitted, "A month ago, I was one of those upset ones, but watching the woman you've become in the face of this adversity is incredible. I'm so proud of you."

Araminta asked, "So if after graduation, I were to go to a celebration at Alexander's house, would you be upset?"

Matilda weighed her daughter's request. She paused, concerned for all the questions she'd have to answer. Araminta's grandmother would want to know where she is, Mrs. Nelson was invited, she'd want to know. "I'll tell you what, you let Mrs. Nelson know where you are going, and Mrs. Nelson and I will personally show up for thirty minutes before we head to the house after graduation."

Araminta's eyes lit up. "Really? You'll show up?"

Matilda wanted to shed a tear. Did her daughter not know that for the rest of Matilda's life and beyond, she would always be there for her? "Baby, I'm only sorry I can't spend the whole day with you."

Araminta's spirit lifted. "Showing up is the greatest gift you could give me."

Matilda continued. "I'm sure that I can get grandma Lucy to stay around after all the guests have left so you two can have some time together."

Araminta hugged her momma. "Thank you for understanding." Matilda wanted to thank her daughter for the selfless act. She had no idea how it lifted the pressure she felt developing over the week.

Thursday morning, the sun rose over the hill from the east, dew lifted and the sweet smell of spring brought in the whisper of summer.

"Isabella, wake up." Araminta shook her sister. "Time to graduate."

Isabella sat up, "It's too early, I want to sleep some more."

Araminta teased her, "Maybe a little less kissing until the late hours and a little more bedtime would help you."

Isabella smiled. "But oh how life would be so boring."

Their new dresses hung on the door. "Look."

Isabella's eyes widened. "They are beautiful, aren't they?"

The girls rose and made their way to the kitchen. Matilda had breakfast ready, and Stanley made a rare appearance at the table on a week day. He'd taken the day off for his girls. "So, you two ready to start a new life?" He winked.

Isabella chided him. "Are you trying to get rid of us before we officially become college students?"

He leaned in, "Well, spending money is kind of important for college girls. You might want to have some before you head over there. A summer job might help."

Isabella turned to her sister with a skewed look. "I hate it when he's right. Have you thought about a summer job?"

Araminta winked. "I have, and I have two offers. I'll give you one of them."

Stanley, Matilda, and Isabella all turned and gave their attention to Araminta. Isabella asked, "Where?"

Araminta took a seat and directed the conversation. "Mrs. Nelson has asked for someone to work on cleaning up the boards, the desks, the windows, everything at the school. She promised it would take the summer, and she offered a decent rate."

Isabella rubbed her hands together, "Ooh, I like that one. What's the other?"

Araminta sat up and a sly grin crossed her face. "The Fabric Barn is looking for someone to work in fabrics."

Isabella smiled. "Something tells me that's the one you want."

Stanley lifted his cup and took a drink. "I'd say you girls have a head start on college."

Matilda broke in. "Speaking of head start, how about you two eat, get those dresses on, and let us get you to the school."

The students were given robes and they donned them over their clothing. The theme for the senior year was--For the Daughters, Fathers...For the Sons, Mothers. Stanley waited in the wings, he'd have two young ladies on both arms as they walked down the row to their seats. Matilda had the honor of escorting Jeff.

Araminta checked over her shoulder and several couples behind her was John and Mrs. Whitney. A smile had returned to his face, but then again, he didn't catch her looking at him. In the back, the newcomer, Alexander grinned with his mother, Mrs. Hill.

Pomp and Circumstance played on the Victrola and like a procession the line moved in unison. This day had finally come. Most these kids had known each other from the first day they'd started school. Some, like Jeff and Alexander, had come through the years, but all of them had no idea that this group of kids would never be together again. They would spread out into the world to try and make something of themselves, some failing, and some soaring to heights they never thought imaginable.

The first speaker was Principal Harris who gave the convocation, formally sitting all the students in their seats. His speech, along with a speech by Mrs. Nelson, laid praise on an exceptional class of grown children, now young adults. Cydra's speech was a tribute to her grandfather, and it praised a man who started his life a slave. It moved the audience, and the man himself stood to the applause of everyone.

Then the moment came. Araminta stood when her name was called and walked with her head down to the podium. She looked out at her classmates:

"I am Araminta Fleming. Many of you know me as the girl with the sister who looks just like her." Her voice grew stronger as she drew from the message she had to deliver. "We may never be back this way again, but the journey from the cradle to the grave is made up of events that shape our lives. From the loves we've lost, to the loves

we've gained, from the children we've raised to the parents we become, we are in that place where the flower blooms. We are the flowers of today. But time doesn't wait for us, we must seize the moment. Time is now, and now is where we live. Never let now go, and you will always live in the here and now." Araminta had a wisdom she'd gained from trying to understand who she was, and why she was here. Matilda held Stanley's arm and wept.

Stanley put his arm around her shoulder and whispered, "We have raised such beautiful children, inside and out."

Araminta continued with thanking all the people who had influenced her through the years, pointing out some of the touching moments in her life. Her classmates and the audience again stood for a speaker. Araminta, who had felt strong giving her speech, felt embarrassed by the cheers.

She smiled. "I turn this back over to Principal Harris." She bowed as she passed Mrs. Nelson.

Mrs. Nelson stood and hugged Araminta. "You were fantastic."

The students were called up one by one, and as they received their diplomas. They filed out to the front yard of the building, grouping together with their tassels switched, where Mr. Whitney worked as the official photographer. What would be most noticeable to anyone who knew the kids well was where Araminta stood and where John stood. They anchored opposite ends of the group. Alexander stood next to her, and in the center of the three rows, Jeff and Isabella had their arms around each other with smiles that offered to set the world on fire.

When they finished, Matilda came up alongside the girls. "Isabella, you are going to ride with Dad. We'll be to the house shortly."

Isabella shrugged. "How are you getting there?"

Matilda motioned to Mrs. Nelson. "Your teacher is giving us a ride."

Isabella looked at her momma. "Us?"

Araminta stepped in. "Yes, us." She pulled her mother along, and the three of them headed out to the parking lot.

As they made it to Mrs. Nelson's car, another car pulled up. A gentleman rolled down his window, "Are you Mrs. Fleming?"

Matilda turned and recognized Millicent Hill and Alexander. "You must be Mr. Hill?" Matilda held her hand out.

Mr. Hill reached out. "Please, call me Emmett."

Matilda carried a large bag. "We are headed to your home right now. I've made an apple pie and have some of my homemade biscuits and honey as well." She held up the bag.

Millicent smiled. "Thank you so much."

The gathering at the Hill resident was much smaller than what was happening at the Fleming house. Just the Hills and a couple of the employees from the Fabric Barn were there. Matilda wanted to invite them with all her heart to the twin's party, but knew it would be awkward for everyone.

Matilda stayed long enough to see the Hills give Araminta a beautiful hat, sophisticated, and something a college girl would draw many the eye of young men with. However, her time was sparing and she excused herself without tasting any of the wonderful food Mrs. Hill had prepared. Matilda knew they understood what a sacrifice it was to leave her daughter there when a party raged at the Fleming place.

She kissed her daughter. "I love you with all my heart, baby."

Araminta wasn't sad, she was at peace, easy, happy. "Go, take care of all my siblings. Tell grandma we will be there before she leaves."

Matilda and Mrs. Nelson hurried out and made their way to the Fleming party.

My eyes were burning. I couldn't keep them open. I knew I didn't have a lot of time to stay awake. It wasn't that late, barely six in the evening, but I felt so groggy. "That was beautiful Grandma, and you sacrificed so much.'

Matilda disagreed. "No, Araminta selflessly sacrificed. She had grown wise beyond her years."

"Can you tell me one more story? What happen at the house?"

Matilda's smile cracked and look of concern overcame her. "Okay, but after this, you need to go home."

I floated in the idea. I had no idea how I'd get home. "Alright."

Chapter 46

Matilda and Mrs. Nelson came to the property drive as Grandma Lucy arrived. The rest of the party was already in full swing. Marilyn had helped Stanley and the kids with the food. A picnic table had been set up as the food staging area, and kids picked at olives and celery sticks. Apple pies laid out like generals, heading the list of wonderful food Matilda had made for all the people arriving. In the center of the table, a beautiful three layer cake, the gem of all the work Matilda had done the night before. Next to it Marilyn had brought a sheet cake.

John's family was there, Jeff's sister, Addrianna, and her husband were there. Grandma Lucy took in the setting of people she knew and didn't know, getting acquainted with the girls' teacher, and Isabella's future husband.

Jeff and Isabella walked to the barn. Jeff had feelings resting on his heart that he had to share. When he found the right spot, he looked at her like he was about to pounce. Isabella stared back, wondering what was wrong.

Jeff said, "Nothing's wrong, baby, I'm just starting to get you into my mind, and now my body is about to absorb you."

Isabella blushed. She stood arm's reach away.

Jeff said in a deep whisper, "Come here."

Isabella hurried to him.

Jeff put his hands under her arms and picked her up and swallowed her lips. Isabella sighed, and in turn, Jeff nuzzled her cheek. Jeff held Isabella close.

Isabella's hands were around his shoulders and neck. Jeff leaned against a post and allowed her to hold him anyway she wanted. Jeff loved how she positioned her lips on him. Isabella kissed his cheeks and wouldn't lift her lips when going to his lips; she just dragged her lips to his. Jeff loved it.

Someone giggled.

The two broke away quickly. Jeff questioned, "What the heck?"

One of John's brothers came out from behind a box. "Sorry."

Jeff shooed him away, but agreed. "I think we should go back out and be with the others."

Isabella blushed. "Yeah, that's probably a good idea." They hurried out and Jeff reminded the little tyke that silence is golden.

Isabella and Jeff met John at the porch. He informed Isabella, "Your mother came back without Araminta."

Isabella frowned. "Even if she had, John, you know how she feels."

John kicked some dirt. "I know, but I'd hoped I could at least spend the last day of the school year with her, and tell her how proud I am of her."

Isabella reached out and took his hand. "I understand."

John scowled. "Do you?" He looked at Jeff. "Do either of you understand? You two are happy as love birds.

My love bird has flown the tree for no reason." He turned back to Isabella, "She's your sister, you should have had more control of her."

Isabella took Jeff's arm and started to move away. "You're feeling sorry for yourself. I said I understand. If that's not good enough, you'll have to take it out on someone else."

Jeff said, "Bella, I'll be right with you, I want to talk to John."

Isabella shook her head and waded into the crowd of people. Jeff turned his attention to his best friend. "John, get a hold of yourself. God can see you through this. God can help you get what you so richly deserve."

John started to tear up. "I can't live without her, Jeff."

Jeff scolded him. "Yes you can, and yes you will. Just like everyone has told you, give it time." He put his hand around John. "For now, just enjoy that you are no longer a high school kid."

Mr. Whitney raised his voice above the crowd. "Hey kids, let's see what's the best food here today!" He raised a chicken wing; I'm going with Momma Matilda's chicken."

John tried to shake off his woes and joined his father. "I'm going with Momma Matilda's biscuits and honey."

As though they ushered in the bell to eat, everyone moved toward the table and found what they wanted to eat. Everyone was enjoying the food when a car that no one knew showed up.

Matilda asked, "Who could that be?"

Stanley shrugged. "Don't rightfully know."

Jeff squinted, "Isabella, look!" He jumped off the porch and waved the car in. He rushed to the door, and when it opened he took a little boy in his arms and waved to Isabella. "It's Natalie."

Natalie and her husband, Crawford, and three more children exited the car. He held his namesake in his arms and took everyone to meet his second parents. "This is my long lost cousin, Momma Matilda." Jeff beamed, "And this is their boy named after me, little Jefferson."

The boy grinned and went into Matilda's waiting arms.

Natalie came up alongside Isabella. "Hi, Isabella." They hugged.

"It's good to see you again, Mrs. Bill."

They laughed. Natalie said, "Jeff, Isabella, I would like you to meet my husband, Crawford Billups. Crawford, this is my nephew Jefferson."

Crawford said, "Nice to meet all of you, Nat told me how you met, that was incredible."

Jeff said, "Yes it was, nice to meet you, Crawford."

Jeff made all the introductions and everyone helped themselves to the food. Addrianna's husband played his guitar, and it was a wonderful outing and a great ending to the day. Matilda asked for everyone's attention and asked for Isabella to come up. Matilda gave Isabella a huge gift box and told her to open it. Inside, the box is packed with a sundry of clothes for all occasions.

"I couldn't let you go to school this September without a new wardrobe." She motioned to Marilyn, "Momma Marilyn helped with this as well."

There was an uneasy quietness as one box remained sealed, and everyone knew it was for Araminta. "There are more but that's all we could fit in your box."

Isabella turned to her mother and Marilyn. "You two are the best. Thank you so much."

Jeff came forward. "Even though this party is for John and me as well, John and I have a gift to give to our momma who has done so much for me and has been there for John. This coming school year we will be going to college and you will not be able to talk to your daughters, so the Wilson Firm has helped us provide you with something."

Matilda and Stanley look at each other surprised. Matilda stepped forward and opened a box to a phone.

Isabella let out a shrill cheer. "We can call!"

Jeff continued, "The phone company is coming Saturday to install this one in your house."

Jeff wasn't done. "Isabella I have something for you. This gift I know you once talked about wanting." He handed her a box. "For you."

Isabella opened the box and stared down into gold earrings she'd always wanted. "I never told you I love those earrings, Jeff, how did you know?"

Jeff winked. "Your momma is my momma too."

Isabella kissed Jeff on the cheek. "I will thank you later."

Jeff squeezed Isabella's hand.

Jeff's sister and Aunt Natalie gave Jeff a beautiful wrapped box. Jeff opened up a box of school supplies. There were folders, pencils, ink pens, and a bag to carry his books to class.

Jeff said, "Awesome, school supplies, this is great, I can use this. Thank you so much, Aunt Natalie, Addrianna." He gave a nod to their husbands.

Mr. and Mrs. Whitney came up to the gift giving area next. Mr. Whitney said, "We are very proud of John, Jeff, Araminta, and Isabella." Mr. and Mrs. Whitney gave Isabella two heavy tote to carry books to class. "Please see that your sister gets the other."

Marilyn hugged Isabella. They gave their son John and his best friend Jeff briefcases. Mrs. Whitney nodded. "Time to start looking professional."

Matilda looked around the group, when she saw that no one else was offering gifts, she stood. "I have one for each of you graduates." Stanley handed each of them a college quilt. They were patches of colors the kids liked, and at the very bottom right hand corner was their first name.

Jeff said, "Thank you for taking care of all of us, Momma." Jeff kissed Matilda on the cheek.

The evening wound down and the guest left one by one. Marilyn offered to help, but Matilda knew the longer the Whitneys stayed, the longer her oldest daughter would stay away. "No, we are fine. You guys are good to go." She hugged Marilyn. "Thank you for being such a wonderful friend, and tell that son of yours, that not all is lost. Time sometimes heals all wounds."

Marilyn smiled, but Matilda could see that she knew that wasn't the case. "Thank you."

The Whitneys packed up and left, and ten minutes later, as the sun was waning, Alexander and Araminta made their way to the house. Araminta exited and saw Grandma Lucy. She ran to her and hugged her. "I am so glad you came."

Grandma Lucy teased her, "I came, but you didn't!"

She sighed, "Long story."

Grandma Lucy looked over Alexander, "And is this young man your boyfriend?"

Araminta pulled Alexander over. "This is my friend, Alexander." Araminta leaned in to her grandma. "I've learned to take relationships slow."

Grandma smiled. "That's a wise woman who says that."

Araminta caught up on what she missed, sorry she didn't see Jeff's aunt. Even though she had nothing to do with the party, she and Alexander helped cleaned up. Araminta has a lot of alone time with Grandma Lucy and they talked about everything under the sun, from her new changing body to the last year's relationship. She was sorry to see her have to leave, but her ride showed up and it was time to call the evening a success. She hugged and kissed Lucy for the wonderful stories and walked her to the car.

Araminta turned just in time to see Isabella walk up to Jeff and pull him to the barn. She shook her head and turned to Alexander, "Hey, you want to go in and have some more of my momma's biscuits and honey?"

Alexander walked up alongside her. "I thought you would never ask."

As they came inside, Matilda handed Alexander a package. Alexander looked at Araminta and she shrugged. "I have no idea."

Matilda said, "I am grateful to you young man, this is my appreciation."

Inside was a fifth quilt. Araminta asked. "How did you make one so fast with his name on it?"

She said, "I have my ways, besides, I know a few people at the Fabric Barn." She winked and they laughed.

It was a hallmark day in Matilda's life, the graduation of her two oldest daughters. She went to bed that night, kissed Stanley for making her the happiest woman on the earth.

Stanley kissed her back. "Matilda, you just don't get it. You are the heart of this family. Without you, happiness would just be a dream from people who don't exist."

Matilda smiled, and drifted off to sleep.

Chapter 47

"That was a beautiful story, Grandma." I couldn't move. My lips were numb, and I hurt in places well beyond sickness. "What's happening to me, Grandma?"

Nellie leaned over me and her face had an angelic glow. "It's time for her to go home."

I mustered enough energy to shake my head. "I can't drive, Nellie."

Matilda said, "You don't have to. We're going to see that you get home, but I want you to promise when you feel better to come back, there's so much more to tell you, and you need to know this information for your journey."

Their voices sounded hollow, as though they were fading. "My journey to where?"

"Your journey to second sight."

"I don't understand."

Matilda smiled. "You will."

Nellie reached underneath me and picked me up as though I was a little girl. She didn't struggle, with ease she carried me to the bed and lay me down. "Time to go home."

A penlight shone in my eyes. "Miss, can you hear me?" I blinked and a gentleman in a white coat leaned over me. "Can you hear me?"

"Yeah. I scanned the room. "Where am I?"

He smiled. "You're in Richmond General."

I tried to remember leaving Matilda's "Was I in an accident?"

He nodded. "Yes, and you are a very lucky young lady. Heavy fog slowed a semi in front of you and you just kept right on going and slammed into the rear end."

I gathered my bearings. "How long have I been here?" He looked at his watch. "About three days."

"So it's Wednesday?"

"Wednesday? No, it's Sunday night?"

"That can't be. I was just at my great grandmother's house in North Carolina."

"Well, I don't know about that, but you weren't traveling north bound, you were traveling south bound on Friday morning."

"I need to call my parents."

"You don't have to call them, they're here." He left and came back with my mother and father, and my fiancé.

My mother leaned over and gave me a kiss. "We haven't left the hospital. We were so worried about you."

"You need to call Matilda and tell her I'm okay."

"We spoke to her, and when we told her you were in an accident, I don't think she comprehended how serious it was, because she said she was sorry you didn't make it down but that she hoped you could make it another time. I tried to tell her this was life and death, and she said, 'Just tell her when she wakes, to come down.' She went on to say, 'I'll keep her in my thoughts.'"

"Mom, I was there. I was in her home."

My mother stroked my hair like I was a lunatic. "You have had a traumatic experience. Your thoughts are playing tricks on you."

I shook my head. "No, I was there. She gave me a history of her family."

My fiancé stepped up. "Honey, you left my place and not more than an hour later you were in an accident. I've been here with your parents since then."

I must have dreamed everything. No, no, I was too involved. I came to love my family from generations before me. Araminta, Isabella, it couldn't have been a dream, could it? I sighed. "Okay. I guess when you are in an accident, and they pump you full of drugs, the mind plays odd games with us."

My father leaned over and gave me a kiss. "It's understandable. Give yourself a few days. The doctors said you will recover. Nothing was broken. It appears you had a severe concussion."

My mother waved a finger at me. "I hope this teaches you to wear your seatbelts."

"Yeah, I'm sorry."

I was dejected. I woke to find out I had imagined it all.

My fiancé said, "The doctor said to let you rest, and maybe tomorrow you can go home."

"Thanks." I rolled to my side and curled up.

"Oh, honey, quick question."

I rolled back to face him. "Where did you get this? You didn't have this in the car when you left. It's beautiful." He pointed to a quilt with beautiful patchwork, cream material with lavender and pink flowers.

Cassandra Garrett is an IT Specialist for the Federal Government. Born and raised in Washington, DC, She has a degree in Sociology from Norfolk State University. She loves romance novels and historical fiction. In 5th grade, a show and tell day allowed her to craft her first story. When the class laughed at her humor, she knew she wanted to write again. After visiting North Carolina and researching her family tree, her deceased ancestors paid her a visit through her heart, and lo and behold, her first book was orchestrated from pen to tablet. Cassandra is the author of a series, including the very first novel entitled, "Matilda."

Cassandra has been a ballerina, tap dancer, jazz performer, modern dancer and a Gymnast. She was the queen of her Pogo Stick in the neighborhood. Jumping down the stairs on the pogo stick to continue a new task by jumping with no hands. She has had many passions in her life. She went from the pogo stick to making her very own skate board, gardening home grown vegetables, quilting, crocheting blankets, knitting and researching her DNA.

You can find all of her books, as well as the other authors from JaCol Publishing at www.jacolpublishing.com

www.ingramcontent.com/pod-product-compliance
Lightning Source LLC
Chambersburg PA
CBHW071426190726
48292CB00001B/131